Chane

Norman Gant

NEW ENGLISH LIBRARY
TIMES MIRROR

First published in the United States of America by Lancer Books Inc., in 1968

© 1968 by Norman Gant

All rights reserved

*

FIRST NEL EDITION SEPTEMBER 1969

This new edition July 1975

*

NEL Books are published by
The New English Library Limited from Barnard's Inn, Holborn, London, E.C.1.
Made and printed in Great Britain by Hunt Barnard Printing Ltd., Aylesbury, Bucks.

45002506 3

PROLOGUE

The young black man sat for a long time within sight of the house of the overseer. It was almost morning when he first stirred, changing from a sitting to a kneeling position beneath the large cypress tree hung with Spanish moss like a shroud.

It was a long time since Chane remembered anyone praying. The blacks of the Dutchman's Place had no religion other than the secret rite, but far away beyond Iwana, beyond the Gulf and the Caribbean, he remembered Piepie the preacher.

He knelt until he found the strength not to kill La-Forge, then he rose and walked quietly away from the plantation through the woodland of the bayou, away from the river and the Dutchman.

It was still dark when he entered the marsh country on the edge of the Dutchman's Place. The first light of morning was still an hour from the sky when he came to the shack in which Clem Bandeaux and his wife lived.

Bandeaux's mule brayed in the makeshift corral. The frogs in the marsh began to croak more loudly and some even to dive with a splash into the waters of the bayou. The cicada's song rose in volume and the roaring in Chane's head which had subsided earlier began again to threaten him.

The chorus of spring stars was still loud in eulogy in the heavens and the steadiness of Chane's breathing began to deepen. His large black nostrils flared and his heart pumped fury through the veins Iwana had given him. The son of Iwana and the high medicine stood in the Louisiana night and felt a great pounding beneath his forehead and behind his eyes. He remembered the white woman who was asleep not fifty feet from where he stood and tasted the heavy saliva that was collecting on his tongue.

Sometime in the night he had rent his clothes in his despair and his shirt hung from his huge back in tatters. The bright light of the stars illuminated his long muscles and shone from his wide forehead. He felt his body tense and relax, tense and relax, as it had before he had succeeded in calming himself.

He had meant to pass the Bandeaux's cabin, to go on into the marsh and never come back. He could not endure another day on the plantation. But he stood transfixed as the first signs of morning began to show in the sky. He stared at the place where the Bandeaux woman had come to him, there on the earth before her cabin.

He heard Henri's last word to him, "De maitre, now he

know you was here, you. You bes' go on straight back, quick man. Maybe he don't tell de Dutchman."

The mule brayed again and Chane tensed, sensing movement within the cabin, but he did not flee. Soon the door opened and a figure came out on the rickety porch.

It was she. She was dressed in a long blue cotton nightdress and her hair was in disarray. She held her husband's long rifle and raised it carefully as she came down the three steps to the soft earth. She looked to the mule and then to the sky.

"*Qui est la?*" he heard Clem shout from his bed within the dark cabin.

"It ain't nobody," she called. "Go on back to sleep."

As she lowered her rifle she caught sight of him standing in the marsh like a giant black statue; she quickly raised the rifle again and cocked the hammer.

"Is it you?" she whispered.

"Who is it?" Clem called again in his rasping hateful voice. "No one, damn it!"

She approached more closely and stepped within the dark of the brush. "Is it you?" she whispered, lowering the rifle. She raised one hand to press her dark hair against her head. Her white skin glowed in the early night.

"You crazy comin' here, you," she said with a smile.

Chane made no reply. He felt the fury rush through his arteries and understood only vaguely that the woman before him was misunderstanding the heat and intensity of his glance. He had no place in his mind for the woman. He thought about her husband in bed in the cabin, of the last time he had seen the man, mounted on that mule coming back from the Willows, grinning.

She approached him and whispered, "He'll go on back to sleep now. You come—what's the matter?"

She stared at him and lifted her hand to touch his face but stopped suddenly short.

"Oh," she exclaimed quietly, "I know, I know, I jus' found out. He didn't say nothin' to me when he came back. He jus' talked about it before, in the middle of the night, like as if he couldn't sleep until he got it clean out of his mind. It's right awful, Chane, I know how you mus' feel, you."

Chane looked at the woman coldly. He was hard put to keep his balance against the roar in his head and the pounding in his veins.

"But, you'll see, I'll make it all right, you'll see," she said sweetly.

She touched him at last on his thick chest, running her white fingers over his coal black skin, then she leaned forward and kissed him between the points of his collar bone.

He lifted his hand to her head, grasped it like a fruit and flung her to the ground by it. She shouted in pain as she hit

6

the ground.

They both waited in silence for another shout from the cabin, but none came. After a moment she looked up at him and smiled. She lifted her nightdress up to her thighs and said, "Gonna get me some poison ivy like as not, but it's goin' to be worth it, ain't it, you?"

He watched her as she squirmed to free herelf of her one garment. He was suddenly amazed and he looked at her curiously for a moment as she returned his gaze with open lust.

"I know what you had once you wants again," she whimpered.

The roaring took over again and the steady pounding of his blood mixed with the sounds of the swamp and the insatiable anger that her husband had helped to kindle. She had her legs spread wide and was offering herself to him in a fashion as vulgar as any the Dutchman could have desired. He thought with distaste how she had blackmailed him.

He knelt, took her neck in one powerful hand and began to choke the amazed, half naked, throbbing woman. Her eyes swelled in her head, a strange small sound left her throat and when he stood up, still holding her by the neck, she was dragged up with him. Her nightdress fell, covering her body again. She shook violently for a moment and then died, a foot off the ground, held in the powerful grip of the infuriated slave.

He let her fall to the earth as if she were no more than a crumpled piece of clothing.

"*Mon Dieu!*" he heard Clem hiss from near him. The man was armed with a pistol but was too shocked for a moment to discharge it. Chane kicked it away and into the swamp before the Frenchman had a chance to move.

The elder Bandeaux backed away from the black man, placed his hands before him with the fingers spread and his palms toward Chane pleadingly.

"Now boy, you git back, you. Git on back or you gonna be whipped bad. You git back, boy!

Chane caught the man by his shoulders and listened with pleasure as the white man screamed furiously into the early morning air, trying impotently to loosen Chane's grip. Clem was a powerful man but he had no chance against Chane. His hands and lower arms although free could not do enough damage to Chane's body to distract his attention. He lifted the man from the ground and walked backward with him.

"Put me down, *cochon!*" Clem spit into Chane's face with all his fury and Chane smiled. The roaring stopped, the swamp seemed quiet, the screams of the humans had silenced the frogs, and even the cicada had let up. He felt actually peaceful for he realized the ordeal of the long night was almost over.

He proceeded to an old cypress tree, carrying the white man before him like a toy.

"I'm sorry, boy, sorry boy, sorry boy. I had to do it," the Frenchman pleaded. "Jes' you let me loose and I'll fix it, you'll see. Jes' you—"

Chane broke him against the ancient tree like so much straw. The first blow silenced him and cracked the back of his head open, the second broke his back.

Chane hurled him into the soft earth of the swamp and was a good half mile away before the Bandeaux cock announced the dawn. From deep within the marsh he could hear the ownerless mule bray repeatedly.

1 : BARBARY

There were four men in the British shore patrol. The officer was armed with a sword, sheathed smartly at his waist. His sergeant carried a short billy stick by a black leather thong.

"You're an American, then?" the officer said.

"That's right, sir," Jameson Cowley replied.

They were standing a few hundred yards below the fortified walls of the Medina, the ancient city of Tangier, on the stone wharf. A four masted vessel of New England construction had moored in the harbor, and the first of her long boats, making steadily to shore, was halfway between the mother vessel and the first land of North Africa. The harbor pilot was still aboard, and a motley group of Arab customs officials was moving slowly from the town to the wharf.

"Southern American?" the lieutenant guessed from Cowley's accent.

"That's right, sir."

"What's your business here, sir?"

The thin man turned slowly, shifting his gaze from the approaching long boat to the face of the officer. It was much hotter at the bay than it had been in the narrow streets of the Casbah. The breeze had let up and a gray haze off the Spanish coast obscured Gibraltar. A Ghibli woman, in the red and white skirts, striped like the peppermint candy they sold in New Orleans stores, burdened with a load of twigs for kindling, was making her way toward them along the bay road from the mountainous peninsula to the east.

"I'm not sure that's your concern, sir," Cowley replied sternly.

The lieutenant was tall, had a thin nose, blue eyes set wide, and the good teeth of the rich. He was in fact, very much like Cowley in appearance.

"If you've any business in the slave trade, would you mind if I put a question to you?"

"I've no business in the slave trade," Cowley replied.

"We're looking for a man who deserted His Majesty's ship, the *Good Bess* while she was berthed at Gibraltar not a fortnight ago. He's a big man with a heavy nose, Hugo James is his name. He'll be looking for work on a slaver."

Cowley turned his attention to the long boat again; the customs officers were nearly to the wharf. Behind him the lieutenant continued to speak.

"His Majesty's government has no official policy against slavers, sir. If you've any knowledge of this man, whom we believe to be here in Tangier, we'd be obliged if you'd give it to us."

Jameson could make out the faces in the long boat. It had been three years since he'd seen that many Americans at once. Behind him he heard the sergeant mutter something to the lieutenant. He heard the odd vowel sounds of his Cockney accent, then the footsteps of the patrol as they left the wharf and confronted the approaching Arabs.

The water in the bay was quiet. The soft waves came in slowly and washed the rock of the wharf without spray or foam. A man was getting ready to leap from the bow of the long boat to the shore. He had a dirty red bandana wrapped around his forehead and he was all but black from the sun of the Atlantic crossing.

"Welcome to Africa," Jameson called.

The man glanced quickly toward Cowley, then turned his attention to the approaching wharf, leaped smartly and held the long boat fast by the bow line while his companions disembarked and then relieved him of its custody.

They were a tough crew, most of them walnut from the sun and salt spray.

"Where are you out from?" Cowley called to the first man to lift himself ashore on the helping arm of his mate.

"Salem."

"Are you from the company?" the man who had first touched shore asked, and Cowley laughed wryly.

"I'm looking for news from Louisiana," he explained.

"Sorry mate," the pilot cried, still in his aft seat. "There's no man in this crew who's been south of the state of New York in a year."

"Well, you're south of it now," Cowley laughed. "If you're in for a few days, come to the house in the Street of the Gazelle, and I'll stand you all to the rotten wine of this dry land. I haven't heard the sweet sound of the colonies since LaFitte drove the English from New Orleans."

He left the men cheering as he moved off. One of the Arabs in the customs detail nodded to him and Jameson touched his hat. Cowley was dressed like a young English dandy out for a stroll along the French Riviera. The hat was straw with a wide blue band.

He passed the Ghibli woman as he approached the open gates of the city where Portuguese cannon pointed menacingly at the bay, big cannon which could be turned on a steel track by a huge windlass.

The noise of the ancient city broke upon him as he passed through the gate. The bell and cry of a water carrier dressed in a short brown jalabah of coarse wool, the clatter of the hooves of the thin legged donkeys, the traditional cries of the market place and the constant music of the long flutes and the short drums.

The wind came up from the bay at last, just before Jameson turned into the small square where a hundred men sat in six cafes chattering over sweet mint tea and where a score of urchins ran across the cobblestones begging.

"*Labas, Monsieur* Cowley," a child cried and Jameson nodded as he passed. The boy caught up with him as he passed.

"How are you today, fine yes, *M*. Cowley?"

"Fine yes," Cowley replied.

"That is an American boat in the harbor, no, *M*. Cowley?"

"Yes, Mustafa," Cowley replied. The boy, who was almost black, reminded him of any number of his father's slaves.

"You will go on him, yes?" the boy asked.

"No, boy," Cowley replied.

He turned into the narrow Street of the Ancients and passed the forbidden door of the old Mosque with the child still at his heels. A herd of goats turned into the street from above, the bell of the bearded leader jangling and the old goatherd, like a figure from the Testaments, crying his wares through the stone streets.

Through narrow, uphill streets and the heavy odors of mint, saffron, goat cheese and kief, under passageways which connected the homes of the wealthy Arab merchants, Cowley and the young boy made their way to the Casbah gates. The Sultan's guards stood with shining scimitars like eunuchs before the doors to a harem. They allowed Cowley and the boy to pass through and proceed to the high sea wall that overlooked the harbor.

"No more boats come in today, *M*. Cowley," Mustafa said.

Cowley looked down at the child's flashing eyes and smile. "Have you seen my English friend today?"

"No, *M*. Cowley, not today. You will leave on the big American ship, yes?"

From behind, Cowley heard the gravel voice of the head of

10

the Sultan's guard. *"Labas, Monsieur.* There is nothing else yet today."

Cowley turned and looked at the man. He was lighter than his underlings and bigger, much bigger. He had Riff blood in him, and the fierceness of that people.

Cowley nodded and made back for the gate. A wail came up from the building behind the palace and the sharp sound of a whip broke the air.

"New slaves for His Highness, the first chosen of Allah. There is no God but God and Mohammed is his only prophet." Mustafa repeated the Islamic articles of faith called five times daily by the blind muezzins from the minarets atop the Mosques.

"Have you seen the British patrol?"

"Yes, sir," Mustafa said. "They are checking all the pleasure houses and hotels, but they have not come this far yet. They are still below the small square."

"So that's why you've been following me today," Cowley said with a sneer.

The boy shrugged. "It was not to tell you of the new shipment of slaves, *M.* Cowley."

"Well, I did not expect to find the English at my door, but here, boy, a dirham for you so that you will disappear like a djini."

The child looked up quickly at the young American and ran off between the pantalooned guards of the Sultan, the first chosen of Allah.

2

Four hundred miles directly south of the imperial city of Marakech in the northern half of the great Sahara, a caravan up from the Sudan had encamped on the oasis of Abdullah ben Mohammed, saint of Islam. It was said that the venerable saint had planted the ten acres of palms that fed on the underground stream whose only surface pool was the refreshment and life of travelers three hundred years before, in the first years of the sixteenth century.

The Arab members of the caravan were heartened, for the trip was all but over. They were on their own soil, on holy ground, and they had lost only a half dozen of the blacks they had bought from the Portuguese agent in the Sudan.

The encampment was light with the sound of the long flutes. A small, heavy man, a light skinned Moor who had become intoxicated with the wine of the foreigners which he kept in a great skin on his camel, was making ever smaller and faster circles before the tent of the caravan leader.

In a small grove behind the tent, the camels who had just been watered were tied, but the wind had shifted and the

11

pleasures of the cool desert night were marred by their vicious odor. It was a reminder that there was still care to be taken, for although they were nearly out of the desert, slaves had been known to die inches short of the market in Tangier.

Hassim Marakeshi came to the flap of the white tent and looked out. He shouted a curse at the drunken man, who ran off to lie near the slaves, perhaps to cut one loose for his own pleasure, if the guards would permit.

Marakeshi looked up over the palm trees. He heard the sounds of the names of the constellations echo in his memory from the days when he had sat cross-legged on the floor of the Mosque and repeated the words of the Koran, the names of the stars, the principles of the geometry and the dates and the places of the history of the people of Islam.

He had abandoned his robes and wore only the loose white silk shirt and pantaloons, his yellow baboosh and the red fez of the intellectuals, as if he were already back in the city. He returned to the cushions and sat down opposite his partner Kassim.

"Halfway between the jungles and the city I am never comfortable," Marakeshi said. "It is neither the one nor the other."

Kassim made no reply. The sound of the flutes stopped and a low mournful wail came from outside. One of the slaves was in anguish. There was a shout and then all was quiet.

Marakeshi continued, "The feeling of disorientation is severe throughout the trip, but most often on this leg of it. Man must earn, however."

"If only to be charitable," Kassim interjected.

There was the sound of hoofbeats on the harder soil of the oasis and Marakeshi stood suddenly and made again for the front of his tent.

"If it is Mohammed your son, see if he has brought any tobacco," Kassim yelled after him.

A stallion whinnied and a camel screamed in response as the hoofbeats came closer. With his robes flowing and the starlight reflected on the silver bands of his long rifle, Mohammed, Marakeshi's eldest son of his second wife, rode into the clearing before the tent and dismounted.

Marakeshi rushed to embrace the young man, and with his arm about his shoulder led him to the tent where they greeted Kassim. The three men sat down together on the pillows in the center of the floor.

"You are looking well, Father," the younger man said. "And you too, friend Kassim. Have you had a good trip?"

"We have two hundred natives, all from the same tribe. That is only six less than we started with after Ramadan. They are fine strong young bucks and females, the strongest group I have ever led through the Sahara."

The three men laughed. Discipline was always easy by the time the caravan reached the Sahara, for the slaves were not led through it. Instead, drink was withheld and the slaves were told in which direction the next water hole lay. That direction was always north.

"After you have rested and eaten, I will show them to you."

"They were once a fierce group," Kassim interjected.

"They are as tame as cattle now," Marakeshi laughed. "What news do you bring from home?"

"Everything is well, Father. I am to marry again when you return, a daughter of the Sherif of Fez. The Sultan himself has approved and will offer the calf."

Kassim made a sound of impressed assent and Marakeshi beamed. "I am pleased," he said.

"Fatima is still the same. My youngest sister takes too much pleasure showing herself on the roof. I have put her into strictest purdah until your return."

Kassim chortled and Marakeshi frowned, and it was not clear whether he frowned at his daughter's rebelliousness or his son's strictness with her.

"Your wives are well, and yours Kassim, and I have brought tobacco from an American boat that arrived in Tangier last month. Another was expected just before I left, so there may be even more for you to smoke when you return."

"A habit of fiends and djini," his father remarked jocularly.

"And the Sultan will require only one slave at his prices, the slave quarters at the palace are full and my marriage has put him in a good mood toward our family. We may sell all but one directly to the highest bidder. Father, perhaps we should give that one to the Sultan as a gift."

"Don't be ingenuous, Mohammed," Marakeshi snapped. "Of course we will give the one to the first of Allah's chosen as a gift."

"Unwind your turban and be comfortable," Kassim said. "All this riding will take the hook out of your nose."

Marakeshi stood and went to the tent flap again. He opened it and looked once more at the constellations. He felt better. His son had brought not only good news, but a feeling of the city with him. In a week they would be in Marakech where he would go to the Mosque. The sound of the muezzin would lighten his heart.

"Abdullah!" he cried into the night. "Bring food. Mohammed is here."

After he had dined on lamb tajeen and upon every variety of olive, Marakeshi led his son out of the tent and beyond the camels to the cool spot in which they had bound the slaves for the night. Eight of Marakeshi's men stood guard. The great black Moor was among them, the only one in-

13

dispensible to the trip because he spoke Swahili and five other dialects of central Africa. He had once been a slave himself, although he was an Arab, not a native; he had been made a eunuch and released by his charitable master. Marakeshi and his son approached him. Marakeshi had redonned his robes.

"Is everything well, Abdul?" Marakeshi asked.

"Very well, master. *Labas*, young master."

"*Labas*, Abdul."

"I will lead you through them, master, young master."

Abdul drew his scimitar and walked ahead. The slaves were tied in groups of ten or fifteen around the trees, with enough slack in the ropes to use their hands, though none had dared to loosen his bonds. There was nowhere for any of them to go in the great desert, for none of them could follow the stars or find water.

They were a healthy group. Most of them were young and the bucks were strong to a man and well endowed. Apparently no weakling had been allowed to survive in their tribe, or else none had been taken by the Portuguese in the Sudan. The women were well formed and many were still young enough so their breasts were not fully developed. There were no children.

But, by the last palm, tied in with eleven of the eldest women, a stately black of twenty-five or perhaps thirty, with a great depth to her eyes, had been given the most room by her sister captives. Those sisters had all turned toward her as best they were able and had begun to chant quiet, morbid phrases as the Arabs approached. The woman was entirely nude, for her swelling belly had outgrown her native garment and it had been cast away.

"Pregnant?" Mohammed muttered. "That is odd, Father."

The chanting continued and Abdul snapped something at them. The blacks persisted however and Abdul snapped again.

"What is it, Abdul?" Marakeshi demanded.

"Is it because she is pregnant?" Marakeshi asked the black Moor.

"No, young master."

"It is a miracle that she is, still," Marakeshi stated flatly. "I have spent each day of this journey wondering when she would drop that child. She has received no greater rations than the others, and look at her condition. She is in fine health. Abdul, stop them!"

The chanting had been taken up by the group of slaves at the nearest palm and seemed in danger of spreading.

Abdul snapped again, and one of the women said something quietly.

"I don't like this, Father," the young Arab said softly.

"Nonsense," Marakeshi snapped, but the chanting continued.

14

Abdul shouted back to the other guards and immediately the air resounded with the sound of their rifles being discharged. The noise was enough to silence the slaves.

"It is not simply that she is pregnant, young master," Abdul began to explain. "Your worthy father can tell you. She is the queen of this tribe. If the child she bears is a son, he will be their king, the highest of kings, and the chanting must persist through his birth. It is the superstition that the events of the day of his birth determine the fate of the tribe and the chanting is to keep away the evil of that day."

"They will have to chant very loud indeed," Marakeshi said. "Their fate is almost certainly sealed."

Mohammed laughed, but quieted again when he looked down upon the queen. There were many things in the depths of her eyes, but none of them was fear.

"It will not be our problem, master," Abdul said. "She will not bear for another month, despite their chanting, and it is more likely that she will miscarry or die before she is sold."

"You keep her alive," Marakeshi said with sudden decision. "If she bears before she is sold, I will have her royal son for myself."

"Yes, master. If Allah wills it, her child will be yours."

3

A restlessness had caused Hugo James to come up to the roof despite the protestations of the girls. It was a blazing white afternoon, but a breeze from the Atlantic kept it comfortable. As he leaned over the wash blue parapet he heard the tittering of women and looked down to see several Fatimas scurrying for cover on a roof below him. He called all Arab women Fatima, as it seemed to be the given name of them all.

The Street of the Gazelle was too narrow to walk two abreast but at the mountain where the women drew water the alleys broadened and the largest of these, the Street of the Weavers, led up a flight of steps toward the Mosque and the Sultan's palace. There he caught sight of the young American's straw hat. Nothing seemed to ruffle the young American and for that Hugo liked him.

The big man looked out across the ancient city as the flags were being raised on the minarets and the blind muezzins began their mournful call to prayer. He could just make out the song from the Mosque by the harbor gate until the muezzin at the Casbah Mosque began his chant and drowned out all but the echo of the other. Hugo was tempted to call to his friend but thought better of it. He watched the washed colors of the Biblical city for a moment and then turned to go back down. The restlessness was still on him.

The dark stairs were steep, built for smaller men than he, and he had to stoop and brace himself against the wall as he descended. He wore no shoes or socks, as was the custom within the house—only the breeches of an English sailor and a white silk shirt Jameson had lent him.

The pleasure rooms in the old house were large and sumptuous, but the individual sleeping rooms were small, although similarly furnished with deep rugs, drapes and sleeping mats and cushions. The girl was still there and the empty bottles of the rotten wine he had finished by himself when she had refused to drink.

She was young, no more than sixteen, and had the eyes of a frightened doe. She had put on a skirt that hung from her hips and her white veil, but her small breasts were bare. The red henna dye in her hair and on the palms of her hands and soles of her feet and around the nipples of her breasts caught the rays of the sun slanting through the small window. Hugo had found the henna very amusing at first.

He heard the American on the stairs. They were both too big for the Arab houses. His friend was ascending slowly because he had to place his feet with care.

"Hugo."

"In here, mate," the Englishman called.

Jameson Cowley walked into the room, bending his head to avoid colliding with the doorway. He tossed his straw hat to the girl who caught it with a start and set it beside her. The light caught Jameson full on the face, emphasizing his shallow cheeks and sharp features, his long nose and cold blue eyes.

Jameson was very much unlike Hugo, who weighed four or five stone more. He was dark for an Englishman, and reputedly the ugliest man in the fleet. He had a nose which had already been broken twice and which reddened like an early flame at the tip.

"Any news off the American ship, mate?"

"None, Hugo. Do you mind if I sit down?"

The big man shook his head and pursed his lips, gesturing to the cushion beside the girl.

"Best ask her to leave," Jameson said.

"Eh? Sure. Get going, lass. Come on, come on."

The girl understood after a moment and fled on the toes of her feet as silently as she made love.

"There's a shore patrol here looking for you, Hugo."

"Aye, I figured they'd be along."

"Aye."

"And you haven't come to a good place to hide. You're too big. You stand out here."

"If we can keep the patrol from this house until the sailors from the Salem ship come along, you ought to be safe. I've

16

invited them all."

"That was good thinking, mate. I'm in your debt," Hugo said slowly, moving his huge hand to Cowley's knee to mark his friendship. Then Hugo stood up and moved to the window.

"It would be the rope sure, evil captain and a worse mate or not, no sight of land for eleven months and a back so scarred from the lash it ought to belong to one of your alligators. When is the next American vessel due, Jamie?"

"A week, perhaps less. This will be the one, too. I've a feeling."

"With the news you've been waiting for?"

"Yes."

"Well, I hope it's in your favor, mate, I really do. I wish you all the best in the world."

"Thank you, Hugo."

"And will you be going back on the next vessel if the news is good?"

"Yes."

"Then I go too," Hugo said adamantly.

"It would be a mistake."

Hugo came back to Cowley's side of the room and bent down to be on a level with him, saying, "How so, mate?"

"You English have nothing against stopping and searching a vessel from the colonies, though the war's been over and impressment's come to an end. You'd be safer traveling by other means!"

"There's a Dutchman that makes for Curacao," Hugo mused. "But it's an awful ship he runs, a slaver known on all the seas for losing half her cargo of blacks on near every voyage."

"A Dutch ship would be safer, Hugo."

"I'd like to travel with you, mate; you're a fine companion. think I'll risk the American vessel, if you've a mind to leave on her."

Hugo watched Cowley raise himself up from the cushions and walk to the door, his straw hat clasped in his hands and a distant look in his eye. Cowley stopped at the door and looked back.

"Does this Dutchman put in at New Orleans on his way to the Antilles?"

"Aye, that she does, Jamie."

Jameson shook his head and bent down to leave. "Dying slaves are nothing new to me, Hugo. If the news is right we'll both travel aboard the Dutch ship. How is she called?"

"The *Zeebaas*," Hugo said.

He watched Jameson leave the room and make back toward the stairs. There was a titter from below and then the American laughed. He was probably teasing or choosing a woman.

Hugo James' sea bag was stowed beneath the window. He went to it and bent over it to withdraw his brace of pistols and check their charges. There was no one who was going to bring him in while there was a breath of life in him, nor would he miss England if he never saw her again.

Voices below in the street attracted his attention and he stood up to take a careful look out the window. There was English being spoken and he cocked his pistols and chanced a look.

But it wasn't the patrol. The little Arab lad, Mustafa, who followed Jameson around had led a dozen Americans up through the Casbah and was depositing them on the doorstep of the pleasure house in the Street of the Gazelle. The tiny, curly haired boy had his palm outstretched and was pretending not to understand the sailors' reticence to pay him for his services. He repeated over and over again in Arabic what Hugo had come to recognize as meaning, "There is no God but God, and Mohammed is his only prophet."

Then the door below opened and Hugo heard Jameson's voice, saw the child reach into the air to pull down the dirham his friend had tossed and heard a shout from down the street. It was the Sultan's sergeant of arms from the palace grounds yelling, "*M*. Cowley, *M*. Cowley, another vessel arrives! *M*. Cowley, she is flying the colors of your free colony!"

4

The pregnant queen was being borne on a litter. They had left the camels behind at the edge of the red city, Marakesh, which the one who spoke a few words of her language had mentioned.

The robed men who had bought them from their captors, and who wore yellow slippers and white cloth beneath their white robes, rode horses while her people walked as they had walked across the great desert.

Of all of them only she was carried, for the one who spoke her language had told her that she was to receive careful care.

They bore her on a makeshift litter of thin wood that the sparse trees bore. Here there was little foliage and although there was no sand, it was more like the desert than like the veld below the land her people roamed. There was no sign of game for the bucks, and the birds were thin with long beaks and blacker than the birds like them in the jungles.

When they came to pass a forest it was not like any other. The trees were planted by design other than the design of the gods for they stood straight and in rows, and the trees themselves were too small and their fruit too small. It was the sweet green fruit they had been given to eat from which they crushed cooking water as the man had told her.

18

These were all things she would keep from her son when he was born. None of these were things a king would know.

The head man with the red hat rode with the young buck who had joined them in the end of the great desert. They spoke little, but that was better than it was with her people who no longer spoke at all.

Nor was this anything she would tell her son, that her husband, the king of kings had been killed by the Portuguese; that their village, the last village of her people, had been burned by the Portuguese; that he was, by his heritage, the warrior of warriors, brother to the lion, master to all the women of the tribe, seed of the gods of thunder, bearer by his actions of his people's fate, their chief in dance and song.

Nor would she tell him that on the journey across the great desert she had carried him without pain for her prayers to the thunder had put her in a state without pain, or of how food of her sisters had been shared so that he might be strong, or that she no longer felt even the weather between the weight of her breasts nor the heat of the eyes of any man upon her.

She would not reveal to him how his father and the high medicine would have run with him to the lair of the lion to capture a young cub to grow with him, to live as long as he lived in the taboo place, nor how his father and the high medicine would hurl his spear to the heart of the deer and the heart of the fish and the heart of the woman he chose in the dance. She would not tell him anything of how it was with her before the Portuguese, or after.

For the first time since the beginning of the long march away from their land the clouds came into the sky and blackened the face of the sun, as they should have done the first day they had seen the white Portuguese. The thunder spoke softly and she felt him kick; she closed her eyes to the sight of the foreign place.

The man who spoke her language rode near her litter. The other, the small one who took her youngest brothers for his bed in the night, rode with his firestick that imitated the thunder pointed like the spear at the brother who bore her and sometimes at the brother who bore her at the rear.

The head man with the red hat called and the man who spoke her language spurred his horse and went up to the front of the train. The small man with the firestick yawned and looked at the sky.

She felt herself fall, but felt no pain as she landed. The child kicked again and she knew it was all right. The two who bore her were racing as only the bucks from her tribe could race, the great runners of the black forest, toward the strange small trees three spear throws away.

The firestick of the small man shouted and her sisters began the chant to keep evil away from the king that was to be born.

The man who spoke her language reared his horse and she saw the great power of the horse in his muscles and watched him leap forward like the light when he came down.

Her brothers ran together tied to each other by a vine two spears in length. They were bound to the same speed as the horses went after them, as the great cats take after deer.

The firesticks shouted again and gray puffs like tiny clouds rose from them and the horses came closer to the running brothers as they came closer to the trees.

The others on horses rode round and round those who were close to her on the path and the chanting women spoke more loudly as they came closer, and the thunder spoke more loudly this time. The god of their thunder in a strange land with a muffled voice threatened the enemies of her people.

The man who spoke her language had ridden his horse between the brothers. He had caught the vine that bound them so that they were both hurled down upon their faces into the stream before the trees. Even from three spear throws distance she saw the red blood rush from her brother's face as first he and then the other rose. At the word of the mounted man they rushed back to the path as fast as they had fled from it.

The head man and the younger man hurled words at each other as the brothers arrived and lay at the feet of their animals, once brave bucks, now prostrate before the feet of animals. But nothing of this would she tell her son.

They were led by the small man with the firestick to the head of the train and tied closer; she was made to rise and come up so that she could tell her people who were at the rear of the train.

The thunder mourned in the high sky from which all the medicine had fled. The chant of her sisters rose but could not shut out the snapping sound of the whip as it tore the skin and raw bone of the brothers who had tried to escape. They fell together and rose together and the thunder shouted. The cries from their lips when the whip of the evil medicine descended to draw raw blood were not drowned by the cries of her sisters. She would not tell her son of any of this.

They had to cut one of her brothers loose from the other for the one whose head was covered with blood like the sacrificial boar at the festival of the hunt had died and the thunder mourned him. The sisters smote their breasts and chanted throughout the day and next night to keep the evil from him.

They marched the entire time until past the fall of the sun from the high sky on the blooded mud.

5

"Dear Jamie," the letter read. It was written in a fine

feminine hand on expensive paper.

"I have not told a soul of your whereabouts. As far as everyone in New Orleans and around Bayou Chien is concerned, you are still in England trying to settle your uncle's estate. Well, I am writing to tell you it is safe to come home at last, for there is no one left to account to. Your father has died.

"I can tell you Jamie that I feel very peculiar writing such a thing, for I know it is a relief more than a sorrow to you. I am not at all sure I wish to marry a man who is a prodigal and a scoundrel. Of course I know that as soon as I see you I will lose all reason and you will have your way with me and I suppose that I wish that that would happen soon. I miss you dearly and it is boring at the Willows without you.

"There is a new crop of rice and it has been sold already by Lawyer Mendes at a profit. The will was read and it was as we all expected. The land is yours so long as you care for Lou-Ellen and your father blesses our union, though you will be glad to hear it is not a condition of your inheritance. I would not want you to *have* to marry me.

> I miss you dearly,
> Love,
> Almira

"P.S. Give the sailor who bears this letter no more than a pound as I have already given him some money."

The noise of the party below drew Cowley's attention from the letter. He folded it and put it in its envelope for the fifteenth time, placed the envelope in the deep pocket of his white silk shirt, and played distractedly with the frills on his cuff.

Hugo's favorite Fatima came to the door and beckoned to him, saying, "You come." As usual she was dressed only in her veil and her hip skirt and she had a way with her hennaed eyes that made Cowley's temperature rise.

"In a minute," he said, smiling.

She did not leave but continued to lean against the entrance to his room, watching him. He had not touched her once because she was Hugo's favorite, but he had a mind to, if only to take his thoughts away from New Orleans.

He could not believe that his father was really dead, that it was at last safe to come home. He had squandered the small fortune his uncle had left the family and for fear of his father's wrath, had stayed abroad. He longed for home, for the plantation, for the chance to prove that he would not make the same mistake twice, that he could run a profitable, a model plantation, with happy, hard-working slaves and a full crop of rice.

"You come," Hugo's Arab girl said again, this time coming into the room and kneeling beside Jameson with a smile both sweet and mysterious playing on her young mouth. "There is surprise for you *en bas,*" she said.

He had half expected something. Since the crew off the *Israel Mather* was still in port—and it had been two weeks—and since they'd been joined by the mate and the boatswain off the ship that had brought his news, the *Virginia,* life on the Street of the Gazelles had been a constant celebration with Cowley at its center. Hugo had done nothing but talk about the way Jameson had saved him from the patrol and how his young friend's smile was proof enough that the colonies had been in the right all along. Cowley himself had added to his popularity as he had done since he left Louisiana by buying everyone in sight as much Arab wine and women as his pockets held money. He was on another splurge; there was no spending it at sea and he'd soon be back home with Almira and Lou-Ellen.

"You want me?" Fatima asked coyly. "I pull the curtain."

Cowley watched her face and reached up to take her chin in his hand. Her brown skin fascinated him and reminded him vaguely of the black girls back home. He ran his finger over the bones below her neck and then let his hand drop to circle her small breast. He watched his white fingers spread on the smooth surface of her light brown skin.

"Or, do you wish surprise?" she asked.

Hugo was a pal. The big cockney slob was dearer to him than anyone he'd known before. He asked nothing of him and admired him openly. His dazed, abstract mood in which he contemplated his imminent return to Louisiana was not unaffected by the knowledge that these fine friends, these wandering sailors and adventurers, would probably be lost to him forever. He was sentimental about Tangier. He liked these little Arab girls.

"What is it?" he asked as he began to squeeze her breast.

"Careful," she said. "You hurt me."

Cowley laughed and squeezed harder until she pulled away and stood up, then he laughed again.

"Come and see," she said hotly, and rushed out of the room.

Still chuckling, he got to his feet thinking that all women were pretty much the same and wondering what his friends had done for him. He came to the head of the stairs and listened carefully.

He heard Hugo-Jim, as he was now called by the Americans, talking loudly to the mate of the *Virginia*. Hugo was imitating crudely the accent and speech patterns of Captain Van Zachten the Dutch slaver who'd sold them their berths to Louisiana that afternoon.

"Und you dink dat it vill be ane goud cherney, yah? Vel

dis isn't ane pleasure schip, yah?"

Jameson laughed as he began to come downstairs carefully on those narrow Arab staircases built for small-footed women.

"Vel, all recht. Ven der blacks dey are loaded, ve sail."

The mate too had found it funny and was laughing uproariously. No doubt the wine helped. Jameson noted that there was as much on his shirt as in his glass as he came into the big room on the ground floor.

A cry went up and the boatswain off the *Virgina*, a small, wiry, almost albino white New Englander, rushed out yelling, "I'll bring the booty on deck, mates; hold him down."

Jameson suddenly found himself surrounded by the American sailors. Hugo-Jim had gone to help the New Englander, his ugly face broken by a drunken smile, a drop of spittle running down his stubbly chin.

Jameson was grabbed on both sides, lifted off his feet and thrown to the floor and a pile of cushions. He heard a piece of crockery break somewhere behind him.

He shouted and asked what was going on, but the men made no answer. Instead they laughed and yelled instructions to one another. He was being stripped, his breeches were coming off fast and his silks after them, leaving him in just his shirt and his shoes, exposed like a black in the fields.

"What the hell is going on here," he yelled at the top of his voice.

There was laughing around him and suddenly Hugo-Jim's booming voice imitating a trumpet fanfare, and then suddenly the men let go of him and stood aside.

Hugo-Jim was holding in mid air between his tremendous paws a screaming, bewildered nude, stunning black girl; he was yelling, "A virgin for you, Jamie, bought for ye by yer friends."

The men let out an uproarious cheer and the dazed slave caught sight of him and stopped squirming. His must have been the first white body she had ever seen unclothed.

"A virgin beast for ye, Jamie," Hugo-Jim yelled. He was bloody drunk as were all the others, only Jameson was sober, it seemed, Jameson and the black girl who was trying again to break away from Hugo-Jim's steel grasp, without success.

"And she be no more than fifteen, lad."

Another roar went up and the near-albino boatswain appeared out of nowhere with a full wine mug which Jameson, to prove he was a sport, sloshed down in one breath.

The black girl had been picked special by the boys: that was clear. Each time she tried to shake loose of Hugo-Jim her great breasts swayed temptingly like tropical gourds.

"Well, gather round then, boys," Jameson yelled. "Bring me my booty here."

2 : THE SLAVE SEAS

The *Zeebaas* was a three-masted vessel, built in 1760 in Amsterdam. She flew the Dutch colors, was under the captainship of Hans Van Zachten, and made the route to the Netherlands Western Antilles, Curacao, Bonaire and Aruba, off the coast of Venezuela, once every three months alternately from the Cape of Good Hope or the Port of Tangier. She was a slaver.

The blacks were stowed, each with enough room to lie comfortably, in the two lower decks and the three smaller aft compartments. Generally the women were stowed aft and the men and children below. Each slave was chained to two of his brethren and to the sea wall. The *Zeebaas* could thus accommodate nearly eight hundred blacks, and a greedy captain could manage one hundred more on the weather deck. Van Zachten, of course, was a greedy man.

Hugo-Jim watched the Dutch captain pace the bridge from the foot of the foremast where he was comfortable with his pipe, quite the passenger for a change, instead of sweating like a black, swabbing deck or hauling line, or risking his neck aloft like a monkey.

Since they'd left the coast of Africa over the distant horizon, Hugo-Jim had felt a new man. He was forever indebted to Jameson Cowley who, presently stowed below like a sack of salt, owing to a bad case of sea stomach, had all but saved his life on two occasions. Cowley had hidden him in with the Fatimas when the patrol had come looking and had then smuggled him aboard the *Zeebaas* with the help of the mate from the *Virginia*. They had gone out three nights previous when only the stars provided light over the medina and the voice of a drunken Arab was lifted in song against the dark. They had made their way out the rear gates of the city, down to the Atlantic coast and a waiting rowboat.

Hugo-Jim puffed cheerfully on his pipe, watching the fat captain stroll his bridge. He laughed to himself when he caught a few words of Dutch, for the language sounded to him like the language of savages, full of grunts and worse nasal sounds than the French tossed about.

It was a bright day and the sea was as calm as the bay of Tangier. A slight breeze gently pushed the sails stiff and kept the *Zeebaas* running true. The Captain seemed cheerful.

He was a ruddy man with a nose as bright throughout as Hugo-Jim's was at the tip. It was a round ball of a nose, great and porous, and certainly the object of jokes among the crew. His weight was over twenty stone, while he was only five foot five or six inches tall. His proud belly preceded him as he strode from starboard, listening to God's calm.

Behind him Hugo-Jim heard the rattling of a chain and felt suddenly bleak. His face contorted for a moment in a vicious frown and then found its normal composure again. The rattling of the chain had reminded him for a moment of the party for Jamie the night before they came aboard the *Zeebaas* and the black girl he and the crew of the *Virginia* had brought their friend. There were ruddy good prices for blacks in Tangier if a sailor could just scrape enough money together to go into business for himself.

It had been all right at first: Cowley enjoyed the girl and then retired with her. But later she had attacked him and he had to beat her down, hurting her badly. Then while she was bleeding and all but unconscious on the floor and Hugo-Jim was standing in the doorway telling him to take it easy with her, Jamie, from the drunken midst of a devil of a stupor, had raped her again. It had not been a pretty sight and Hugo-Jim blamed himself for it.

The friends hadn't spoken of it since it happened but the girl had been left behind at the house on the Street of the Gazelle, sold for room and board for both of them to the dirty Arab that ran the place.

Hugo-Jim had never had much to do with blacks. He'd thought it a fine idea when the mate of the *Virginia* proposed the idea of buying Jamie a virgin, but as he listened to the occasional rattle of chains from the poor bastards stowed on the weather deck, he wasn't sure he liked any of it. Of course this was the messy end of the business. The buggers could be safe and happy once they'd been bought in the new world.

The English frowned on slavery, but they didn't do anything about it and he didn't see why they should. There was talk on the fleet that the high courts were considering cases protesting that slavery was piracy; but that was clearly absurd.

A dolphin leaped from the water at the bow and cleared the starboard side for a moment where the water was closest to the rail. Hugo-Jim smiled and drew on his pipe. This was the life! To have a good friend who paid your passage and promised you a future in a new country, away from mad sea captains and the biting lash of his sadistic mate. Nor was it a one-way bargain: he had plenty to watch out for Jamie's sake. He had to keep him out of trouble, look to him when he was drunk, discourage his excesses with women and blacks before he got into trouble. Of course Jamie was a lad away from home who would calm down right enough as soon as he got back where he belonged. When that had happened, he'd just been sowing his wild oats. Hugo-Jim would leave him and move on.

The dolphin and several of his friends jumped again and Hugo-Jim found his pipe had gone out. He stood up and spread his legs to keep his balance on the deck. The wind in the topsails had picked up and in the distance ahead the water had changed color, indicating a swell. He laughed aloud as he considered what would happen to his friend's stomach if they hit any real weather. So far it had been like a ferry crossing in a picture book.

He walked forward and nodded to the mate who nodded in return. The mate said the Dutch word for hello which sounded to Hugo like the spitting of a horse.

"Dag yourself mate," he answered back.

The mate was a thin blond man, about thirty-five, with very thin features and brown eyes wrinkled at the corners as they should be from staring at the sun.

"You find it a funny tongue, Dutch, eh?"

"Aye, but your English is good, mate," Hugo-Jim said with good cheer.

"Learned it in school," the mate replied.

Hugo-Jim nodded and looked over at the captain, nodded again this time at the chief officer and asked the mate, "He don't mind if I stay up on the bridge, do he?"

"No, I don't think so," the mate replied. "He's taken your passage money; make yourself at ease."

Hugo-Jim moved off and stood behind the man at the wheel for a moment, but he began to feel restless as a result. He had piloted many a sea under the ferocious captain from whom he had finally run when the *Good Bess* last moored in Gibraltar.

The swell was coming in sure so Hugo-Jim turned his mind dutifully toward his friend, nodded both at the mate and at the captain, and turned to go below. It would be best to have a little talk with Jamie about seasickness. He'd have to get the lad to eat something, and then to work until his stomach quieted.

He walked slowly midships packing a new pipe and watching the sky. The white gulls were still with them, circling over the stern and occasionally lighting on the stays, squawking and then taking off to ride the updrafts and glide down. Sometimes the birds stayed with them clear across, though it was a popular myth that they never left the sight of land.

He stepped into the forward compartment where it was dark, cooler than it had been on deck, and lowered himself down the stairs to the crew's quarters where he shared a cabin with Jamie. He was just about to open the door when he heard it. It was coming from aft, from the hold where they'd stowed the female blacks and it sounded mournful and vicious. It was a low murmured chant and it put the fear of

26

God in Hugo-Jim's soul.

Jamie came to the door and opened it, and found Hugo-Jim standing there sucking on his pipe, bent as if to knock but frozen silly, looking aft.

"What is it?" Jamie asked. "What the hell those niggers doin' back here?"

Hugo-Jim just shook his head a few times and then shrugged. "Listen, there's something I want to speak to you about," he muttered to Cowley. "I think you'd be better off to get out of that sleeping gown and come on deck."

"What are those niggers chanting about?" his friend persisted.

2

After Hassim Marakeshi had delivered them to the Dutchman and they had been mixed with the other groups, it had seemed for a long time that they would become separated from Iwana, the Queen, who was about to give birth. Then they had been put together, all of them, along with many of the others, in a closed space on the water. There were only the women, for all the bucks had been put elsewhere in the great ship—but there were also the women from the other tribes.

They could not understand one another, but the Moor, the man who had driven his horse after the bucks who had run and who had brought them back to be whipped and killed, the man who spoke their language, also spoke the language of the women of the other tribes.

He had spoken with them a long time, explaining things. She did not understand that man, for all the others who had come in with the women had made the fertility rite with them, trying to put them with child. But the big man of their own color who spoke their language had not tried. Iwana had said he could not even if he wished it, but she did not understand that either.

All that she understood of all that had happened was that everything was changed and she was afraid. She had one duty left, to help with the birth of the child, for if he was to be a boy he would be holy. It would be worse than death not to do her part in the chant and the dance that was to follow. Still, she feared the time when the baby was to come, for it would not last long and then there would be nothing left to think about. After that there would be only the rocking movement of the great ship and the closed room in which they had to lie flat.

So far she had been lucky, for she had been allowed to remain with her queen and her sisters. One of her tribe, a young girl of fifteen summers, had been cut out from them

27

and given to the large man of white skin by the head-man, and another, the strongest of their brothers, had also been sold.

The Moor had told them that he had been sold to the chief of all Allah's chosen, the high Sultan, and that they should all be proud. But she did not believe him, nor in his Sultan.

She lay against the sea wall under the square hole through which the light came in dazzling streams to fall in the center of the hold, as it sometimes came through a clearing amid the trees to illuminate the grass or the shrubbery in the forest. She lay there and kept up the slow chant for the high queen who had begun her labor.

She had not seen Iwana's face lose its high strength in all the time they had walked, or even in the time she had been carried between the great desert and the red city, but as she watched her queen other marks of the beginning of the birth were on her. Iwana was in a sweat and her breath came to her infrequently. She was staring at the low ceiling of the wooden hold and every half hour her eyes would light with the pain.

When they had been chanting for a few minutes the yellow haired officer came in and looked carefully about him. He watched her especially as she was near Iwana and therefore in the center of things, for the eyes of all the women were on Iwana.

She knew she was good to look on. She was at the height of her youth, and had been mated with a son of the chief's brother, so that she was family to Iwana. Her full breasts showed her pride and, like Iwana, her body had been made by the high medicine for the fertility.

She felt the heat behind the officer's eyes as he watched her and then he went away.

The one with yellow hair came back later, when Iwana was resting and the spirit of the chant was low. With him came the short, fat man, the chief with the strange hat who glared at them and shouted and then smiled a fiend's smile when he was near her. He said something to the one with yellow hair and laughed; the other laughed with him.

Iwana awoke and the chanting increased, and the fat one shouted from under his red nose which was a nose unlike any she had seen among her people, or among the Portuguese or Arabs. But the chant did not stop. No chief could command the high medicine and the high medicine proclaimed that the chant must continue until the male child screamed in the first light. The evil must be kept away from him in the day of his birth or the fate of the tribe would be evil.

The chief with the red nose spat beside him and strode to the center of the hold, glaring at Iwana. He raised back his foot to kick her stomach and the chanting raised to a furious pitch. The one with the yellow hair shouted and the chief stopped. He spat again and this time the white phlegm came to Iwana's belly and ran down the curved mound that held her child. The chanting stopped and behind her one of her sisters sobbed.

The chief came to her and bent down and put his hand between her thighs, laughing. The one with the yellow hair spoke. She looked at him as he pinched her flesh and touched her hair and probed with thick hairy fingers, ugly as the evil medicine in their whiteness, a whiteness tinged with the red of blood, like his nose, and then she looked away as he laughed again.

His voice when it came was like gravel but she could not understand the words and when she looked again his eyes did not hold the heat of the young yellow one's, but something else that she had never seen before.

He began to rise and she saw it was difficult for him because he was so heavy. They stood at the end of the hold and looked back, not at her but at Iwana, and then they went out, closing the light out with the door.

In the forest, the bucks who had made the fertility rite with her had placed there not their fingers but the sacred parts of the oldest dead, so that she would not bear out of turn. And when she had been mated at the dance with the son of the chief's brother, the women had come to her in her hut with the fishes' mouth and the sacred parts of the old chief. They had placed the fishes' mouth there and opened its jaws and pushed through it the sacred parts so that she would bear. Then her buck had lain with her but she had not borne.

What the white chief had done was not like that. It had given her no pleasure. She had no thoughts to pleasure, not even to food which came first. She had no thought to food nor even to dance, which came first, but only to the new king and the chant and the prayer that there be no evil while he was coming into his first day.

When the white chief had gone and the yellow with him, and the thought of his color and his hairy fingers had left her flesh, she turned once again to Iwana and leaned toward her to remove with her palm the spittle the evil white chief had cast upon their king. She removed it entirely and smiled at Iwana. All about her sisters began again the chant of the high medicine.

The fervor of the chant increased and this time no whites came to them to stop them. The pains came faster to Iwana. She knew because she too could feel them, as could each woman in the compartment, and then, from the depths of the great vessel, from some place below them, she heard the others also chanting.

It began to become dark and the great ship was thrown

harder upon the water.

"Do as you're told, Jamie; you have no knowledge of the sea."

Jameson Cowley watched his big friend and tried to say something but stopped halfway there for fear of retching in the lap of the cockney idiot.

Then he summoned his courage and said, "I can't Hugo. I can't be expected to eat in this condition."

"It might be best to force feed him. There's a blow coming down from the north," the mate said in almost accentless English.

"Dammit. Just leave off!" Jameson barked.

"Jamie boy, if you don't eat you'll pay hell just as sure as you feel evil as sin now."

It was not just his stomach, but his head as well. It had proceeded to get worse and worse since the damn noise from the nigger holds had started. He cursed the officers under his breath for letting them scream and howl. If it were his ship he would throw a few overboard for a lesson.

"Eat Jamie," Hugo-Jim prodded.

The crossing to England had not been as bad. Perhaps he had become soft while living high on his uncle's legacy. His stomach felt as though it held ten gallons of bile. He raised a forkful of salt pork to his lips and stuck it in his mouth in a rush.

They were at mess in the officer's quarters. The captain had decided to eat alone. There was only the blond mate who spoke English and the blond one who didn't. The latter looked as evil a son of a bitch as he had ever seen. Jamie wished to God he'd left Hugo-Jim to the British and sailed a decent American vessel.

"It'll be a bad night, Mr. Cowley, but the worst will probably be over by morning," the mate said.

"Aye," Hugo-Jim agreed and Jameson watched as the big idiot shoved a huge hunk of brown meat into his oversized jaw and began to chomp on it like it was fish fry time on the Bayou.

Every time the sea let up for a few minutes and the noise of the wind and the waves abated, the sound of the niggers chanting in the aft hold washed forward. He wished to God the trip was over.

"And if you'd let me walk you a bit around the deck when you've swallowed some food," Hugo began with his mouth full, "you'd probably feel good enough to sleep."

Jameson groaned. The ship heeled again and pitched, and the kerosene lamp swung violently from the ceiling as water spilled out of the big pitcher on the table. The evil mate laughed with his mouth wide open enough to see all his bad teeth. The lines, like a jackal's, around his jaw deepened and his black eyes sparkled.

"What'd 'e say mate?" Hugo-Jim asked the other Dutchman.

"He said your friend ought to be glad he isn't tied on deck like one of the blacks, or stuck in the hold on his ass. In the one case he'd drown and in the other he'd lie in his own puke til morning."

Jameson groaned and watched Hugo-Jim keep chewing with his mouth open like an ignorant savage.

"How is it the old man isn't eating with us tonight?" Hugo-Jim asked.

The chanting seemed to pick up in intensity, although it might easily have been a trick of his head. He felt a pain behind his right eye that drove him near to distraction. He forced down another mouthful as the ship righted itself for a moment and then heeled again. On deck he heard an order being shouted in Dutch.

"They're rigging for worse weather," the mate stated without stopping his meal for a moment. "That was the captain telling them to rig the foretop sail. We'll just ride this out I expect; no point getting blown to Cape Hatteras."

Jameson groaned inwardly again; he bit on his lip and swallowed the disgusting mouth full of sea fare. He watched the bowl of bananas that was rocking in the middle of the table and swallowed again.

"Shove it down, mate, shove it down," Hugo-Jim advised.

"Captain Van Zachten often prefers to dine alone," the Dutchman explained. "He's a lone man. I wouldn't be taking offense at it if I were you."

"Oh no offense, no offense," Jameson managed to say. "Weather like this, surprised he dines at all."

The evil-looking mate began to skin a banana with glee, smiling blackly as he watched Jameson watch the fruit come naked.

"There's a good market for blacks in Williamstaad?" Hugo-Jim asked.

"Aye, friend. But a better one in New Orleans. These below are headed for Curacao only because our owners have a contract with the nationals there. There's more money now in your friend's country."

"And the naked buggers on deck?" Hugo-Jim asked.

The mate just raised his brows and smiled. So that was why Van Zachten put in in Louisiana. The owners of the *Zeebaas* probably had no idea that their Captain carried an extra hundred blacks on each run.

"Have another piece of meat," Hugo-Jim suggested,

slapping Jameson on the back with his bear paw.

Jameson shook his head.

"Banana?"

He shook his head again.

"All right laddie, come on. Twice or three times around the weather deck and you'll feel a new man."

Hugo-Jim rose and waited for Jameson who struggled to his feet. It was a wonder the English bastard could keep his balance at all aboard the heeled vessel but he stood steady as a colossus in the small cabin.

"Come along," he repeated.

Jameson let Hugo-Jim take his arm as they came outside. The door flew open and a wet wind washed his face and left the sting of salt.

"It's probably impossible on deck," Jameson shouted. "Here's good enough."

"Up you go," Hugo-Jim shouted.

He was unable to argue. He climbed the ladder and stuck his head into the night.

He felt immediately relieved. He found his balance and held on and felt the wet wind. He took a deep breath but nearly gagged as the bile rose in his stomach.

"Best to keep it down," Hugo-Jim suggested.

He nodded, and they began to make for the bridge.

"Only go as far as the ladder. Don't want to lose you to the deep," Hugo-Jim shouted.

The seas were high, higher than they had been when he'd come the other way, but he knew they were nothing new for his friend. They walked toward the bow and the ladder to the bridge and the foremast. All but the forestaysail had been lowered as the ship had been rigged for the storm.

There was a light in the captain's cabin and Jameson glimpsed a view of the man bent over an empty plate when the ship rocked. He seemed immobile in there, evil in the crude yellow light of the kerosene lamp.

"Back now," Jameson said.

They turned from the ladder and the outside door of the captain's cabin, and for a moment Jameson thought he was lost, for the ship hove and he slipped. But Hugo-Jim had firm footing and held him fast.

As they made their way midships again he heard the chant from aft. He saw faces of the blacks who were tied fast to the rail along the weather deck. They were all young bucks. Van Zachten had chanced exposing only the heartiest.

Jameson nearly retched again but caught himself. The sea rose and threw him to his feet and Hugo-Jim stooped again to help him.

As he rose on the man's arm he stared long and hard at a black nigger who was watching him hatefully from the rail.

the man's curly short hair was soaking wet from the sea. His only garment was useless and outlined his body as if he were buck naked, and his thick lips were pressed firmly in hatred. The negro's eyes flamed toward Jameson, who looked quickly around at the other blacks, most of whom were huddled and shaking with fright.

"Can't," was all Jameson had a chance to say to his friend as he made for the heeled rail and threw his dinner into the sea. Hugo-Jim held him steady and the sound of the chanting rose like a curse around him.

4

Captain Van Zachten pushed himself up from his table and went to the porthole. The seas were heavy but the *Zeebaas* had been through heavy seas before and would again. He looked out over the weather deck and frowned. Some of the blacks were shivering with fright. If they weren't careful, they'd drown in their own tears.

He went through his cabin into the chart room and stared bleakly at the lines he had drawn that noon. Soon it would be time to step out on deck again with the sextant and take a reading—assuming there were stars enough in that black sky to give him one.

The kerosene lantern rocked and cast an uneven light about him, throwing his face first into shadow and then into a yellow pallor, emphasizing the lines which separated his several chins. He spit at the spittoon near the chart table and missed, heard someone at the door and turned to shout, "Come in."

The steward entered and lifted the tray from the table. A rush of wet wind came in with him.

"Send the first mate," Van Zachten barked after the man as he left.

"Aye, sir."

He had a hell of a crew. Every man of them was wanted, and every man of them capable of murder or worse. Soon he would retire from the seas. Soon he might have to.

In a little while the mate came.

"How are the passengers?" Van Zachten asked when the other had closed the cabin door and stood dripping beneath the lamp.

"The thin one is sick from the weather. The other is as hearty as you or I."

Van Zachten grunted. "The thin one looks rich. When the seas are calm I must speak with him; you will listen in case my English fails."

"Aye, aye, sir."

"He owns property near New Orleans."

"Aye, sir."

"Do you know New Orleans, Carl?"

"We've put in there twice now, sir."

"Aye. A healthy port. And good land for privacy and plantations. That new nation is a fine refuge for men who—"

"Who have reason to seek refuge, sir?"

Van Zachten grunted and turned to the porthole again. The ship was firm under the one foresail. There was no reason to chance more sheet.

"How are the blacks?"

"They are secure," the mate answered. It was the young mate, the nicer one. The other, the thin one, made Van Zachten ill at ease at times. He always seemed to be laughing behind his jackal jaws.

"Shall we break out the rum, Carl?" Van Zachten joked. He spit once more, this time hitting the spittoon dead center.

"Aye, sir."

Van Zachten brought two mugs and poured the heavy liquor from a jug. He recorked it and said, "It's on nights such as these that the sea makes me restless."

He watched Carl empty his glass and smiled at him a long time before saying, "Carl. Go below."

"Aye, sir."

"The nigger wench near the pregnant bitch."

"Aye, sir."

"Bring her to me."

Carl returned his glass and then turned to make for the door. At times Van Zachten hated him. He was high birth, too good to work on a slaver, the sort of man that might talk to the owners.

"Bring her to me."

"Aye, sir."

"You know the one."

The lad went out and Van Zachten finished his rum. It warmed him well and brought a content smile to his lips. He spit again and missed again.

He had finished two more rums before he heard the knock on the door. He called and the mate opened it and brought the wench in. Her hair was short, down about her ears. She had probably worn it close to the scalp back in the jungle.

"How are things down there?" Van Zachten asked.

"They're still at it, sir, louder than ever. Has something to do with the pregnant one, I figure."

"Has it?" Van Zachten snorted. "Of course it does, you fool. Check the deck again. Now get out."

The mate left hurriedly and Van Zachten examined the girl. She was young and firm. Her skin was black as coke. He pinched her and looked at his fingers. It was to show her color would not come off. It was a joke he always used. He poured more rum and handed her the mug, but she refused it.

Instead she sat down at the table in the corner below the porthole and pressed against the wall in fright. He watched her and smiled.

Ripe. Prime young black flesh. She was no virgin either. He'd checked on that. He didn't break cherries when they were worth so much in New Orleans. They weren't any good anyway.

He approached the girl, still forcing the mug on her, and she finally took it. She held it in both her hands and sniffed at it then handed it back. He thrust it at her again and she drank from it reluctantly and then spit.

Van Zachten laughed. He threw the mug away and grasped her lip between his fingers. It was a thick lip, moist and red. There were good teeth behind it and he kept his fingers around it, daring her to use them on him. She didn't take the dare and he laughed again.

He turned and opened a seachest, and withdrew a loaf of bread which he handed to her. She sniffed it and then ate it greedily. It was better stuff than they got in the hold.

When she'd finished eating the whole loaf he replaced the mug from which he'd been drinking on its shelf and approached her again. Her eyes were like the eyes of an animal. They were black and they darted from his face to his stomach and back to his face. From the aft compartment he could sometimes catch snatches of the continuing chant of her wretched tribe.

She didn't resist when he came up to her and took hold of one of her breasts, squeezing it hard. Then there was a sudden banging on the door and he sprang to it and hurled it open.

"What in God's name is it?" he shouted into the face of the mate who was standing in the weather.

"Sorry, sir," Carl said. "One of the blacks broke loose with the help of the sea and is either on board or has been tossed over the side."

"Well, he hasn't sprouted wings and flown off like an angel, eh?" Van Zachten screamed at the young man. "Search the ship and don't bother me again." Van Zachten flung the door to, bolted it and approached the black once again.

He very nearly made a bad mistake. While his attention had been averted the girl had found a crude table knife and had hidden it behind her back. She was standing as Van Zachten approached and made at him, raising it ferociously above her head.

He caught it with a quick motion in midair and forced it out of her hand by twisting her wrist viciously, then he spun her about, yelling foul Dutch at her, throwing her half over his table so that the jug of wine which had been sitting on it was knocked over and fell to the floor. It broke and spilled its contents over the cabin.

He reached above him quickly, grasping the line he kept on the wall, and tied her so quickly it betrayed practice. He kept her bent over the table by holding her down by her firm shoulders. She was bent so completely over the table, and her hands were of so little use to her lashed to her sides, that her mouth was forced open against the wood.

She had a hearty rump and Van Zachten laughed as he stripped her of her only garment. He knew her breasts, forced against the table by his powerful arms, were hurting her, still it took him several minutes to make her complain and even longer to make her scream. When the wind and the sea were quiet he could scarcely hear the continuous chanting from the aft compartments.

5

Jameson heard the screams when he came on deck to relieve himself again. He thought he had heard them before, in his sleep, but he wasn't certain. The evil looking mate was standing watch on the bridge and the pilot was an old man with a healthy shock of white hair. The sea had quieted and the stars and moon lit the deck with a pale glow. From the aft compartments the steady chanting continued, but it was hushed and the phrases of the ritual were being uttered more slowly.

As he climbed the ladder to the bridge he chanced to see into the captain's cabin. Through the yellow porthole Jameson made out the prostrate form of a young black woman whose back had been severely lashed. He stood with his mouth open for a moment and then rushed ahead to the deck.

"Hello," he said to the mate and his voice broke. He chastised himself for being weak-kneed, but forgave himself as readily because of his recent illness. Only since his last trip to the rail had he felt human again.

The mate nodded to him and moved off. Neither spoke enough of the other's language to make conversation possible.

The screaming started again. Jameson worried that it was his tread above the captain's roof that might distract Van Zachten's attention and he was frightened.

The ship was rigged for better weather and lesser winds and heeled only slightly to starboard as she proceeded on her reach. The pilot kept his head and eyes straight forward and never once faltered while Jameson watched him.

After a few moments he again heard movement in the cabin below, and a long, plaintive wail, then nothing.

He thought he heard the captain's hammock creak, but it might have been any of the old beams in the fine ship. He felt peaceful and did not deliberate long on the goings-on

36

beneath him. There were plenty of men he had known in his youth who had mistreated their slaves. They were frequently men whom he had come to respect.

The ship plied steadily eastward. At the sound of the bell beaten four times the other mate came silent on deck, as the night itself, and whispered something to his comrade. The latter shook his head and went below.

"Hello, Mr. Cowley," the mate said.

"Hello. You've a dour face tonight, man," Jameson answered.

The mate looked at Jameson but said nothing. He moved off toward the rail and stood framed by the darkness behind him. There would be first light soon. Jameson hadn't been awake to see the dawn since his days on the plantation. His father, who had managed to live and to thrive in the Louisiana territory under the French, had been a stern man. Everyone in the Cowley household was up at dawn in the old days.

Jameson clasped his hands behind him and began to pace the bridge. It felt good to keep moving and he hoped to work up an appetite for breakfast. Of course Hugo-Jim was right; he had to keep something in his stomach.

Below him he heard the black girl complain softly. The sounds carried too well on the sea at night for any of it to be lost. The captain was apparently roused again. Behind him he heard the mate called Carl spit meanly. He turned to look at the young Dutchman but kept his face stern. He wasn't sure how he felt about what was going on three feet beneath him. Niggers were property and right now they were Captain Van Zachten's property. He had a right to treat them any way he damn well pleased. The feelings of compassion the captain's conduct touched off in Jameson he was able to dismiss by thinking of it as foppish sentimentality, unmanly and un-desirable.

Gradually it began to get lighter. Jameson strolled to the ladder and looked out over the deck. The blacks were quiet. He looked for the spot where he had stood at the rail when he had been sick the night before and found it. But the place was vacant, the black who had been tied there was no longer there. Jameson turned to seek the mate.

"Mr. Leeun," he called.

"Aye, Mr. Cowley."

"There's a black missing from the deck."

"Aye, sir," Carl explained. "We know that, sir. Afraid he was washed overboard during the storm."

Leeun held Jameson's eye as he pronounced his English words coldly, emphasizing, perhaps in subtle sarcasm, their lack of passion.

"Mightn't he be hiding on the ship?" Jameson queried. "He

37

was a tough-looking one."

"You remember him?"

"Yes, sir, I do," Jameson proclaimed.

"Aye, he might be hiding, but I doubt it. A party searched the deck last night and checked the holds. When it's a bit lighter we'll look again."

Saying that, the mate moved off and scanned the horizon blankly. It was becoming just light enough to make it out. Below him he heard the captain grunt and then sigh deeply.

Suddenly there was a resounding crash below. Jameson turned to look at the mate who stared back. Neither moved for fear of disturbing the captain below unwarrantedly, but waited for some further sign that something was wrong.

The sign came soon enough. Something in the cabin beneath them had been thrown over and Van Zachten was cursing. Jameson saw the mate hesitate, read something in his eyes which he could not and then ran for the rail, leapt over it and down from the bridge the ten feet to the weather deck. He righted himself and rushed for the captain's cabin. The door had been battered down. The huge black buck who had freed himself of his chains had smashed it in the one blow that had alerted him above. Now the buck had his huge black hands around Van Zachten's throat and was strangling the life out of the naked fat man.

Jameson rushed into the cabin and made for the black. Above him he could just hear the mate begin to descend to the weather deck and there was a call by the pilot for aid. The buck turned as Jameson entered, kept his hands on the captain's throat and smashed Jameson in the midsection with his elbow.

The negro was moving Van Zachten around as though he carried only one-third or one-quarter what he weighed. Jameson lost his wind and was thrown back against the captain's hammock. He righted himself quickly.

Van Zachten's eyes were popping. The black's forehead was beaded with sweat and his thick dark lips were forced ferociously against his white teeth. Heavy chains dangled from his wrists. He was within an inch of snuffing out the captain's life.

Meanwhile the girl had been thrown to the floor where she lay watching the attack. Her hands were bound behind her back with a length of line and she was naked and bleeding from several places. She looked more dazed than frightened.

Jameson found his wind and grabbed an empty rum jug from beside the captain's hammock. He raised it over his head and rushed forward again. He saw the captain's eyes watching him, and then the big buck's stared down at him with the same strength and ferocity that he had seen the night before when he had been sick. He heard the captain gargle and watched the buck decide, too late, to release his hands from the Dutchman's throat in order to protect himself from the descending jug. It broke in a thousand places over his head and drew a long line of blood from the black man's scalp.

Jameson had saved the captain's life and won for himself another friend.

6

The *Zeebaas* made use of a morning wind from the north east to proceed due west on a broad reach. The sun had been in the sky for over two hours and at last the chanting from the aft compartment had stopped. Captain Van Zachten, with a white silk scarf tied around his throat, paced the bridge steadily, his eyes fixed dead ahead.

On the weather deck, hands were at their positions among the negro slaves ready to change sail. The two mates held prisoner the buck who had escaped during the night's storm and who had hidden in the shadow of the bridge. The ravaged girl had been returned to the aft compartment where she lay panting and in pain next to Iwana. Hugo-Jim and the young Louisianan were far aft among the waiting crew.

The crossing from Tangier to New Orleans was always made south of the Azores so that only in the worst months of February and March was the Atlantic less than pleasant. The sun was already strong enough to give a hint of a blistering day and the sea seemed unconscious in its calm mien of the pall which had settled on the ship.

Once before in the year previous, the year of our Lord eighteen hundred and nineteen, Captain Van Zachten had been forced to punish his charges severely by whipping and then throwing overboard a half dozen blacks who had tried to kill the second mate. That had been done in full view of five blacks from each hold and compartment, as a lesson to them to resist any rebelliousness, either of want or of fear, which stirred in their breasts.

Captain Van Zachten came to the edge of the bridge and, grasping the rail, shouted the order to the first mate to bring a representative number of slaves to the weather deck again. He shouted an after thought, naming the pregnant queen in the top aft compartment specifically. He thought she would have the most influences among her fellow slaves.

The quiet seas whispered along the flanks of the vessel. Hugo-Jim pulled thoughtfully at his pipe as the minutes passed and Jameson stood determinedly staring at the spar of the main mast from which the rope had been hung. In an aft compartment an old woman comforted the ravished girl and, apparently having released a demon of talk by her long chanting, was giving further release to it, explaining in a hoarse voice the fate of their people. She spoke slowly, as if it were all part of a script, something she had said many times before and knew by heart, but of course she had never said nor thought it before.

"When the first dawning day of the new king whom Iwana has refused to name and shall refuse to name any of the names of his fathers the kings for he is in a servitude beneath those names, nor any other name befitting a king, when that first day begins with the rape and torture of one of his sisters, no, when the birth of the day is timed with his birth and both times proceeded from that pain, no amount of high chanting will help. We are lost, we are now a lost people. And he is lost."

The old woman shook her head several times and watched the naked child, still slick from his mother's belly, for there had been nothing with which to wash him. He was lying against his mother's breast, breathing softly. She turned to the queen and wailed, "Oh, Iwana, Queen to the high medicine!"

The girl shuddered as the old woman's hand came down on her shredded back and she heard the old woman begin again, first the chant of the healing and then the new words which sounded as if they too had come down from old or from high.

"And what will they do with your husband who tried to save you, with the brother of the king who is still alive, whose breathing I can even now hear on deck, and when will they do what they will do. They must wait for the second day of the child's life or that too shall affect the fate of us all, and our fate shall be in revenge and he with no name shall revenge, and our people will be revenged."

Iwana rose and the old woman hushed. The queen stared straight at her, holding the king at her breast, having found in the ordeal of the trek across the desert and the birth in the great ship a strength beyond even that strength the queens are expected to have and Iwana said, "No. The child will never know any of this."

In the back of the hold one of the women sighed deeply and began again as if she did not know the child had come, the high chant which must precede its birth.

The door was cast open and a pale glow of the light of the early morning entered with the one with the yellow hair who had yesterday come for the girl who lay broken beneath the old one's touch.

He strode into the center of the hold, extended his arm for Iwana and moved his head meaning that she should rise. Then he bent to help her and she let him. The old woman collected spittle in her mouth for when he would leave.

He bent and released Iwana's chains and led her from the compartment to the deck where the old woman knew the brother of the old king, the one who had failed to kill the white chief, was kept.

"Look!" Hugo-Jim said. "Look what the hell that damn fool is doing."

Jameson looked forward and saw the mate lead a number of savages up to the weather deck. Among them was a woman fresh from childbirth, with stains of the afterbirth still on her thighs, and holding to her breast a naked child.

"Damn fool!" Hugo-Jim said and spat over the rail into the weather.

On the bridge, Captain Van Zachten waited until all hands were silent. Then he motioned to the mate with the jackal jaws. He pulled the rebellious savage toward the main mast and the waiting spar. The man who had been their pilot during the storm, the old man with the white hair, fitted the thick line around the buck's neck. Jameson agreed in silence. An example had to be made, and justice would have to be swift.

The mate gave orders to the seaman closest to him. They grasped their end of the line and pulled at it until it was just taut. The great main mast creaked beneath the weight of the morning breeze and the spar tightened slightly as the sails bent. The Captain murmured something to the pilot who kept the wheel steady as he nodded in response.

Then, as Van Zachten gave the order, the three seamen hove to on the line, lifting the buck by his neck halfway between the deck and the spar. The old woman in the aft compartment felt the life go out of her son and groaned. The others about her took up the chant from fear instead of purpose. The ravaged girl shuddered under the fresh wave of pain across her lashed back and the new king, the child to Iwana and the high medicine, cried hysterically into the morning sea air.

3 : THE CARIBBEAN

Iwana came to the door of the mud hut and looked out. Up the slope, beyond the double row of giant prickly pear cactus, the dull orange house of the master was lit in the first, even light of day. It stood boldly, its peaked façade mirrored by two peaked side façades. The bold front portico, upper balcony and short, squat balustrade gave it a look of substance. To the right and left were two fortified out-buildings made of the same orange clay. A mad cock behind Iwana's hut crowed on despite the late hour.

For sixteen years, Iwana had lived in the same mud hut near the great house with a succession of men, bearing and rearing their children and helping in the master's kitchen. Since her first born had reached his tenth birthday, she had also become the teacher of the slave children, for she had been among the first to learn the language of the whites.

The first slaves in that part of the world had been from unruly southern tribes, mostly from the Gold Coast and from the deep jungles above the Cape of 'Good Hope to the west. They had made good workers but had to be treated severely, were a constant threat and never learned anything of their masters' ways. They died young and their progeny, often mixed with the weak blood of the indigenous Indians, were usually slow-witted to the point of stupidity.

One of these halfbreed blacks, a tall, lanky, brown-black man with long, thick hair and a stoop like a flamingo, named Piepie, had absorbed something of the white religion, and, with the master's permission, preached to the other slaves in a mud church at the base of the wall each Sunday morning.

The wall was a miracle of industry, although Iwana never thought of it as such. It stretched for over eighty miles, running around pastures, slave villages and Indian towns, so that the island, if seen like a bird from above, would appear to contain a labyrinth of chaotic design.

The wall, which had been completed a generation before Iwana came to the island, had been built entirely by the Gold Coast and Cape slaves and was meant to keep the goats and poultry away from the gardens and small farmed areas and away from the houses of the masters.

Iwana looked from the main house to the wall and followed it along the road which it separated from the slave compound of the Opzeelands, her masters, looking for Piepie, the tall preacher. Chane had, of late, taken to spending much of his time with Piepie and Iwana wished a discussion with the halfbreed.

Chane was becoming insolent. A fire burned in his loins which no amount of covering the young slave girls seemed to extinguish. It had been an evil day when he'd been born and an evil day when he was sent to work in the great house. Iwana wished to speak to Piepie of the high medicine which she had not mentioned to anyone since the day of Chane's birth, when her husband's brother had been stretched by the neck from the low spar of the great mast of the great ship.

Iwana spoke little. Piepie would immediately understand that she had something important of which to speak with him, for she never wasted words. She had never explained why she had named the child Chane, nor why the burden she carried seemed to everyone to be so much heavier than the burdens of her fellows. She kept silent, moved silently, kept her face cool and expressionless and taught the children to speak Dutch so they might understand their masters directly.

The rooster began to crow again, and Iwana, able to see neither Piepie nor Chane, turned and went back inside the hut.

On a straw mat beside the cooking hole the child slept easily. He was still only two and had not yet to work in the salt flats or in the great house. She wished silently that the high medicine would help her keep him out of the flats, where Chane was about to begin for the first time.

He was a strong baby, called Hanny by her friends and by his father, so much stronger than Chane had been when he had been born. But, she had been weak then, and her milk had barely sustained him until the Opzeelands bought her and saw to it her child was well cared for. Chane had grown into so powerful a boy, however, that Iwana had learned not to put too much emphasis on an infant's appearance in its first months. Chane's blood showed clearly. He was like a prince who, until that day, had roamed the island like a free man. No good would come of it.

Iwana bent beside the child and touched it lightly with two extended fingers of her right hand on the center of its forehead, chanting under her breath one of the old chants. She did these things secretly because the masters disapproved.

She always compared her children to her first born. None of the others had grown up so fine in form and face. Three had not grown up at all but had been taken to the high medicine before they could walk. Comparing her young had been like a test for Iwana, a test to see if the breeding of the ages of royalty would show, for her other mates had all been strong bucks.

The child stirred and fell into a deeper sleep and Iwana rose. This would be her last son. Her milk was already weaker, her large breasts had descended so that they hung half way between her navel and where they had stood when she was a young girl, and her thighs had become great from child bearing. She had had enough of it and would make the rite to stop her fertility forever at the next dark dance in the cactus grove.

She went to the door again, crossing the lengthening rectangle of light that broke the floor of the mud hut, bringing her shadow into it. Around her head she wore a bright scarf to absorb the sweat and around her body a huge dress of calico the mistress Anneke had given her. She had worn the dress for five years, letting out more of the seams each winter as she fattened. She had made it even bigger the winter she was pregnant with Hanny and then had never taken it back in after she bore him. For Iwana had become a huge woman, although she did not think of herself as such. She moved easily and with grace, and was smaller than her mother had been and her mother's mother. The queens of her tribe had always been of great proportions.

Finally in the road she saw Piepie coming toward the great house, leading the milk goats. His three goats were Mistress Anneke's favorites and Piepie brought them six days a week. Piepie belonged to Baas Corver whom he admired greatly.

Iwana left the shelter of her hut and walked slowly toward the slave wall. At its end, where it came to the fortifications at the sides of the great house, it was only five feet high, and it was to that point that she headed.

The side fortification, like the fort overlooking the river in Williamstaad, had been built against the French and the Spanish. The English had already come once and taken over the island when the Dutch were busy celebrating the New Year. They had not been gone for many years and the masters did not want that to happen again.

She came level with the wall just a moment before Piepie arrived, but he had seen her approaching and would have waited for her. The large iron bell on the lead nanny goat clanked noisily as Piepie arrived.

"Hey dag," Piepie shouted far too loudly.

He always spoke too loudly. It was why they had made him preacher.

"No parlo tro aki," Iwana said in Papiamento, the island dialect, a bastardization of the mainland Spanish.

It was amusing that the first thing she said, she who spoke so little, was "Don't talk too much here."

"Hey, what you want, Wana?" Piepie asked.

"Where is Chane?" Iwana replied, coming directly to the point.

"He my place, Wana."

"Piepie, when you done here, you come right to my place, hear!" Iwana commanded. Nor was Piepie about to disobey her.

"Yes. Good so," he said, and moved away toward the portico beyond the fortified outbuilding.

Iwana watched him for a moment, and before she turned to go she saw Kitty, the Opzeeland's daughter, the fifteen year old redhaired girl, come out to the porch instead of Mistress Anneke. Kitty's eyes met Iwana's for a moment and the young white girl blushed.

Iwana returned to her child in the hut slowly, pondering the weight of the shadow she had just felt come over her.

2

Eli Opzeeland stirred when he heard the bell on Piepie's goat and thrust the covers away. He sprang to the floor and put his hands into the basin on the commode next to the bed, throwing the water over his face and hair.

He was a blond boy of seventeen, lean and handsome in the unassuming way the Dutch have. His bone structure was good so that the lack of meat and bulging muscle on his body did not detract from his appearance. He strolled to the window wiping his face with a towel and blinking the sleep out of his eyes.

Kitty was below with Piepie and Iwana was walking slowly back to her mud hut. From below he smelled the sausages frying and could already taste the chocolate he was in the habit of smearing on his toast. He was in the mood for some old cheese with his sausage too, and plenty of goat's milk. He had a huge appetite.

When he had dressed he went down to the kitchen with a rush. Neither his mother nor his father were about. His father was probably already in Williamstaad, for word had come the night before that a Dutch man o' war, recently home in Rotterdam, had put in at Aruba and was expected by morning or the next day at the latest. The word had been carried by the Indian peddler from the Spanish coast whose eighteen foot yawl brought bananas, oranges and mangoes once a week in good weather.

The fire in the hearth and the sausages in the pan were unattended, and Eli yelled for Moira, the house servant. The old woman quickly came in with Kitty, both carrying a pitcher of goat's milk.

"Sit down, children, sit down," Moira said. "Everything's all done, hear. You jes' sit down."

Eli threw a leg over the chair in front of his place and pulled himself up to the table as Kitty sat down, somewhat more decorously, on the other side of the table.

"Ma asleep?" Eli asked.

His sister nodded. They were close and didn't need many words.

"Pa in town?"

She nodded again.

"Going in?" she asked.

This time it was his turn to nod. They looked across at each other circumspectly as Moira put the cheese, the sweet jam, the chocolate toasts and sausage on the table and went back to get the pitcher of milk.

"I saw Wana at the fence," Eli said.

"Oh," said Kitty looking quickly at Moira whose back was turned.

"Seen anyone else?" Eli asked.

Kitty frowned and shook her head quickly, looking down at her plate. They were talking about Chane.

"He's supposed to start work in the—"

45

"I know," Kitty said.

"Now you children hush up and keep eatin', hear!" Moira said.

She didn't want to listen to anything about their doings with Chane. Both Eli and Kitty knew that, but they couldn't help talking about it anyway.

"Piepie say anything?"

"No."

Kitty dove into her breakfast again, smearing a heavy blackberry syrup on a piece of thick round toast with a heavy silver knife. She was a pretty girl with many freckles, a small sweetly built nose, a mouth that seemed to double its size when she smiled, and bright green eyes. She took Eli's lead in everything, especially with the blacks, and until recently, very recently, she had been more of a tomboy than a young lady.

It was since the change had come over her that Eli had begun to worry. He was trying very hard to remain steadfast and strong willed. It was easy because Kitty brought out his manliness, his protective instincts. He smiled at her understandingly and she returned his good cheer.

"Come on," Eli said softly. "Let's hurry with breakfast and get the cart."

Kitty smiled and dug into her sausage, cut her toast into small sections with her knife and fork, and ate each one carefully but quickly.

"What you hurry for?" Moira asked. "You children take your time, hear?"

They washed their food down with sweet goat's milk and left the table quickly. Eli smiled when Kitty laughed at Moira's loud protestations which were still emanating from the kitchen.

Instead of waiting for the stable boy who would have to be roused and probably reprimanded, Eli put the pony in harness himself and helped Kitty to the seat of the small cart. He got in beside her and they trotted off around the road which circled the house and then led straight out to the main road to Williamstaad in one direction, and the salt flats and the Indian side of the island in the other. They took the latter route.

It was a fine morning. The trade winds which blew across the island and kept it cool were coming in at just the right speed to keep the sweat away from Eli's arms and forehead as he whipped the pony. The thick cactus on either side of the road flashed by. They passed three of Baas Corver Indians returning from Williamstaad on foot with fruit from the yawl from the Venezuela coast.

Eli flicked the whip lightly again to put greater distance between them and Baas Corver's household crew. They would have to move quickly. The pony picked up speed.

They took a slow turn in the road and looked ahead. About one hundred yards up the road the cactus jungle stopped and the wasted flats of Baas Corver's acreage began. Ahead even further they could see the white gleam of the sun off the salt works. Eli pulled to a stop quickly.

Kitty was ready. She leaped off the cart, whispered, "Quickly," and disappeared into the thick cactus. Eli whipped up the pony again and kept going.

The salt flats ahead had once been his father's exclusively but in 1827 financial reverses and the prospect of greater rewards had convinced his Dad to go in with Baas Corver on a fifty-fifty basis. It hadn't worked out. Corver was a tough, vindictive man. His overseer, Greuer, was too tough on the blacks, and although production increased, slaves were lost, and slaves were expensive and becoming more so. If things got much worse, Papa Opzeeland would have to sell out to Corver completely, or sell a large number of his own servants and field workers, which he was unwilling to do.

Eli's cart hit a small rut in the road and he lost his balance on the seat for a moment. It was then that he realised he was going too quickly. He drew back shortly on the reins, slowing the pony down, and looked carefully ahead.

If Chane were not at the flats where he had been ordered to begin work there was bound to be trouble. His father was not a mean man, not at all like Corver, but he could be strict when he had to be. The Opzeeland half of the working contingent had to be maintained if he was to get half the profits. It was Chane's duty to do his work.

Eli turned the cart onto the small road that led off the main one about two hundred yards to the heart of the flats. Only fifty yards away the salt was already piled in long pyramidal stacks on either side of the dirt road. Fifty blacks were raking the salt into piles and shoveling it into baskets within whip distance of the overseer who walked above them on the road. The salt was manufactured by running in sea water from an estuary, blocking it off, allowing it to evaporate and then scraping it up. It sounded easy, but it was hot, evil work. The salt got into the feet, the calves, and even into the lungs. The beneficial effects of the trade winds were lost in the pits and the lash of *Heer* Greuer cut deep.

"*Minheer* Greuer," Eli called as he stopped the pony and got down from the cart swiftly. He walked over to the overseer slowly, watching the work in the flats.

"*Hoet* Morgen," Greuer said. He was a short squat man, bald under his Panama, and he chewed tobacco voraciously.

"Good morning," Eli replied. "I see the entire field is cleared already."

"Yah."

47

"Very good," Eli said. It pleased him that Greuer treated him with deference, but he was not pleased with himself for feeling lifted. He was better than that.

"Are all the Opzeeland blacks working well?" Eli asked.

"Yah, *Minheer* Eli, all but one," Greuer replied, spitting a great wad of tobacco juice into the center of the road and then returning his gaze to Eli. "The young Chane had best be ill indeed, eh?"

Eli looked sharply at the short powerful man. "How so?"

"Well, *Minheer* Eli, he did arrive this morning."

"Chane?" Eli asked, pretending incredulousness.

"Yah, *Minheer,*" Greuer said, turning to look over the flats where the toiling had not let up since Eli's arrival and where none of the blacks had even averted his attention for a moment from the gruesome work. "Chane."

3

Behind the thick stand of cactus lining the road to the north was a narrow path, and on the other side of the path a thicker wood. Kitty crossed the path quickly and entered the wood. She followed a trail she knew for several hundred feet, crossing the gnarled, dead bodies of fallen trees until she came to the clearing the blacks used for their dances and forbidden rites. She crossed the clearing and continued along another trail equally well hidden to anyone who did not know it was there.

After a few minutes she came to the edge of the hills which line the north coast of the island, behind which some of the Indians still lived. She followed the line of the base of the hills until she came to a cave.

"Chane," she called, but there was no answer.

She looked into the mouth of the cave but her eyes were not yet accustomed to the light. She called again but this time his name reverberated in the dark caverns and echoed in the old places of the Indians.

She was afraid, but she ventured inside. She had never come there alone, but had always been accompanied either by Eli or Chane or both. She climbed down the rock stairs and entered the center of the cavern.

It was there in the high, vaulted, natural chamber that the ancient ancestors of the Indians had once come to bear their young, alone with their magic in the damp earth. The white people on the island never came there, and the Indians and those of partial Indian descent did not dare, for a high taboo was on the place and the pure African blacks and mulatto blacks respected the taboo of the Indian.

In the center of the vaulted chamber was a natural couch of stone surrounded by larger rocks which had been moved there hundreds if not thousands of years before by the Indians' medicine men. Kitty went to the couch to sit down and wait. It was there that the Indian women had suffered the pains of birth, alone, without midwife or doctor.

She could not relax. The thought of bats far above her kept her stiff and nervous. She did not like the place, but it was the safest spot on the island.

She swallowed and thought of Chane, pronouncing his name with the hard, guttural intonation of her language. In the dark cavern the name only added to her fear, for spelled in Dutch it was the negative word, the word which meant no or nothing. *Het slaav met hein naam* meant the slave with no name. The boy with no name. It was a mystery to her why Wana had called him that.

She hoped that Eli would hurry. She hoped that her brother had found him working under *Heer* Greuer and would soon come and tell her. But she knew better. She knew he had not gone to the salt flats but was hiding as he had sworn he would, rather than work under the lash of Baas Corver's overseer.

It was quiet in the vast cavern, and cooler than any place else on the island, and she bit hard on her lower lip as she waited. If Chane had done as he had promised and not gone to the salt flats he would be lashed, he would be broken. But he was not like the other blacks. There was a strange dignity about him. Wana was not like the other blacks. She had a depth and solitude and majesty in her bearing. Kitty had never been so frightened.

Far above, up the ancient flight of stone stairs, the light of the morning filtered in through the entrance to the cave. At the very top of the vault, over far to the left of the chamber, another thick stream of light entered from the top of the hill. Behind her she knew the cavernous corridors led to the coast side through devious passages whose secrets were no longer known even to the Indians who had once kept them in the body of knowledge of their magic. A small bat screeched far behind her in the depths of the cave and she shuddered with apprehension.

Suddenly she sensed something near her and looked quickly to the mouth of the cave. The light was partially blocked. He was there, becoming accustomed to the light, standing with his legs spread and his arms on either side of the entrance. He was tall and lean and powerful and her heart leaped toward him.

"Chane."

He heard her and came to the head of the stone stairway, rushed down it as she stood, came toward her with great speed and stopped suddenly. They stood looking directly at one another for a moment, she within the great circle of magic rocks and he between two of them, higher than any of them.

"You didn't go?"

"No," he said and his voice filled the vault.

"You fool!" she said.

"I could not go."

She sank again to the natural couch and lowered her head. She was trembling far worse than she had been when she was alone.

"I could not go," he repeated.

"What will happen to you?" she asked.

She heard his feet on the stone ground and felt his presence closer to her. She looked up and stared into his face, black eyes and short curly hair, a strong wide brow, unfurrowed, a nose of surprising length and strength, and a wide mouth which could make her intensely happy when it lengthened into a smile. His black neck was like the trunk of a young tree, the muscles and veins in it thrust through the skin with vitality.

She took his hand when he held it toward her and put it hard against her cheek.

"Don't worry, my Kit," he said.

She stood up quickly and embraced him, pressed close to him for fear that he would soon be gone. She *knew* he would soon be gone. She tried to find courage by clutching his young strength.

He ran his free hand through her hair and murmured, "Red hair, red, white skin."

They sank to the stone floor and kissed. She ran her hands over his body and pressed her breasts against him, kissed his eyes and felt the iron muscles of his arms. They sank still closer to the floor and she whimpered, "Yes, yes Chane."

His long black body came over hers and she tore at his shirt to expose his chest, ran her hands over it, kissed it, kissed his neck, kicked free of her silk underthings, hurried to free his body from his pants, ran her hands along his powerful flanks, tried to touch every handful of him and kiss every handful of him.

For she knew somehow that they would not have another chance. She desperately embraced him and in her youthful faith, she almost believed that she could capture him with her love and keep him with her forever.

She grasped the steel blackness of his thighs with hers, her pure white, thick thighs and screamed with despair and joy and fright and hope and obstinacy and faith as he found her vagina with his massive sex, the sex she knew, the sex she had slavered over, and although it was not the first time, there was great pain in her cry, too, a real, almost physical pain that this might be their last time, that their youth would end

50

with the end of that throbbing, spiritual, innocent, shattering act of love.

4

"You understand, Piepie, huh?" Iwana asked.

Piepie nodded and brought his knees up closer to his chest. He was seated in Iwana's hut, had been there already for some time while she had nursed the child Hanny who had begun to cry. Iwana had brought one of her great breasts out of Mistress Anneke's dress and offered it to the child who had grasped it greedily, and as the child had suckled Iwana had told Piepie of her life in the country of the high medicine.

"Yes, Wana, I understand," Piepie said.

"Swear on your Jesus Christ and on the medicine of the Indian people and on your old gods, swear on them all."

"I swear on them all, Wana," Piepie said not without fear and sincerity.

"Then understand that the high medicine is strong. It has brought the truth to my son to whom the truth has been withheld. I tell you he knows, in his heart he knows, and I will tell you, Piepie, vengeance he shall take unless we keep him from it."

Piepie crossed himself three times and looked at the roof of the mud hut as if to heaven for guidance.

"I do not understand, Wana," he moaned.

"Chane is the true prince of my people, a descendant of the royal in a straight line from the high medicine."

Piepie's face lit with color, his white eyes popped out even further. His mouth opened revealing a cavernous pink area wholly without teeth. Somehow he managed to knock off his straw hat which fell to the ground. He was too busy crossing himself and moaning oaths to pick it up.

"Hear me man, you Piepie," Iwana threatened him. "He must not be given special treatment, he must be made to think himself a black and no more than a black. He must not be gettin' ideas in his head. You don't understand any of it man, you Piepie." Piepie stopped crossing himself and looked at her frozen. His eyes were like the glass in the house of the Baas.

"Hah?" he said involuntarily, "Hah?"

"The fate of the child of the high medicine is sealed on the day of his birth. It is Chane's fate to kill. Do you understand, you man?"

Piepie nodded fiercely and moaned slightly. The hand that had been busy crossing himself was held over his heart in a fist and frozen there. "You are wise woman, Wana," Piepie said.

"So you must not give him shelter, Piepie. You must take him with you to the salt flats and let Baas Greuer whip him. He must think no more of himself than he is a black man, worth nothing. Fit to be whipped and no more."

Piepie let loose with a louder moan than before and clasped his hands on his forehead saying, "Ayeee, Wana, he will not let Baas Greuer beat him. Last week only Baas Greuer beat a man of Baas Corver to death in de salt, Wana. Chane know dat, Wana."

"Worse will come to Chane unless he goes."

"I know dat Wana. I tole him dat. What we gonna do, Wana?"

"You bring him to me, black man. You bring him to me here."

"Yes, Wana."

"And you swear again you don't mention his birth to him nor anyone else, you Piepie."

"I swear again, Wana. I bring him back to you."

Somehow Piepie managed to get to his feet and get his hat straight on his head. He looked once more at the gigantic woman sitting with the child on her lap, her huge black tit in the child's greedy mouth, and he ran, out of the hut toward the wall on his way back to the road where he'd left the goats.

"What's all that about, Wana?" Moira asked.

Iwana turned to see her in the doorway to the hut looking after the fleeing Piepie. "You sure put the fear in him."

Iwana said nothing. She had spoken enough for one day. She simply lay the child on his mat and rose, tucking her breast back inside her dress.

"If the child he done, you let him sleep. Come help in the kitchen, Wana," Moira said. "Baas Opzeeland maybe he come back from the ship with company."

Iwana nodded and followed Moira out of the mud hut. She turned once to look at the child, but Hanny was already asleep with a full belly. She started up toward the great house after Moira, with a heavy heart for the thought of Mistress Kitty's expression that morning was still on her.

"Big ship come into the harbor this morning, sure," Moira was saying. "Else *Baas* back by now."

They went around back and into the large kitchen. Immediately Iwana went to the center table and picked up a knife. There was a huge pile of freshly picked vegetables that needed cleaning and dicing.

She felt a great silence descend upon her, as once before. When she had first come to the island, been bought by *Baas* Opzeeland and put to making children and helping in the house, she had not spoken for a long time. She had not spoken since her husband's brother had been stretched on the spar of the great ship. It was the same fear and feeling

52

which kept her silent then.

But Moira considered silence a waste of space. "Yes Wana, a strong chile that Hanny. He goin' to be your strongest chile."

She chattered and chattered and Iwana tried to think of where Chane was and what he was doing.

The vegetables were nearly done when she heard a sound on the stairs outside and soon Mistress Anneke entered the large kitchen.

"Oh, it's hot in here," she said.

She was a thin greying woman. Iwana liked her. She was good with her children and with her blacks. She had a large heart and was most always joking, but she had been sick lately with the ague and had been sleeping late.

"Where are the children, Moira?" she asked. "Good morning, Wana."

Iwana nodded gravely and Mistress Anneke looked at her for an extra long time.

"What's the matter, Wana?"

Iwana just shook her head and went back to work.

"Children done took the cart, Mistress Anneke," Moira said.

"Where to?"

"Williamstaad, I speck, after the master."

"I rather doubt that," Mistress Anneke said and sat down at the breafast table.

"*I rather doubt that,*" Iwana found herself repeating in her head in exactly the same tone and accent, exactly the same voice as her mistress had used.

"They won't be chasing their father on a nice day like this," the mistress said smiling. "Moira, what is the matter in here today? What is the matter with you? You look like there's a ghost in here."

"Nothing, Mistress Anneke. Jes' feelin' a bit ill."

"Well, you go on to . . ."

"No, Ma'am," Moira said firmly. "I'm okay."

"Well . . ."

"Here's your cocoa, Mistress Anneke, you drink it up now, you hear?"

The mistress laughed and Iwana looked up to watch her for a moment. You could see she had been a beautiful woman once. Kitty's features had come from her, if not her coloring.

"What's that?" Mistress Anneke said suddenly. Iwana pricked up her ears. A horse was galloping up the path.

"You finish your cocoa, Miss. It's the master, he'll come right down here," Moira said affirmatively.

There was a shout outside, for the stable boy had raised himself when he heard the master's horse, and then the sound of heavy footsteps crossing the floor overhead and the tread of heavy boots on the stairs.

"You down there, Annah?" the master's voice came into the kitchen like a cannon shot.

"She's here," Moira shouted for her.

He came in. A tall man, dripping with sweat from a heavy ride from town, garbed in heavy leather riding boots and carrying a leather thong he used to whip up the horse. He seemed somehow drawn. Iwana sensed immediately that something awful had happened. His wife rose, leaving her cocoa on the table. She seemed to move toward him for an answer without actually moving laterally at all.

"What is it, Jan?"

He stood stark still for a moment. His cold blue eyes went from Moira to Iwana to his wife and rested there before he spoke.

"It's the salt. The *Moie Dag* went down not three days out from here. The whole ship lost. The year's work."

5

The hollow light from the oil lamp lit the interior vault of the cave. Outside it was night. An owl in the nearby bush hooted every few minutes and the flutter of bats' wings overhead was constant. Chane was standing at the far end of the chamber, staring ahead into the interior of the cavern. Behind him they were waiting for him to speak.

He did not have to turn to know they were waiting and watching him. Eli and Kitty were standing together near the lamp, their shadows drifting, wavering on the high wall. Piepie stood as if in church, with his hat in his hands, bowed, humble and waiting.

Finally Eli spoke and each of his words pierced to Chane's lungs as if they were darts of fire or salt.

"Father has already decided and there is no going back on it or protesting. Should we protest, it would all come out, you know that. It is New Orleans or *Baas* Corver."

"I would rather work for *Baas* Corver. I would work under *Baas* Greuer. I will stay."

"You can't," she cried.

He could feel her reach out to him across the darkness. He did not know what would happen when he was too far away to feel their bond.

"You mus' go, man," Piepie said softly.

"Your mother and Hanny and the others, all are going. He will not sell you to Corver. There is no place to hide on this island. You must go. Do you hear me, Chane?" Eli asked.

"I hear you, Eli," Chane said.

"Oh," Piepie wailed. "*Baas* Eli, forgive him."

"Take Kitty back now," Eli said. "I will stay with Chane

and bring him to the dock in the morning."

Finally Chane turned. He saw her in the shallow light. White, white as a spirit. He looked at her and knew he had to go, and something within him turned and died. He knew it had happened to her at the same moment.

There were no words. She moved toward him half a step, turned and ran out. Piepie followed.

He went after her quickly, but Eli reached out and stopped him. The white boy grabbed him about the chest and held him and he stopped. He looked into the blue eyes of the white boy and stopped.

"How?" was all he said. Then he sunk to his knees and listened. He could not hear them leaving, but he knew they were going back. All he could hear was the owl and the bats and the emptiness of the vault.

Eli knelt beside him and kept an arm over his back. They stayed motionless for a long time and finally Chane stood and walked back toward the interior of the cave, toward the north coast. He stopped and sat upon a rock.

"Wana never told me anything of Africa," he said. "I know only what I have learned from you and from . . . I mean to say that it has been nice here," he said.

"I want you to listen to me, Chane."

"Why, Eli? What more is there?"

The owl had stopped its regular cry. It was hunting. It and the bats were feeding in the long night.

"We are poor now."

"Yes," Chane said.

"But we will not always be poor."

"Don't be a fool," Chane said turning on his friend. "Don't give this black man hope."

He lowered his head and watched the cold ground.

"The salt will get through the next time as it always has, and the price for it has risen. In a few years we will have money again."

"Don't!" Chane said.

"I am not promising her!" Eli shouted and his voice reverberated in the depths of the caverns and came back to them.

When it was quiet he continued, "There is nothing there."

"God pray there be nothing there," Chane whispered.

"But I have an oath to make to you, given freely and from my love for you. When we are rich again, I will come after you. I will find you and buy you again."

"I will never come back here again," Chane said. It was cold suddenly. He longed to be on the beach or among the cactus.

"I will free you and send you to the north, to Canada."

Chane went limp. He tried to draw circles on the cold

ground but there was no soil, just the hard rock of the hill.

"Thanks," Chane said softly. "But not for the promise, for I won't count on that. Thanks for . . . for everything else."

He heard Eli move toward him and take a seat on a rock nearby. The owl took up his hooting again. He had fed.

"In the morning you'll take your first sea ride."

"Uh huh," Chane agreed. "My first sea ride. Not even you have done that."

"No," Eli agreed. "Not yet."

"Here, somewhere in this cavern," Chane began, "the spirits of stillborn Indian children and women dead in childbirth . . ."

He didn't finish. Then he said. "I have a child, you know, Eli."

"Who?"

"The mother is Anna, *Baas* Corver's Anna. See to him if you can."

"All right. I didn't know."

"I think he is mine," Chane said.

"All right."

"And, I have a favor to ask."

It was a long time before Eli answered. "What is it?"

"Something has ended tonight."

"Yes."

"No, something greater than that. I don't have the words."

"Our youth, perhaps."

"Her youth, yes. Yes, our youth. I feel a man. More than when I gave Anna a child."

"Yes?" Eli asked.

"Let me go kill Greuer."

Again there was a long silence. The light of the lamp began to flicker and Eli stood and went toward it. Chane knew that there was something in the atmosphere of the cave he would never know again. It was not any of the things that were already gone: not Kitty, nor even his childhood, but something new which was passing just as quickly and finally.

"I could be back here in a few hours. I could be on board before anyone knew."

Eli returned from the lamp. "It will go out soon," he said.

"Let me do it, Eli."

Eli came over and sat down beside him.

"No," he said. "Corver would kill ten blacks. The truth would come out and they would send word after you. All of it might come out."

"Well," Chane said. "At least you didn't say that it was wrong."

"No, I didn't say that," Eli said. "But, if you want to protect Wana and Hanny, and if you want to live to the day I can come for you, for you all if I can, you must forget that we were ever friends, that we ever spoke like this, that you

56

ever knew my sister. You must never rebel. It would ruin it all. You must be a black slave, stupid, humble, obedient."

A bat dove out of the loft and swept over their heads, another followed it, and then it was quiet.

"It is not bad in Louisiana," Eli said. "You will probably not be taken far from New Orleans. And when you get wherever you are, you must get word to New Orleans, for this Dutchman, for the day he will arrive there."

"I will have trouble with the language," Chane said.

"No, you are a quick learner, Chane."

Then Eli explained to him what his name would sound like in English and what the meaning was of that word and they both barked with ironic laughter as the lamp burned down and out.

Neither of them stood to refill it.

4 : THE WILLOWS

The big man came down the gangplank easily, as though he were well accustomed to travel. He was dressed in a smart light suit and silk shirt and tie in the gentlemanly fashion, but he was an exceedingly ugly man, and more than his huge bulk betrayed a lower birth. There was too much swagger and strength in his walk, as though he had once worked for a living.

Behind him his tiny man servant struggled with three heavy valises. A small troop of beggar children, mixed breeds and coloreds, rushed to offer their services, but the tiny man shooed them away in a high, shrill, frightened voice. The smaller man had never been to New Orleans before, had, in fact, never before been to sea. The voyage had discommoded him tremendously and had removed from him the little spunk he had. Hugo-Jim had foreseen that and upon hearing the fright in his valet's voice he barked once loudly with laughter.

"Come along, Mathews," he called behind him.

Eyes turned to watch the strange procession. The larger man seemed capable of carrying the smaller as well as the luggage if he had a mind to, while the smaller was barely able to manage his burden.

A thin, hawkish white man dressed like a waiter from one of the better establishments, the Charles or the Louis Quinze, approached them as they made their way quickly along the wharf at the sea reach of the great Mississippi.

"Hi there, sir," the young man said to the gentleman with the flaming nose who stopped suddenly, removed his hat and mopped a completely bald pate with his white silk handkerchief.

"Is that one of your river boats?" he shouted at the thin man.

"You bet it is," the man said turning to glance at the boat. When he turned again the large man and his huffing valet had moved off again. He hurried to catch up.

"Say," he said, but the man just kept walking inland toward the Esplanade. "She's one of the new ones. A beaut, eh?"

"She'll do," the gentleman replied, but did not slow his pace.

"You seem to know where you're going," the younger stated as he hurried to keep up. The valet's breath was coming shorter and shorter all the time.

The ugly man made no reply.

"Might I suggest a hotel?" the younger offered.

"No, you might not."

"Best leave off," the valet managed to call out from behind.

But the man in waiter's black moved closer to the gentleman so that they were shoulder to shoulder and whispered into the gentleman's hairy ear, "Listen, sir, this is a fine town for amusement, if you know what I mean, sir."

Hugo-Jim didn't slow his speed but he was becoming angry with the young hustler and said softly, "I know what you mean, lad. Now move off before I move ye off." He often slipped into his cockney accent when he was annoyed.

"Young girls, sir. Black, white or Injun. Mixed breeds. Virgins available sir, for a man who has the—"

Hugo-Jim turned to look at him for the first time. A phaeton bearing a lady of quality slowed at the corner of the Esplanade and across the street. The sounds of the wharf were still loud but were becoming mixed with the noise from the carriages hurrying through the crowded streets, the voices of men calling to one another, and the shouting in the saloons.

"Anything you like, if you know what I mean, sir. A good house, clean it is, young lads there too—"

There seemed to have been very little movement. The lady in the phaeton saw it all and raised an eyebrow, not because she had never seen a brawl before, but because she had never seen one over so quickly. Hugo-Jim had simply lifted his left fist upward in what would have been a sweeping arc had the younger man's stomach not been in the way. The latter was shortly lying on the wooden sidewalk in a ball.

The valet, who had caught up, took the opportunity to reassert himself in the eyes of his master saying, "A gentleman never strikes an inferior in public, sir. Very unbecoming, sir."

Hugo-Jim snorted and moved off again. The waiter made no attempt to get up and the lady in the carriage moved off, although she leaned out the side of the phaeton looking back until it became too much to hold her parasol against the wind.

The two men continued up the Esplanade until they were were under a lane of cypress trees filled with Spanish moss. The stable Hugo-Jim remembered was just ahead.

He found it just as he remembered it and turned into the building. A large man, stripped to the waist and wet with sweat, came toward him.

"*Bonjour*. What can I do for you?"

"Goin' up north for a week," Hugo-Jim stated loudly. Mathews caught up again and stood close by panting. He set the baggage down with evident relief.

"You'll want a horse, then, sir, and one for—"

"A horse!" Hugo-Jim said. "Rot! It's a buggy I want, a carriage. And two horses. In a half hour's time."

"Yes, sir," the blacksmith said.

"Wouldn't be caught dead on the back of a horse," the gentleman exclaimed loudly.

"He can't ride," his valet added in a whisper.

"What?" Hugo-Jim shouted, turning.

"It'll be a fine ride, sir," Mathews said.

"You stay here with the baggage, Mathews," Hugo-Jim said with pride. "My throat is parched."

Meanwhile the smithy had turned to the interior of his establishment and was calling orders in broken French to someone hidden inside.

"*Deuz chevaux, une phaeton bien et fait-le nettoyel!*" he shouted.

"I'd as soon come along with you," Mathews said.

"The baggage," Hugo-Jim said, looking sharply at the tiny man who was still out of breath. Then he moved out onto the Esplanade again.

He remembered it all quite well. It was one of his favorite towns. He would spend a week up the river with Jamie and then return to town to see to his business. He was in importing, and there were new markets opening up as the western frontier pushed quickly toward the Pacific Ocean. He meant to continue to operate out of Massachusetts, where his goods were brought from England, around to New Orleans with ships of a Boston fleet, and then up the river by river boat. He was sure Jamie would be surprised and more than happy to see him and he was glad he had not written to say he was coming.

He walked back toward the wharf and turned right at the corner where he had left the hustler in a bundle. Everything was normal there and there was no sign of the waiter.

It was a clear spring day with just a chill of winter left in the air. It had been cold in the south that winter. The Georgia and Carolina crops had suffered and he hoped Jamie had made out all right with his sugar cane.

He found the saloon he remembered and entered through the open door. The big bar room was drafty, a heavy chandelier swung from the center of it, and a half dozen dock workers were standing at the bar over half empty glasses of beer. He noticed that the bartender was huddled in conversation with a short man nattily dressed in black who wore long mutton chops and a bushy moustache.

"A beer," shouted Hugo-Jim as he came up to the long bar. There was a giant picture behind it of a nude blond holding a rose in her teeth and a cup and saucer in her hands.

"Comin' up," the bartender said moving away from the short man. The latter paid no notice of his departure but kept on with his talking. He chatted faster than anyone Hugo-Jim had ever heard.

"And I oughta know," he was saying rapidly. "I've sold more than ten thousand blacks in my time from the blocks on the wharf, right off the old slavers many of them were, and now, I tell you, the price has never been so high. The govinment's doin' it. Yes, sir, they are indeed! A thousand gold dollars for a healthy nigger ain't nothin' nowadays. Julius LaForge come in jes' the other day, said he was lookin' for stud material. Gonna make 'em himself he is. Lot cheaper than buyin' the labor for out the Dutchman's place, it is. Yes sir, never seen nothin' like it."

"Have a drink, friend," Hugo-Jim said to the natty little man.

"Why thank you stranger, don't mind if I do."

"Where's the Dutchman's Place?" Hugo-Jim asked, apparently to make conversation.

"Why, it's up a ways past the Cowley Plantation, over on Bayou Chien, the Frenchies call it, if you know where that is."

"What do they grow besides niggers?" the big man asked politely.

"Why cane, of course, and more," the man said pausing for effect. "A bad mess of trouble right enough I expect," he said.

Hugo-Jim could not get any more out of him even with the bribe of another drink, and soon the auctioneer left. It was time the phaeton was ready at the livery stable. He put a dollar down on the bar, took most of his change and left.

Hugo-Jim had wanted to know why they called it the Dutchman's Place. He had a peculiar interest in a certain Dutchman whose path he had crossed years before, for he had long ago taken an extreme dislike to whippings.

2

Jameson Cowley came out of the large house, took a seat

on the porch, and lit a cigar carefully, keeping the flame of the heavy wooden match away from the tobacco. He relaxed and looked out across his plantation.

Although the property was known as the Cowley Place, and rarely by its formal name, there was one. It was carved into a sign on the river road near the ten foot high white wooden gate posts. That name was The Willows.

When Jameson's father bought the land from the governor-general he received not just the land, but papers that said it was his forever, signed by the King of France with his seal in the lower right hand corner. Then he went out again to the place where he had decided to build the main house and planted a row of weeping willows on either side of what was going to be the main drive. By the time the house was completed and the last coat of heavy white paint had been laid on the brick and on the wood framing and on the pillars of the porch, the willows were five years old.

In those first few years, while the trees were growing and the drive was being worn down to a good road surface by the builders wagons and the house itself was growing by the side of the great river, Jameson's father drove the slaves himself. He cleared what bayou country was not already cleared by nature, and planted rice, the crop that made The Willows its first fortune.

When Jameson was a boy he often went out to the fields and looked out, to see nothing but more fields where more of his father's rice grew clear to the horizon. As he grew older he learned that he had been fooled, that the fields did not go that far, but only seemed to. The land actually fell off to the north into bottomland, only some of which was his father's. To the south were heavy woods between The Willows and Bayou Chien where an old and dying Frenchman named LaForge had his place.

Nevertheless the Cowley lands were extensive. It took an hour for the slaves to walk from their hovels to the farthest fields. Often many of them would go out that far and sleep and get up to work again in the morning, and do that until the harvesting or the pruning or the planting was done. That was how the low place beyond the plantation had first come to be used as a refuge and hiding place for any of the blacks that did not want to be caught doing whatever it was they did when they did not want to get caught at it.

Meanwhile, *Monsieur* LaForge, whose son had run off to get into trouble in New Orleans, and then in every port to which his wanderings led him, was growing near poverty as well as death. He had not planted rice at first, but had experimented with sugar cane and failed. Another kind of sugar cane later proved workable and even more profitable than rice, but by then *M*. LaForge had been long dead.

He lost his place to a holding company in New Orleans that did not find a buyer for it until Jameson returned from his wanderings in Europe and Africa. About the same time the LaForge son found his way back. The difference was that the younger LaForge had nothing, no money nor any land to come into, while Jameson had The Willows, already one of the richest plantations in Louisiana.

The LaForge boy, who had as much lust as Jameson to settle back on the land and bring it along, went to work on his father's old home for the new owners. The plantation, which became known as the Dutchman's Place after it was purchased by a gentleman of that nationality, finally started to turn a profit. Meanwhile, Jameson settled down with both Almira, whom he married upon his return, and his father's ward, Lou-Ellen.

Jameson found out about the new kind of sugar cane and tried it on half his land in 1823 and on all of it by 1825, so that looking north, all that one could see, seemingly as far as the horizon, was the tall sugar cane that was bringing so much money up north and in the markets in England and Spain.

Often Jameson would ride out in the mornings to look at the crop. He would do that even though he had a Scottish overseer who got paid to do his worrying for him, as well as to see to it that all the work was done by the slaves. But Jameson counted his frequent rides as the main thing that accounted for the difference between his place and the place the LaForge son ran. The Willows turned a healthy profit each year and every year Jameson's accounts in the New Orleans banks got fatter. The Dutchman's Place kept going but they were always a little late getting the crop in and always produced an inferior product. It was Jameson's opinion that if the Dutchman wanted to make more money out of his land, or even make that amount which the land ought to bring in just because it was land, he would have to quit his absentee ownership and come to live on it. He would have to give it the love and attention it deserved and required. LaForge had never been much more than a stranger to it and the fact that he no longer owned it did not help.

Nor did the way LaForge drove the niggers. Cowley's blacks stood in constant fear of their master only because the Dutchman's Place was so close they could hear the snap of the whip and the screams of the women whose sons were being sold down to New Orleans. In that way LaForge did Cowley a service. He provided constant incentive to the niggers of the Willows to work better than those at the Dutchman's Place. The niggers at the Willows had to keep it out of Cowley's head that his leniency was losing him money.

There was a death or a runaway or an incident of some

sort, not all of which Cowley liked to think about, let alone talk about, almost every month at the place next door. At first Cowley stayed away from it. He trusted his blacks and respected them. He had learned in his travels that they could sometimes be smarter than they looked and he had learned that they could be as sensitive as whites, or as white women, when it came to bed. He tried to keep the whip off their backs and when he thought of the incidents in Tangier and aboard the ship when Captain Van Zachten tortured the young slave girl for his own sexual pleasure, he changed the facts in his memory. He thought that he had looked askance at what was happening while the girl was being whipped and raped and the buck hung. He changed the way he had felt about it to understanding, mixed with contempt, instead of sympathy, for Van Zachten.

It was his marriage to Almira and the constant presence of Lou-Ellen that made him hide from himself his real feelings. He did it so well that he was at first both loved and admired by his blacks.

It was not until some ten years after Cowley had come back to New Orleans that his friendship with LaForge started again. They had known each other as boys. It was from LaForge that Cowley had learned what he knew of French, and it was with LaForge that he had experienced first the pleasures of black flesh, the stuff on which every young Southern gentleman of the era was weened.

Cowley had first avoided LaForge because he recognized in the man a threat to his marriage and to the vow he had made upon touching Louisiana soil, the vow to prosper and to be a respected gentleman. But dissatisfaction grew after the Willows was thriving better than it had done under his father's hand, after Lou-Ellen had become old enough to go to the convent school in New Orleans, leaving Cowley alone with his wife and his household servants.

Once a day, the Scottish overseer, who kept pretty much to himself and to his black family, would come to report. Then Cowley would mount up and go off to call on LaForge.

He knew as well as his wife did that it was because their marriage had stopped being a marriage.

He crushed out the butt of his cigar on the bottom of his boot and called for Mac to come out and bring him a drink. The mistress of the Willows heard her husband's voice from her sitting room. She smiled to herself and returned to her petit point. She was making an embroidered bed sheet for her cousin Jane-Anne in New Orleans.

Almira O'Hallahan Cowley was a thin woman with shallow cheeks and a bosom she did not take much pleasure in displaying at social functions or to her husband. She thought highly of herself, knew her place and what was proper, and, in her own words, was endowed with a clear sense of right and wrong.

When Almira was first married she had been extremely happy. Jameson Cowley was not only rich and about to take possession of the most famous, largest and most highly respected plantation in the territory but he was strong and handsome and kindly disposed toward her. Furthermore and about this she was brutally honest with herself, he had sown his wild oats. Almira O'Hallahan had no illusions about that. She knew perfectly well what Jameson had been up to in London and Tangier. It made him all the more worthwhile a conquest, for he was not liable to be terribly demanding of his new, fragile, blue-blooded wife.

Almira's hair was the color of straw; her eyes were, like her husband's, wash blue. Her complexion was wan but even and she knew how to move gracefully about the house from stately room to room at the Willows, or between couples dancing at the homes of Creole society in New Orleans. She knew how to do the latter only too well. She was tired of the demands of New Orleans society and had been all the more anxious to retire with Jameson to the country when they were married.

For the first few years, everything had gone exceedingly well. Almira had been a model wife and Jameson had been so busy with the plantation he had had little time for her. When he returned from his tours of inspection at night he was usually exhausted and, although they frequently made love, she did not become pregnant.

Almira first attributed her failure to conceive a child to her passive role in their sex life, then to the presence of the child Lou-Ellen in their house, and finally to charms of the niggers in the household service. The servants were sent back to the fields and new ones were found, then the same process would repeat itself and still other maids, mammies and butlers were found to work indoors. They were bought new in New Orleans and taken out of the fields and taught to cook and serve. It kept Almira quite busy but no results were obtained; she remained barren.

Eventually Jameson stopped coming to her bedroom at night. He stayed out late in the fields or at the Dutchman's Place where Julius LaForge was overseer. Almira spent time in New Orleans with her parents; when they died she simply spent time in New Orleans. Pregnancy became a subject which one did not mention in her presence.

In fact, as far as the subject of children was concerned, Almira had become quite mad. Like many people, she knew there was a small but complete area in her life where reason no longer ruled. She began to miss Jameson and tried to lure him to bed, succeeding with increasing difficulty each time.

Finally in the year the sugar cane brought the highest returns ever recorded at the Willows, Almira and Cowley stopped sleeping together at all.

The Cowley house fronted on the line of Willows old man Cowley had planted the day he received the papers from the French governor general. The house was in the old style, square pillars lined the verandah and supported the upper storey. The verandah itself was wide and comfortable and sported many chairs and chaises longues, but Almira never sat on it. In the summer when the heat became intense she would sit outside and watch the Mississippi. In all other seasons she would remain either in her sitting room upstairs or in her sewing room on the ground floor, and most of her time she spent doing petit point. She had never been close to Lou-Ellen.

For one thing, Almira had her doubts about her ward's parentage. Needless to say she had always kept them to herself; she was not a gossipy woman. But when the child had appeared out of nowhere and old Mr. Cowley had simply announced that she was the child of a dear friend who had died, Almira had guessed that she was actually his.

All that happened while Jameson was away in England. Jameson's mother had been long dead. The woman had never had the stuff it took to survive in those days. She had died of the typhus when Jameson was still a child, a fact which Almira sometimes used to explain her husband's frequent chilliness.

Almira had at first tried to be a mother to Lou-Ellen. Even if she was old Mr. Cowley's illegitimate daughter, she had to be cared for, to be loved and looked after, and Almira rightly considered it her duty as the mistress of the Willows to see to it. Then, as Almira's attempts to have a child of her own proved unsuccessful and Jameson became distant, she found she disliked Lou-Ellen.

It was not that she thought Lou-Ellen's presence was in any way responsible for her lack of fertility. Lou-Ellen was through and through white. Whoever her mother had been, she had not been colored—God forbid even the possibility of that! No, Lou-Ellen was not to be blamed for the failure to conceive. It was just that she got in the way. And she took up too much of Jameson's time.

He doted on the girl. He bought her a pony and as soon as she was old enough he took her riding across the plantation on his daily tours. The three of them—Jameson, Lou-Ellen, and Big Mac, the house eunuch Jameson had taken—would go out and not come back for hours. Big Mac had become his body servant.

Frequently, when Jameson went into New Orleans on business, Lou-Ellen went along. Big Mac would drive the carriage and Lou-Ellen would sit beside Jameson where she, Almira, should have been sitting. The two were thick as molasses. They had a slew of silly, personal jokes and were always laughing together.

Nevertheless, Almira did not dislike Lou-Ellen. It was just that she did not take to her company. Since the girl had come back from the school in New Orleans she had not spent much time with her.

It was not that Almira had anything to be jealous of: Lou-Ellen was not a pretty girl. Although it was true she had many suitors, more even than Almira had at her age, that was due to the scarcity of available women in the territory. Lou-Ellen was almost fat, much too fat to be thought of as pretty.

Almira had enjoyed the company of only three suitors. Jameson, of course, had been her favorite; a man who had died helping LaFitte defend the outposts during the battle of New Orleans was the second; and Julius LaForge had been the third.

There had never been any possibility of her marrying LaForge. Even before his accident he was ugly. There had always been something slimy about him. Further, her mother had told her that old man LaForge was not doing well. Events had proved her mother right of course; they always did. LaForge was a miserable overseer and she was mistress of the Willows.

LaForge's accident was something Almira often thought about. The story was that it had happened at sea, that he had been burned by being thrown against a firing cannon by an English bullet. It had marred him for life, however it had happened. The right side of his face was scar tissue. Whenever Almira thought about it, she shuddered. She wondered what Jameson saw in him, and why he had spent almost every evening at the Dutchman's Place, until Lou-Ellen had returned from school.

After that, Jameson had been too concerned with Lou-Ellen's suitors to leave the Willows more than twice a week. He spoke to them all deliberately, trying to find out how they thought and what stuff they were made of. After all, one of them would someday own the plantation. Jameson could not be blamed for being overly cautious in the matter. The Willows was his life and love.

Almira looked up as Clarissa entered with her afternoon tea. She smiled wanly at the big, young Negro woman who placed the tray silently on the rosewood table, waited for instructions, and receiving none, backed timidly out.

3

Mathews put the bags carefully on the back of the

phaeton, one at a time. The carriage was in good repair and the horses were well matched. It took him several minutes to think of something about which to complain to the stable hand.

Finally he tested the step of the carriage with his one hundred and ten pounds and when he heard the springs squeak slightly he turned to the man and said, "Mr. Morocco weighs close to three hundred pounds. What makes you think this old carriage can bear his weight?"

"*Ca marche*," the shirtless man said quietly.

"What's that?"

"*Ca marche, ca marche*. It works good enough, little man, for you, your Mr. Morocco and two more like him."

Mathews was about to continue to complain when Hugo-Jim entered the stable and bellowed at him.

"No trouble now, Mathews, jes' ye get up there and handle the reins."

"Me, sir!" Mathews balked. "Me? Best hire a colored—"

"Up!" Hugo-Jim shouted and the French blacksmith laughed.

"Twenty dollars deposit," he said.

Hugo-Jim paid him. The big man had adopted the surname Morocco because he had found freedom there from his majesty's service and the threat of a noose. He paid the Frenchman and climbed easily into the phaeton. He had to scream again at his manservant to climb to the driver's seat, and they were finally off.

At Hugo-Jim's instructions, they took the street by the roadstead. Hugo-Jim wanted another look at the river boat he had seen. He was still a seaman at heart.

Mathews turned around to say, "There's that fellow again, sir."

"Keep yer eyes on the road."

"Yes, sir."

But the fellow was there, all right, leaning against the side of one of the wharf saloons, smoking. His clothes were brushed clean from his little roll in the gutter.

He didn't see Hugo-Jim until the phaeton was abreast of him, then Hugo-Jim turned to starboard where the hustler was moored and smiled down at him. The hawk man's newly rolled cigarette dropped clean out of his mouth at the sight of the big man.

They were nearly clear of the traffic when they came to the commotion at dockside. The man whom Hugo-Jim had tried to pump at the bar earlier was finishing tacking up a notice.

"Hold it a minute here, Mathews," Hugo-Jim called out.

He got out of the phaeton and crossed the street. Most of the men gathered around the poster seemed to be gentlemen. It was an auction notice. "Stud material" was written as descriptive information after several of the names. The auction was scheduled for the following Thursday. Hugo-Jim retraced his steps and climbed back into the carriage.

"All right, Mathews," he said using the deep tones of his business voice. "Follow this street out of town, then turn left back toward the river road, then straight north thirty-five miles."

"Thirty-five miles!" his valet exclaimed.

"Get on with it. On with it!" Hugo-Jim bellowed and the little fellow in the driver's seat hunched further over his reins, raised them high and brought them down hard on the horses' backs. They started off at a fast trot for the edge of the city.

It was two o'clock in the afternoon and the southern sky was clear and blue straight back to the horizon. Mathews found the river road easily and turned the carriage north along it. There was the levee for the first five miles or so, but then the river and the road ran level and Hugo-Jim kept his eye out for traffic.

They trotted past several small plantations, much smaller than the Willows, and watched the darkies in the fields busy with the spring planting. Most of the small plantations grew their own vegetables and the majority of them planted rice, not sugar cane. The land near the river was perfect for it, as was the bayou country further north.

Hugo-Jim stretched, loosened his tie, opened the first three buttons of his shirt, and put his feet up on the door of the carriage. Mathews saw it, mumbled something, straightened himself and returned his attention to the horse with a sharp snap of the thick reins. He was learning.

A barge train piled high with baled cotton floated into view. Then from behind him Hugo-Jim heard the fast hooves of a galloping horse. He turned around in his seat and looked over the back of the carriage.

The bay was coming fast and the man on its back held well to the saddle. He didn't kick his steed, but encouraged it when it sighted the phaeton by slacking still further on the reins. The horse understood and did not slow its pace. Horse and rider flashed by.

The rider was a young man, blond, with skin darkened by the sun. He wore a gentleman's white linen suit and shoes instead of riding boots. Whoever he was, he hadn't planned on a horseback ride when he dressed.

As he flashed past, the rented horses became excited and Hugo-Jim leaned over and shouted at Mathews, "Better haul in on your line, mate. She's liable to run away with ye as there's too much wind for your sail."

"What?" Mathews asked turning around again and by then it was too late.

The matched mares the stable man had given them took off after the gentleman's stallion, causing Mathews to all but tumble back into the passenger's portion of the phaeton.

"Steady yerself, mate," Hugo-Jim bellowed, righting his valet with one foot and bursting into laughter at the same time. "Steady yerself and haul in on yer line."

The carriage picked up speed along the dirt road and was soon running fair into the stallion's dust. Mathews shouted and tried to rein in but it was too late. The mares were too spirited.

Laughing boisterously, Hugo-Jim kept his valet in the driver's seat with his boot and held on with both hands as the carriage began to bump its way along to the Willows. Finally the stallion so badly outdistanced the anxious mares that they slowed and Mathews was able to bring them to a complete halt.

"What're ye stopping for, ye lily-livered colonialist!" Hugo-Jim shouted. "Get goin', get goin'!"

Unheeding, Mathews descended from the phaeton and stood calmly at the side of the carriage. Hugo-Jim was forced to stand up in the carriage and reach over to the driver's seat to get the reins and maintain control.

"Get back up here!" he bellowed.

"Mr. Morocco," Mathews began.

"Get back!" he shouted again.

"I should like to tender my resignation," the valet finished.

His carefully combed hair was flying in several directions, his tie had come as loose as his master's, and his face was covered with the dust the stallion raised.

"I shall walk to New Orleans and seek passage immediately to New York," the little man said with finality. With that he spun on his heel and began to walk steadfastly south.

He took six steps when he stopped dead in his tracks. The bullet from Hugo-Jim's revolver had brought the dust flying at his feet and the sound of the report was full in both his ears.

"You'll what?" Hugo-Jim bellowed.

He was carefully holding back the mares with one hand while pointing the revolver in the other straight at Mathews.

"Nothing, sir," the valet said. "Nothing at all, sir."

He climbed back in and they made off at a quick walk along the river road.

4

Jameson Cowley came out onto the porch of the Willows to light another cigar. He held a long wooden match in his hand for several seconds before lifting his foot and scratching it on the bottom of his boot, then he drew in through the cigar slowly, keeping the flame from the tobacco at the tip. He had spent the afternoon mulling over his accounts in his office.

It was several hours before sunset, an hour and a half before dinner, and already the sky had taken on some color. A line of cumulus clouds had come peeking out over the horizon like a flock of sheep, about an eighth of the way across the blue fabric of the heavens, and the bravest of the herd were already tinged with the sun's red. In a few hours, the whole half the sky would be afire and streaked with deep purple.

Lou-Ellen was walking with Lafayette Neile who had appeared suddenly and uninvited on the pretext of bringing Jameson the news of the auction on Thursday. As if Jameson hadn't already known about it. Of course, Almira had insisted he stay for supper. Lafayette was an effeminate lad and Jameson did not like him, but Lou-Ellen seemed to favor him.

Mrs. Cowley was sitting out there with her petit point, keeping an eye on the two children and humming softly strains from the music she used to dance to when she lived in town. Jameson laughed ironically when he thought that Almira had hated those balls with all the fury of her young southern heart.

Far off in the fields Jameson heard the gong mark the break for supper for the men. Soon McKenzie would give his final orders for the day to the foreman and come to the house to report.

Jameson walked over to a wicker chair and sat down in it softly. He drew back on his cigar and watched the heavens. They always seemed especially still at this time of year. He closed his eyes for a moment and just then he heard Big Mac open the front door. He didn't bother to turn his head.

"If there's nothing ah kin do fer ya, Mr. Cowley, suh, ah'll help out t'kitchen."

"Go on, Mac."

"Yah, suh, Mr. Cowley, suh."

Big Mac closed the door behind him and Jameson was alone again. He sat quite still, looking intently down the avenue of Willows and listening to the low chorus of cicadas. After a few minutes he heard the door open again and, sensing an alien presence, he turned. He thought somehow it was Lafayette, but it was Almira. He hadn't seen her out on this side of the house since the last time they had gone into New Orleans together.

"Well, good evening, Mrs. Cowley," Jameson said, addressing her formally.

"Good evening, Mr. Cowley," she replied.

She was dressed in yellow that evening. Her hair was drawn back in a bun emphasizing her shallow cheeks. As usual, she wore an unfashionable high neckline and her shoulders were

70

covered by the short sleeves of her frock.

"This is an unexpected pleasure, Almira. Won't you sit down? I'll call Mac and have him bring you a drink."

"That won't be necessary," she said softly and her voice had a distant ring, as if she were only half thinking about what she was saying. "I've come to ask you for something, Jameson."

"Yes, Almira?"

She didn't take his offer of a seat, but continued to stand before the closed door of the Willows, gazing down at him distractedly.

"I want more help around the house," she said.

"You have Clarissa and Melody and Mae, Almira. What would you do with more help—or are you thinking of sending one of the girls back to the fields?"

"Oh, no," she said quickly. "Nothing like that. I just want more help, Jameson. I want more help."

There was urgency as well as distractedness in her tone and Jameson did not want her upset. Whatever she wanted she could have. There was money enough.

"All right, Mrs Cowley," he said. "If you want more help, more help you shall have. I'll find someone for you shortly."

"Thank you, Mr. Cowley," she answered, obviously relieved. Then she bowed ever so slightly from the neck and went back into the house. Jameson's cigar had gone out and he stared at it blankly. She upset him, she upset him terribly.

He heard McKenzie coming and looked up, but he could not see him yet. The Scot was coming along the river bank and was hidden from Jameson's sight by the house. He heard Lafayette shout a greeting to him and the hooves of his horse as he drew up at the side of the plantation house and walked around front. When he came into sight, Jameson was busy relighting his cigar.

"Come up, sir," Jameson said.

"Thank you, Mr. Cowley," the redheaded man answered. "Kindly of you, sir. Been a hard day, but most of the plantin's done, sir."

"Good," Jameson said.

"Some of the boys are down with the typhus, Mr. Cowley." McKenzie took the seat next to Jameson. He was a ruddy man with clear green eyes and a thick face.

"I know that," Jameson said. "As long as they're quarantined."

"Oh, they are, sir, they are."

"Then?"

"Could use some more help out there. Sure if we're going to open another field next year. Might be best to think of it now."

Jameson frowned. He had tried to avoid the conscientious

71

family planning the other plantation owners had begun with their slaves. It was too much trouble keeping after them. But it looked like he would have to make up for his decision by making new purchases.

"You thinkin' what I'm thinkin', McKenzie?"

"Might be best to get a stud or two by June so the women can be back in the fields for spring planting next year. Though they'll miss the winter harvest, most likely we'd be looking ahead, sure enough. Prices going up all the time, best to keep our own breeding pens. Know what we got, if you follow me sir."

Cowley drew on his cigar and watched the sky. It had reddened intensely just as he had predicted.

"No, sir. Still think it's too much trouble. Leave the raisin' of niggers to the Dutchman; we'll just work as we know best, turnin' the land to use."

"As you say, sir."

"See what I can do about getting you some help."

"'Preciate that, Mr. Cowley. Good night."

McKenzie rose and walked back to where he had left his horse. He nodded at Cowley a last time, mounted and rode off toward his house. Cowley's father had built an overseer's quarters in the woods near the plantation boundary by Bayou Chien. It was there that McKenzie lived with his mulatto woman and her children. He made an especially good overseer because his concubine and her children were Jameson's property.

"Uncle Jameson, Uncle Jameson," Lou-Ellen shouted, appearing suddenly from inside the house. "There's someone coming. We saw him turn off the river road from the back porch. He'll be turning into the drive any second now."

Cowley turned from his pretty ward to the young man standing next to her wearing an idiot smirk on his face, to the avenue of willows stretching out toward the road.

He heard Hugo-Jim's great bellow of greeting before the heavy clatter of his matched team.

5

"A Dutchman up Virginia way had 'em on his place, didn't speak a word of English," the short man with the mutton chops said.

"Rubbish," interjected Hugo-Jim.

"For strangers to the language, you're askin' too much money, Bentley," Julius LaForge remarked from the corner of the auctioneer's big desk where he had pulled the heavy red leather chair.

"I have to agree, sir," Jameson Cowley added.

Chane stood at the back of the room. Although he had

been on dry land over two days, he still felt weak. He stared at the men and listened closely, trying to gather from their expressions and their inflections what their meaning was.

"Now the woman and child in here before, that's his mother. She is trained and house broke and cooks, and the little son looks right healthy. Now, the two of them together you can have for eight hundred, whichever of you gentlemen wants 'em. This is sheer favor, Julius, Cowley. I could put 'em onto the block where they'd bring a thousand apiece."

The big man with the bald head and the red nose snorted.

"And this here boy is the best stud material I have seen in all my days in New Orleans markets. On the block he'd bring two, maybe three thousand dollars. Julius, I'll give him to you gladly for fifteen hundred."

The lanky man with the scarred face turned to the stern blond gentleman and said, "We would be saving a pretty penny, Jameson. You said Almira's been after you for help in the house and I could use this boy. He's fancy material, right sure."

The blond man drew a long cheroot out of his white linen jacket and struck a match on the bottom of his boot. He lit up carefully and tossed the match across the room into a spittoon. Then he said, "I don't deal with illegals, Julius."

The man with the mutton chops who had been sitting behind the desk, the one who had examined both Chane and Iwana when they were taken off the boat at night and brought to that place, rose and bent forward toward the others gesturing openly with his broad hands.

"Gentlemen, gentlemen, these aren't runaways, I assure you."

"No one said they were, sir," Jameson Cowley assured him quickly.

"Why then—"

"Why then the bargain?" the big bald man said. His voice sounded like fifty frogs.

"Because I—"

"Because they all aren't from Virginia, sir. They're from the Dutch Caribbean," Cowley stated.

"I—"

"Never mind, never mind," the one with the scarred face said. "It's no one but the U.S. Government we'd be goin' against, Jameson. It's not as if we agree with the restriction on slave traffic."

"Aye, it's brought the prices up sure enough for ye," Hugo-Jim snorted.

"I don't know," Cowley said standing.

Chane shifted his weight and stretched his muscles, listening to the strange language, trying to make it out was tiring.

"Slavers can't get past the English patrols anymore, anyway. It's not just the U.S. Government that's brought up the prices."

"Aye," the big man muttered. "Never thought they'd call it piracy."

"But they do," LaForge said, also standing. "All the more reason to take advantage of this." He made a sweeping motion toward Chane who met his glance and found he disliked it.

"Perhaps," Cowley muttered and Chane watched the eyes of the man with the mutton chops gleam for an instant and sensed that he had been bought.

"Look here, Jameson," LaForge said. With that he walked over to Chane and unhooked his pants which fell in a heap. Chane bit down on his teeth and watched the wood floor. "Look at the size of the boy. And I won't take him for my pens unless you take his mother, for I've no need for her. What do you say, Jamie?"

The man called LaForge looked Chane up and down again and then put his hands between Chane's thighs, lifting his testicles.

"There's weight here enough for a thousand screaming brats," he muttered.

Cowley was watching with interest, the man with the mutton chops was smiling and the big one, the oldest one with the bald head and huge chest, was staring blankly at Cowley.

Chane concentrated on his breathing and waited. Soon LaForge dropped his testicles and walked back to the desk. He stooped to pick up his pants.

"It won't fill my need entirely," Cowley stated, and listening to his tone, Chane suspected he was hedging, looking for an additional incentive, not really backing away. "I need two or three more field hands as well."

"Tell you what," the man with the mutton chops whispered conspiratorially, leaning forward across his desk and eyeing the three men one after the other, then letting his squinting eye rest on Cowley. "Help me out here by giving me the price I have to get on these Dutch 'uns and I'll see to it you get three farm hands at the best prices at the auction this afternoon. Fair enough?" he concluded straightening up and smiling.

Cowley nodded. "All right, Bentley. I'll take the woman if Julius has a mind to have the boy. Appears good enough, though you're always takin' a chance with a stud, Julius," he concluded, slapping his hand on his thigh and looking at LaForge.

The man with the scarred face laughed. "Sure enough, Jameson." Then he turned back toward Chane and looked at him hard. "*Zo younger hoe oud ben yea?*"

Chane flashed a fierce look at the man. He had not

74

imagined he could speak Dutch.

"*Seventeen yaar*," he answered.

"*Hab yea been kinderen?*"

Chane nodded.

"You see, Jameson?" LaForge said turning. "He admits to being a father. You see to it that they get on our wagon after the auction, Bentley."

The big man with the mutton chops rose again smiling broadly. "Thank you, gentlemen," he said. He shook hands both with Cowley and LaForge and went to the door to see them out.

The big man was the last to walk out the door. He looked at Bentley a long time before smiling and taking his leave.

Chane stood in the center of the room and watched the man with the mutton chops as he turned to face him. He was no longer smiling but had assumed a purely businesslike expression.

He went to the rear door which led to the place in which Chane had been kept with Iwana and the others.

"Through here," he said. "Through here, boy!"

"*Minheer*," Chane said.

Bentley turned and looked at him and then said, "*Yah?*"

And then Chane tried to make the auctioneer understand that his old master would someday pay well for the identity of Chane's new owner, but the young black was never sure that the white man had understood.

5 : THE DUTCHMAN'S PLACE

The owl which had been hooting regularly since midnight had been quiet for a long time. A few hundred feet away, through the underbrush and sparse juniper trees, the outline of the abandoned overseer's house just the Dutchman's side of the Bayou Chien became more distinct against the grey sky.

Behind them the old wooden bridge, built by old LaForge and Jameson Cowley's father, covered by fifty years' growth of moss, soft and tropical, creaked as the tide far away in the gulf was reflected through the waters of the Mississippi and into the still bayou. A frog croaked and hit the water from someplace far above it.

They were just off the path the owners had built by laying nearly even logs from both sides of the bridge the length of the soft ground. The logs too were hidden by soft moss and grass. They might as well have been there for centuries.

"Best I get back," Clarissa said. "Soon sure Mr. McKenzie

be up and checkin' the cabins."

"He be all right," Chane said.

"I still better get," Clarissa said.

There was just enough light to make out her body. She was naked and leaning against the trunk of a juniper tree on a soft mound of earth. Her heavy breasts swelled and shrank slowly as she breathed comfortably.

"You give it to Clarissa once more and then we run," she said, stretching out her hand and running the heel of her palm over Chane's sex, bringing it straight and full.

"Change your mind, gal?" Chane whispered.

"Quick," she said.

She stretched out flat on the soft ground and spread herself wide. Chane came over her, balancing his weight on the palms of his hands so that just the tip of his sex touched her body. She was wide open and ready and he slipped into love easily and started the pace hard and fast.

She whimpered and stretched so that she could get hold of as much of him as she could and then she bit hard on his shoulder so as not to scream as she thrust her hips hard enough to get help from the soft earth to maintain her rhythm.

She left him with a deep mark in his neck.

Chane swung away from her and lay on his back breathing heavily. He listened to the sound of her breathing and the whisper of the morning air in the bayou.

"You git home now," she said huskily.

He saw that her breasts were still thundering with life.

"Uh, huh, here I go," he said, but he stayed where he was.

"LaForge catch you he whip you good," she laughed. "Spillin' yo seed in no account Cowley girl."

"Uh huh," Chane said.

"You git."

"Tell Iwana I done thought about what she said."

"You git."

"Tell her," he began still short of breath, "I'm a good nigger."

"Git," she said.

He didn't bother to get into his denims. He grabbed them with one hand and broke into a trot right from the ground. There was just enough light to see clearly where he had to duck to avoid the branches of the juniper. When he got to the sugar cane fields he kept his head low and broke into a run.

The summer sun peeked over the flat horizon and the cock at the McKenzie house let loose. Within fifteen seconds every rooster on both plantations was barking and singing.

Chane bent still closer and increased his speed. The early morning wind felt good against his naked body and he ran with his legs spread wide so he could feel the cool air in his groin. Suddenly he tripped over something and went flying into the soft fertile soil before the row of cane.

"Wha . . ."

There was someone on top of him with a knee in his back. He knew better than to resist until he found out whether it was a white man or a black man.

"Who dere?"

"Jes me, Mr. Chane, sir," a deep voice growled sarcastically.

"Blaze!" Chane whispered.

"Uh huh, boy."

"Git off my back."

"Oh sure, sure I git off, Master!"

"LaForge catch us and we both be whipped."

"He won't catch me, little man."

Chane squirmed hard and freed himself so that he could turn. But it did him little good. He wound up in the same position except on his back, staring up into the giant negro's face.

Blaze was the strongest man on the plantation and LaForge's favorite stud. It was his duty to cover as many of the Dutchman's slaves as he could, unless he was getting ready for a fight. Then he wasn't allowed to cover any and he got mean, real mean. That was the general idea.

"Who you been with, boy?" he asked Chane smugly.

"No one of yours."

Chane watched the black man's eyes. If they darkened, he would fight. If they didn't he would be better off lying where he was. There was still a chance he could get back safely and undetected.

"Who you been with?" Blaze repeated.

Chane stared up into his face. The giant's nose was flatter than an iron and his jaw was as broad as the jaw of the huge white man friend of Mr. Cowley, only it was shiny black and Chane knew he could break a piece of pine over Blaze's head without more than dazing him.

"Woman from the Cowley place."

"Why you liar, little Chane," Blaze said and moved his thick knee and the two hundred and fifty pounds he could put behind it lower on Chane's stomach.

"I get caught and whipped, likely you will too," Chane tried.

"Maybe, maybe so, little Chane," Blaze whispered and set his knee still lower. Chane knew he would have maybe one chance to get free and break away and he knew Blaze knew he knew it.

"No woman of yours, Blaze."

"What?" Blaze whispered bringing his face and the smell of his breath and the feel of his spittle he coughed through his teeth right up to Chane's face.

"No woman yourn."

"Liar, sweet little pretty liar," Blaze said and this time his knee made contact and Chane stiffened. If the giant negro let his weight down he might cause Chane serious damage despite the soft ground. "You had your eye out for Edie. You met Edie in the bush back there behind the seer's place, ain't it Chane, ain't it?"

Chane sprang, hitting him in the adam's apple once but hard, with knuckle pointing straight out, and at the same time slid far enough out and up to get his knee between Blaze's and his groin. He hit him again hard with his cupped hand over Blaze's bad ear and then took off like lightning.

Most of the crowing had stopped. The light was already high enough to shorten the shadow of the cabins to the edge of the sugar cane field.

He ran low and fast.

There was no one in sight. Big Blaze had not come after him. But the giant black man had his pants and he would have to get them back. He would look pretty damn silly picking cane in the fields without his pants.

Then it looked like he had it made. There was no noise and no one in sight outside the slave cabins. He ran behind the four that preceded the one he shared with five other young men, all without families, and dove through the back window.

He landed in a somersault on the floor, all but laughing, proud of his young speed and his young beauty and his night with Clarissa.

"Get up," a voice said.

A shiver ran through Chane. He stood quickly and felt a cold hand on his testicles.

"Who have you been with?" LaForge shouted. "Who was it?"

"No one, sir, no one, Mr. LaForge!" Chane shouted.

"How would you like to be like Big Mac, boy? How would you like to lose these here, boy?" the dark overseer hissed into Chane's face. "You gonna be one fancy whipped nigger! Git!" the white man ordered.

2

Chane walked out the door of his cabin. Behind him LaForge gave a quick order to George, the oldest of the men that shared Chane's cabin, to get the men to work. Up the length of the dirt path to the trees that hid the main house black people were coming out of their shacks. Children were running around naked and women, all of whom wore calico cotton dresses, bright bandanas and were shoeless, were busy cooking breakfast and shouting at their children. A hush fell when they saw the naked black boy marching with his head bowed toward the whipping post. LaForge walked directly behind him.

"I ought to hang you for this, nigger, you know that?" he growled. "Next time it happens, I will. It would be better for you than letting Blaze loose on you. You hear me boy?"

"Yes suh, I hear you suh," Chane said softly.

"Git between 'em," LaForge ordered.

He meant the two pillars which Chane approached. They were stuck firmly in the ground like two fence posts and they were five feet high. At the top of each a long chain was set in a heavy iron eye. Obediently, Chane put his hands against them.

LaForge walked to the other side of the posts and locked his wrists in place, while Chane watched him dumbly, waiting. He knew he was about to get a speech as well as a whipping and he tried to keep Iwana's imprecations in his heart. He had to do as he was told, and do it humbly. He had to survive.

"You are going to grow into a fine looking animal," LaForge began. "In two or three years you'll be finished growin' and you'll be fit for one or two things on this plantation. You'll stud or fight, or you'll do both. I didn't buy you to work in the fields. I didn't pay that much for a lousy field hand. If you don't work out I'd as soon see you hang as put you to work like an ordinary nigger."

"Yes, suh," Chane said.

"Don't you talk, boy," LaForge barked. "Jus' you listen. I've been watching you. I've been watchin' you close since you came here. You're going to pay for your disobedience today, but if you get smart and do as you're told, you could be a house nigger. How would you like that, boy?"

"I'd like that fine, Mr. LaForge, sir," the black boy replied.

"You could be a real class nigger, boy. Make your mammy over to the Willows real proud. Would you like that, boy?"

"Yes, sir."

"Who you with last night, boy?"

"Nobody, sir, nobody t'all," Chane replied.

LaForge's face grew dark. He walked behind Chane and watched him closely for a moment. He let his eyes run over the fine animal lines of the boy's body. He stared at his muscular rump and gritted his teeth.

"Who you with last night, boy?" LaForge repeated.

"I tell you, I wasn't with nobody sir. I just got cramped up in the cabin."

"Where'd you lose your pants, boy?"

"In a fight with Blaze sir. He thought I was out with one of his women sir, but I weren't. I swear I weren't, Mr. LaForge, sir."

LaForge raised his whip and brought it down sharply enough across the black boy's back that the sound was like the report of a gun. Chane slumped between the two posts, but he didn't scream.

79

The whip came down again and Chane slumped further. Again the report echoed down the line of slave cabins.

There was a hush on the blacks' dwellings. Everyone had come to the front of their cabin to watch. A ten year old boy with wide eyes popping out of his head shoved a handful of hot grits into his mouth and started to chew.

"You jus' goin' to stand there today, boy," LaForge said and brought the whip down once more, connecting the two red running lines on Chane's back with a third. Then LaForge turned and went back toward the house. It was a long time before anyone came over to Chane.

When someone did it was Gusty, the old man who saw to the wood for the fires in the house and who ran the house servants, bossing them like an old woman. He was a short stocky man with close cropped grey hair and big black flappy ears. He was as black as coal and was bent from his years of carrying cords of wood and from age. His thick arms were veined like the leaf of an oak and he had square feet with only four toes on the left one. He had lost the other chopping by the bayou.

Gusty let some of his burden of logs fall to the ground so he could bend in front of Chane without causing a lot of talk. He looked up and saw the boy was watching him with a slow, heavy stare. He was breathing hard and his black nostrils flared with pain.

"No sense," Gusty said.

Chane didn't reply. He just kept looking at the old black man.

"No sense at all."

From over near the main house they heard the sound of a horse or a mule. That would be Mr. Bandeaux or his brother come to help Mr. LaForge. The Bandeaux brothers and their white trash women were the only society LaForge had except for old Mr. Cowley, and on Saturdays when they fought Blaze, the men and ladies from three counties.

"Been here a year all told, whole year, don't know enough not to dally when Mr. LaForge says so."

Chane still remained silent. The folks began to go about their business and the chatter started again at the cabins. Soon the work teams would go into the fields and the women would present themselves at the main house for Mr. LaForge.

"Learn to talk quick, to cover quick, don't learn to listen though. Gonna see few more days you keep it up."

Chane's glance finally left Gusty's face and went to the cord of kindling he had set on the ground before the whipping posts.

"Blaze after you, too," Gusty said. "Who'd you cover?"

"Clarissa," Chane said.

Gusty looked back toward the cabins. "He don't think so,"

he said. "Me, I watched the whole thing. Seen you runnin' from the bayou. Seen it all. Watch you real close. Whyn't you be good, be a house nigger? Mr. LaForge like for you to come to the house."

Chane spat and the large glob landed just short of Gusty's wood pile.

"Too good to show the white man a good time, that it? You crazy, nigger, you right crazy, boy."

Gusty stood up lifting his wood with him. A log fell to the ground and he had to bend again. "Best forget your high ideas, nigger," the old man said and then started off toward the house again.

Before he was out of Chane's sight, two small boys, both children of Cass's, one of LaForge's favorites, came to the whipping posts and stared up at him with wide eyes. They were light skinnned boys and both showed a resemblance to LaForge, though the younger might easily have been Cowley's or Bandeaux's. Chane watched them with a glint he knew was unbecoming for a whipped man.

"What you do, Chane?" the eldest asked.

"Why, nothin' boy. I didn't do nothin'," Chane said softly and something in his voice made the two children freeze in their questioning postures and then hightail it away from there as fast as they could run.

Chane heard the field hands move off to work at the sound of the big bell at the Cowley's southern field, the one closest to the bayou, and then he heard the soft tread of the women approaching.

He turned as far as he could although the pain bore down hard when he moved, until he could see them coming.

Gusty's youngest was among them, Lulu, who was no more than fifteen. There was something about the girl that reminded him of Kit even though she was black. It was something about the way she walked, and the heavy grace of her limbs.

"All be better," the girl said when she saw Chane's eyes on her. "All be better when the Dutchman comes back," she said with a smile. Then she looked at Chane's naked body and the bloody cuts on his back a long time before she moved off toward the trees and LaForge.

3

Clem Bandeaux swung off his mule and lighted on the soft earth outside the Dutchman's place. LaForge was on the porch already, waiting for the foremen to come by for their morning instructions. He was also waiting for the women, the ones that wouldn't be working in the fields until LaForge released them, to see if there was anything special the master wanted of them.

"Morning, Julius," Clem said smiling, revealing a wide space between his upper teeth.

The elder Bandeaux was a thin man of medium height and a dark complexion. His dark eyes were set close together and he was clean shaven although he wore his sideburns down to the line of his small nose.

"Mornin', Clem," LaForge replied. "See you sellin' quail this mornin'."

"Right you are, Julius," the Frenchman replied. "Got her all loaded up and I'm only chargin' a dollar for a half dozen."

"That so, Clem?"

"Uh huh," the other said, shaking his head. He held in his hand a two barrel shotgun he loaded with bird shot once or twice a month whenever he needed some money for something he had an eye to have from New Orleans, or whenever he got the idea that it might be nice to buy a bottle of mash liquor.

" Gonna stop by Cowley's?" LaForge asked.

"Uh huh."

"Tell him 'bout the fight Saturday, then. Tell him to bring the women if he has a mind to. I haven't seen him much since Lou-Ellen announced she was goin' to marry that LaFayette."

Clem Bandeaux came up onto the porch and laughed.

"What's funny?"

"Nothin', nothin'. Don't see what a good lookin' piece of beef like her see in that LaFayette crittur. Bet he don't know what to do with a woman, Julius."

"Maybe not," Julius agreed. "Jameson hasn't said 'go' to them."

"Have him over some time?" Clem ventured.

"Not on your life, boy, not on your life."

The other laughed and then Julius squinted into the rising sun to see the women walking up from the woods.

"How's your wife, Clem?" he asked.

"Fine Julius, jes' fine. *Va etre mouille* later."

"Uh huh," LaForge agreed. "It'll rain this evening. Best time for shooting jes' before the rain."

"Put you down for a dozen then, Julius."

"Half," LaForge said.

Bandeaux nodded and walked down off the porch as the women came by muttering their good mornings to the white men. Old Gusty, dressed for the house, came out of the front door and asked, "Good mornin' Mr. Clem. Is you stayin' fer breakfast?"

"Cain't, Gusty," Clem said mounting his mule and swinging his rifle over his knees. "Goin' shootin'."

"Yessuh," Gusty said.

Clem eyed the line of black women and smiled. He loved the bright colors of their bandanas. In all there were twelve women, the youngest and prettiest of the Dutchman's lot.

"Breakfast ready anyhow Mr. Julius, sir," Gusty said.

"Be down in a minute, Gusty."

"Yes sir, yes sir," the old man said. "Mr. Clem goin' to bring us back some bird?"

"Yes he is," Clem replied, but his eye had fallen on Lulu, who stood humbly in front of the porch, her eyes on the ground. The women were waiting to be addressed.

He took one last look at Lulu and then turned his mule, kicking it twice hard in the rump before he got it to move in a fast walk. Behind him he heard LaForge begin to talk to the women. He would choose one or two to work in the house and be generally available and the rest he would assign to the fields or send back to the cabins. LaForge watched the women carefully because he always suspected they were mating behind his back, ruining the blood lines he was trying to build and fooling with the psychology he was using on Blaze, the pure Mandingo stud.

Bandeaux looked at the sky as he rode toward the old Bayou Bridge, cutting across the Dutchman's Place through the cane fields. With any luck he would be able to fill his pirogue with quail before the rain came in from the north.

He heard a voice from deep in the fields and turned to see the top of a colored man's head swing as he cleaned the cane. Then he heard the voice again. It was the gang foreman Georgie, complaining about the speed with which the men were working. If they didn't work well it was Georgie's head that would roll.

Bandeaux entered the grove of junipers that bordered the fields from the soft land of the bayou and put his mule on the old mossed over log trail old man Cowley and old man LaForge had lain years before. Soon he was crossing the creaking old bridge and was on the Willows.

He passed the place Chane had lain with Clarissa without noticing where the grass still lay flat and shiny. He didn't look once toward LaForge's abandoned overseer's house, though when the Dutchman came, Julius would likely have to move back into it.

Bandeaux turned his mule under a low hanging arch of Spanish moss, taking a short cut off the trail and over by McKenzie's house. Through the underbrush he could make out the slow moving shape of McKenzie's mulatto woman and he reined in softly on his mule and sat quiet.

The large graceful woman was bending in the garden behind her house. She was wearing a red and yellow cotton dress through which Bandeaux was sure he could see the movement of her heavy thighs and rump. She was a good looking woman, maybe the best looking negro on both plantations.

Bandeaux dismounted softly and brought his hand around

his mule's nose to keep it from snorting. Then he softly approached the back of the McKenzie's garden.

When he stepped on a twig he froze; his mule, feeling the urgency, also froze. But the woman had heard and had straightened. In one hand she held a long spade and in the other a fistful of radishes.

"Who that?" the woman called.

Clem smiled to himself and mounted again. He looked back just once to see her peering helplessly into the underbrush behind him, unable to see him because of the glare of the early morning sun and the dark shade of the bayou. He cut back into the log path and yelled, "Hayah," just loud enough to let her know who it was that was watching her. If McKenzie looked at him cross eyed the next time he saw him he would know he had to go carefully; if not, he might just call on his woman. Maybe he would bring her a nice bird the next time he went shooting.

The mule clopped along the log path and then stepped out stronger when it came to the south cane field of the Cowley place.

Clem Bandeaux and his younger brother Pierre were descendants of some of the earliest residents of Bayou Chien. Their people were originally French, creole white who had come to the new world with the first settlers. They were not of the French who had begun to come down all the way out of Canada since the English had made it difficult for them there.

Clem and his wife Cora lived about a half mile from Pierre's stilt house which was right on the bayou where it was widest, about five miles in from the river. Clem's place was on dry land. He had two kids, a mule, a goat, a cow, ten chickens, a rooster and no slaves. Pierre had nothing but two pirogues and two rifles.

Up ahead Clem saw a team of Cowley niggers working the cane. The foreman was talking to Mr. Lafayette who was mounted on one of Jameson's purebred stallions. It looked to Clem as though Mr. Lafayette was already right at home at the Willows, though his marriage to Lou-Ellen hadn't yet been announced.

4

Jameson Cowley stood up. He had been sitting behind his working table which was heavy mahogany, ornately carved in the fashion of baroque France. He handed the gold across to McKenzie and frowned.

"I don't like doin' it, but I suppose you've rightly earned it," he said.

"Thank you, sir."

"The papers will be drawn and given to you and of course all her children, whether by you or any other man, will be your property as well."

"Yes, sir."

"And she will go on tending your place only so long as both you and she are still at the Willows."

"Yes sir, thank you."

"That'll be all, McKenzie. Best get to the fields."

Mr. McKenzie smiled and went out. Jameson had not lied. He did not like parting with his property. In point of fact he had resolved never to sell a slave, and he had only managed to keep his word on that point by giving McKenzie the mulatto woman and refusing to take her price out of his wages.

There was a knock at the door and Jameson shouted, "Come in." He walked over to the sideboard and opened his box of cheroots, placing one carefully into the cutting machine and removing a piece from the end.

"It's me, Uncle Jamie."

"Good morning Lou-Ellen."

"Can we go Saturday, both LaFayette and me?"

"Why I . . ."

The question took him by surprise. He had naturally assumed that Lou-Ellen would want to stay at the Willows with Almira.

"You know how your aunt despises the games," he said.

"Yes sir, I do," Lou-Ellen answered, "But LaFayette . . ."

"LaFayette asked you to ask me?"

"Yes, sir."

Jameson sat down behind the great desk again and lit his cigar. He watched his ward over the flickering flame of the long match. She had become an extremely beautiful girl and, except for some of the Dutchman's nigger women, she had the best figure in the south of Louisiana.

"Hasn't he enough gumption to ask me himself?"

"Of course he has, Uncle Jamie. It's just that he thought if you knew I wanted to go . . ."

"Do you want to go, girl?"

"Yes, sir."

"All right."

Lou-Ellen let a wide smile break across her face. Her freckles wrinkled up and down her nose.

"You know the cock fights are pretty bloody, girl."

"Yes, sir," she replied.

"And that Mr. LaForge is going to match Blaze against that town nigger of Judge Riley's, what's his name?"

"Boon. Yes, I know."

"Huh," Jameson shrugged. "All right then. Leave me to my accounts now."

"Yes, sir."

There was a rustle of petticoats as Lou-Ellen took her leave and Jameson stood again. From the window he saw Clem Bandeaux coming across the fields from the Bayou Chien with his bird rifle on his lap. He knew the man would be after an order, cock sure he could fill it without difficulty. That would mean they were due for a spot of rain. It would do the crops good. It had been a dry summer.

Back at the sideboard he poured an inch of brandy into a glass and swirled it around. He drank when he got restless and he had been restless for a week. He didn't like to leave Almira alone in the house with Lou-Ellen and LaFayette. He was afraid there might be a scene and if there was anything he hated it was being involved in a fight behind his back. If Almira was going to take the opportunity of the children's presence at the Willows to break loose and say what she'd been wanting to say for years, he was going to make sure he was around when it happened.

He downed the glass of liquor in one gulp, replaced the cork in the bottle and the bottle on the shelf.

"Mac!" he called.

"Yessuh," Mac answered.

The big black man hurried toward the door to the study and opened it.

"Yassuh, Mr. Jameson."

"Where is Mrs. Cowley?"

"Miss Almira, she in the sittin' room upstairs, suh," Big Mac replied in his high voice. "Suh?"

"What is it, Mac?"

"May I say somethin', sir?"

"What is it Mac?"

"Suh, I been with your family a long time. Your daddy, that fine man, ah never held it against him he made me what ah am. Ah am grateful to him fo' takin' me out a da fields, suh."

"Yes, Mac?"

"Ah understan' cain't have no full blooded nigger aroun' white women, we niggers bein' animals, suh. But this black man he loves you and he loves Miss Almira suh. An' he ain't never been so worried about you both."

Jameson looked carefully at the big man. Mac was looking at the ground. His palms were turned upward and his fingers spread wide and the position of his head indicated that he was both trying to look at Jameson and not look at him.

"Since Miss Lou-Ellen and Mr. Lafayette aroun' all the time, and you haven't gone to see Mr. LaForge of late, there is a tension, an unholy tension in this house, suh."

"Well, what is it you expect me to do about it," Jameson barked.

"Don't you be down on me, master. Ah mean well, ah do. Ah jes' want you to be pleased. Ah could get your stallion saddled and you cculd ride over there to pay a call on Mr. LaForge."

"Mac?"

"Yessuh, Mr. Jameson, suh."

"I don't ever want to hear you talk about any of this again, you hear?"

"Oh, yessuh, Ah am sorry, suh."

"Go up and tell Miss Almira I would like to see her here in the office."

"Yessuh, right away."

The big eunuch backed out quickly and shut the door behind him. Jameson stood again and went to the sideboard and poured another drink, swallowed it quickly, poured again, swallowed and drew on his cheroot. Miss Almira was a long time in coming down.

When she finally did come in she didn't bother to knock. She entered silently like a ghost and stood for a moment by the heavy armchair and at the side of the desk. Jameson said nothing to her and finally she sat down.

It took her several minutes to speak but Jameson had all day.

"What is it, Mr. Cowley?" she said finally. "I do not like being summoned like a common servant."

"There is nothing common about you, Almira," Jameson said sarcastically.

His wife let the comment pass. She folded her long fingers in her lap and waited. He stared at her shallow, almost transparent color, and at her neck where the blue veins protruded as if she were tensing the muscles of her neck constantly.

"Got one of your headaches, Almira?"

Again she remained silent. In twenty years he had come to hate that woman so that he could have strangled her blue blooded neck on the spot. She had given him neither children nor peace, and he had to fight to keep her from ruining their reputation and the reputation of the Willows. That reputation was all that Jameson valued in life.

"What is it, Jameson?" Almira whined.

She knew he had been waiting for her tone to become plaintive.

"Lou-Ellen wants to go to the Dutchman's on Saturday."

"Oh," she said. She brought her hand to her flat chest and then let it touch her brow gently. "Oh."

"I do know how you hate social functions, Mrs. Cowley, and how you tolerate them occasionally only because I insist. But I will not have Lou-Ellen and her fiance appear at the Dutchman's with me unless you are there, and you know I intend to be there, Almira."

"Jameson, I will not, I will not, I will not go," she said firmly.

"Oh, but you will, Almira. Indeed you will," he said, and they both knew he was right.

5

It got hot early on Saturday morning. A brace of Bandeaux quail were still hanging from the back wall of the kitchen at the rear of the main house. All but the men working the fields and the handlers of the Dutchman's fighting cocks, and, of course, Blaze, had been told to stay down at their cabins.

The sun had done much to heal Chane's ripped back and Mr. LaForge had seen to it that Blaze had left him alone. It had not been for Chane's sake but so that Blaze would have all his hate left to spend on Boon, Judge Riley's big town nigger.

"Why he want me to stay to the cabin with the women?" Chane asked.

Old Gusty shook his graying head and wiggled his black ears like he always did when he wanted to be funny.

"Now Ah don't know, mighty Mr. Chane. Surely Ah don't."

"Don't fun me, Gusty," Chane said fiercely, and the old man looked up at the boy, frightened.

"Ain't funnin' you."

"Why he want me here?"

"Ah tole you. Ah don't know."

Gusty went out and left Chane in the cabin alone. The other men were working in the fields. He could hear scuffling among the poultry as the fighting cocks who were being blindfolded alerted the others of their fury.

The heavy pine door swung open and suddenly Mr. LaForge entered. It took Chane by surprise. He straightened and looked quickly at the floor, as much from fear of setting off his own feelings as from fear of the overseer.

"Don't you say good morning, boy?" asked the overseer, darkly.

"Good morning, Mr. LaForge, suh," Chane answered.

LaForge slapped his hand against his thigh. He was dressed in a white linen suit instead of the usual working costume which always included his whip and high boots.

"Got an idea this morning," the white man began. "How would you like to show yourself in front of the white folks today?"

"Yassuh, Mr. LaForge, suh," Chane answered obediently. He was still looking at the floor. The places where the whip had torn his back began to itch and to burn.

"You are going to be a fine addition to this plantation when you are full grown and broken right, boy. You got the makings of a good show fighter."

"Yessuh."

"You know I treat my black folks proper, boy. If you prove yourself, I'll turn you to stud every wench on this place. If you don't . . ."

"Yessuh."

"You think you got the nerve to fight, boy?"

Chane looked up for the first time. He looked into LaForge's face, at the pale shallowness of his cheeks and the indistinct line of his mustache and at the scar tissue of his right profile.

"Yessuh, I do," he said.

"Last black man to face Blaze lost half his jaw. You know that?"

"I heard it, suh."

"Judge Riley is bringing his biggest, meanest nigger and Blaze is going to kill him this afternoon. The Judge is also bringing a boy about your age. The Judge says he is real pretty and real strong. We are going to put you against him. I don't want you to kill him, but I want his nose broken and his teeth knocked out of his head, do you understand? I want him ugly as sin by evening tonight."

Chane looked hard at the white man. Something inside him clicked, a phrase or an understanding, and the feel of the last time he had spoken to Eli in the cave was close to him. The burning stopped on his back.

"Yessuh, I understand."

The overseer was smiling strangely. He patted his thigh several times and looked perplexed as if he were trying to think of something else to say. Finally he brought his attention back from wherever it had been and snapped, "Go to the back of the house, to the kitchen door. Gusty'll give you a pair of tight pants. Can't have a nigger fallin' out in front of a white woman."

"Yessuh."

"Go on, git."

Chane hurried past the overseer and into the morning light. He hurried past the whipping posts and up through the trees to the back of the main house. Gusty was waiting there with Blaze who was staring dully into the distance across the cane fields. He did not turn when Gusty greeted Chane.

"Here's your pants, boy. Git into 'em. Surprise fer you inside."

Chane looked at the old black man and took the white trousers he had been handed. He stripped out of his denims and put them on.

"Ah'm supposed to go inside?" he asked.

"That's what Ah said," Gusty declared flatly.

"In the house?"

"Nobody's in there but niggers, boy. It's jes' the back kitchen."

Chane stiffened and walked to the door. He didn't know what to do about his bare feet. White people wore shoes, and so did black folks that worked inside. He almost wiped them against his fresh pants.

He felt odd and filthy. He had not bathed since he rolled in the bayou waters before he met Clarissa the night he had been caught. He felt especially naked, stuffed like a wedge of black cheese into his new pants as he was.

He entered despite himself. There behind the large chopping table Iwana was dicing vegetables with a speed and detachment that made Chane blink.

"Wana," he said.

His mother stopped working and looked up quickly. She looked beautiful to Chane. Her chocolate color shined beneath her bright red kerchief, her massive body gave off a human warmth unequalled by any other in Chane's experience. When she smiled he felt better than he had since they left Curacao.

After they had embraced his mother asked him whether he was going to fight. They spoke in Dutch, the language in which they were both most at home, and the language which Chane was able to express himself doubly as well as he could in English.

"And you have been whipped, child. What have you been doing?"

"Well, which question shall I answer first?"

Chane smiled. He held Iwana's hands and looked about the huge paneled kitchen, nodding as he recognised or understood the purpose of each thing he saw. He had never been in a white folk's kitchen.

"*Baas* LaForge caught me after comin' back from Clarissa," he explained. "And he wants me to make a pretty black boy ugly today or to be made ugly myself."

Iwana raised her thick hand to her face and held her fingers against her lip. She nodded gravely, turned and walked a step toward the far wall.

"There is a good deal of evil on this place, Wana. It isn't like . . . like it was. You have never seen a man as cruel as LaForge. He is restrained only because he does not wish to experience all his pleasure in one day."

Iwana nodded. "I have heard . . . from the others. Why did you not speak to me of these things before?"

"There was no point."

"Listen, when you win this fight, ask *Baas* LaForge for permission to see me at night. You will not have to do it secretly and be caught and whipped."

"He will never let me. It is important to him to control our sex. He says it is for the breeding."

"Tell him you want only to see your mother. You must win his faith."

"How?"

Iwana looked blankly at her son and then shook her head. She rubbed her hands against the side of her huge apron.

"Hanny asks for you," she said changing the subject. "He wants to come to see you."

"Send him."

Iwana nodded and then looked at her son a long time, especially at his white pants. The inspection made Chane's back itch again.

"You look like your father," she said. "Now get out before someone catches you here."

6

Julius LaForge pulled deeply on the cheroot he had just taken from Jameson Cowley and excused himself from the group of men still standing about the corral. The Judge and Jameson were hotly arguing about how the Supreme Court of the United States was dealing with the problem of runaway slaves. LaForge didn't much care how they dealt with it. He had never had a runaway yet that the Bandeaux brothers couldn't track down and bring back alive inside of two days.

The Bandeaux men were also at the corral. They were standing there like the white trash they were, with Clem's woman. She was clean and neat in a fresh calico dress but she didn't dare go near the other women who were sitting on the porch and gossiping. That was her problem. LaForge's gatherings were not formal occasions and all the white folks were invited and welcome.

Lou-Ellen and the Judge's daughters were closest to the door and LaForge stopped to greet them politely before going inside. Almira wasn't there, but he suspected he knew where she was. The Cowley ward and the judge's daughters excused him with equal politeness and he went through the door. He knew full well that they despised him thoroughly.

The buffet meal was almost completely laid out in the dining room. From the main hall LaForge watched the huge woman the Cowleys had sent to help move about, adjusting the plates and putting a final touch to some of the decorations.

LaForge entered the Dutchman's study and closed the door behind him quietly. She was standing at the mantle, her thin hand on the large globe.

"Good day, Julius," she said flatly, when she saw who had come in.

"Good day again, Almira. It surely is a pleasure to have

91

you here."

"It is all different, Julius, isn't it?"

"Pardon?"

"None of these things were here in the old days."

"These are the Dutchman's things, Almira. Ours, mine, are at the place in the Bayou."

"Of course . . . of course," she said distractedly. "It has been a long time since I've been here."

"You haven't been here in ten years, Almira."

She strayed away from the mantle and went to the wall of bookcases. "These were your father's," she said.

Julius didn't answer her. She was right, of course. The Dutchman had bought them as well as the old house.

"Living like this," she said. "It's so odd."

"And how do you live, Almira?"

She turned and shot him a fierce look. These frail southern ladies, he thought, so tough when you offended their honor.

"I saw you run off back there during the cock fight. You have missed the whole show, Almira."

"It was disgusting."

"But you saw none of it, dear. Blaze broke Judge Riley's nigger's neck like it was a twig."

"Shut up, Julius!" she snapped. "I do not wish to hear any more."

"And my pretty boy Chane, the son of your kitchen woman . . ."

"Did he fight?" she asked quickly.

"Why, didn't you know, Almira? I do declare, you women have a fancy interest in that boy. I thought that Bandeaux woman would never get her eyes unglued from his pants."

"She is trash," she snapped viciously. "As are you."

"Appears to me your ward found him handsome as well. Hardly anyone rooted for the other fellow."

"What happened to him," she asked breathlessly.

"Why, Almira, I'm right, aren't I? You like him."

"You pig, Julius LaForge. You low skunk, you are worse than a cur, sir! I will find out myself!" she barked and went quickly toward the door.

Julius rushed and placed his hand against it so that it would not open.

"Don't be upset, Almira; you must see how it appears. And how it would look if you—"

"Idiot! He is my woman's son. Of course I want to know if he was hurt."

"Well, he wasn't, so you can relax. He wasn't touched. I believe that boy could even whip Blaze. Give him another year to fill out."

He could see that she was relieved. She turned from the door and walked back to the globe. She picked up the sextant that lay on the table beside and replaced it distractedly.

"I declare, Julius LaForge, I do not know what has gotten into you."

"Why, Mrs. Cowley."

She suddenly surprised Julius greatly by turning toward him and smiling coyly. He had thought surely she had forgotten how. Then she sat down in one of the two huge armchairs by the cold fire place. Julius strode over and took the other.

"I hope my cheroot doesn't offend you, Almira dear. I could leave."

"Oh, do stop it, Julius. You were always brazen and no one expects you to change."

LaForge laughed. He looked over at her. She was wearing a brocaded blue frock, a rather matronly one, but he still thought her attractive. There was something unreachable, fragile and obscure about her that he wanted. He always had.

"LaFayette seems a fine young gentleman, Almira," he said at last.

"Lou-Ellen seems to think so, Julius."

"When will they announce?"

"That is up to Mr. Cowley. He has not yet consented, you know."

"Oh. No, I didn't know. They say that the young man is constantly at the Willows."

Almira sighed. "Yes, so he is."

Julius looked over at her again and pulled on his cheroot, then blew the smoke out in a smart stream toward the empty fireplace.

"So you don't approve either, Almira."

She turned and met his glance. "He is a weak boy," she said. "Weak."

"Yes," LaForge laughed. "You should have seen his face when Blaze drew the first blood. I am surprised that cool young southern gentleman managed to keep his breakfast down during the cock fight.

Almira laughed. LaForge had the idea that it was the first time she had laughed in a long time. Jameson and Almira were the most dour, somber people he knew. Her good cheer raised his hopes. He continued to talk about the boy.

"There's nothing wrong with his family."

"Oh, no," Almira agreed readily. "Not at all."

He leaned over further so that he could see her closely. Her glance was full on him; she was staring unabashedly at his scars. That was fine.

"Almira," he said.

"Julius?"

He looked once quickly back to the door. In a few moments Gusty would ring the luncheon gong.

"I want you to meet me in New Orleans next weekend. At the Carter Inn where you stay when you go into town."

He had whispered his words hotly so that there could be no mistake and he stared into her pale eyes as he waited for an answer, keeping his glance firm.

"Julius," she sighed. "Thank God you asked me."

6 : THE DUTCHMAN'S RETURN

Chane lay abed beyond the first light. Although he was awake he did not care to move. He looked at the wooden roof over his head and savored the darkly content feeling of keeping all thoughts from his head.

He had the upper portion of the new cabin to himself. Three black girls shared the bottom. They were all wide hipped and big breasted, and heavily muscled from the double drudgery of working in the fields and rearing children. Two of them were pregnant and the third probably was. A year previous the cabin and the women had belonged to Blaze by permission of Mr. LaForge. Chane had won them in battle, and Blaze, broken and ashamed, had been sold at the New Orleans market. He was of pure Mandingo stock and had brought the Dutchman a good price.

Below Chane could hear the women moving about. Soon Claire would go on outside and start a fire. There was no fireplace inside the wooden cabin. A few minutes later and she would call Chane to breakfast.

The morning light filtered in through the cracks in the roof. He would have to tar it before the summer rains or he would spend a lot of wet nights up there. He stretched beneath the single rough sheet, filled his chest with air, and breathed deeply.

He had grown, as had been predicted, into the largest black on the plantation. He was so large he could lift a full grown cow and lately, instead of fighting at the games, he would perform that and similar acts of strength for the amusement of the white folks. That was just as well as far as he was concerned. Blaze had almost killed him before Chane had finally won in the big fight.

The overseer had not removed Chane from the games because he had a distaste for death and violence, however. LaForge had done it because the money he might make if he won a bet was not worth the risk of losing a two thousand dollar black. That was how high the price of proven studs had soared on the market.

The women were chattering below. One of the children had come running in and had to be shushed. None of the children lived in the same cabin with Chane's women because none of the women stayed very long. When they were pregnant they moved on, or at least they were supposed to. Claire and Talmy and Anne-Belle hadn't because there were no other women on the Dutchman's place that LaForge was ready to have Chane cover. Chane had already sired ten infants and felt nothing for any of them. He spent most of his time without a thought in his head, feeling the breath in his lungs and the sap in his veins.

He smelled the grits frying below and stirred. He was satisfied that he could eat. Way up at the house the work gong was being hit. The teams would have to be on their way. Like Blaze before him Chane was not the favorite of the black men on the plantation because, like Blaze before him, he was excluded from the roughest work details. He was kept like a prize stallion. His energies were spent as a stud and sometimes as a show animal.

"*Baas*, you *baas*, you *maitre*," Claire called up mockingly. "Time you git down here, *baas*."

Chane filled his chest and let the air out again. Then he sat up and looked down at his brown palms. He threw his sheet aside and looked at his sex, languid after just waking. He stood straight up and went over to the ladder.

Outside he could hear one of the work gangs passing the cabin. One of the young bucks was calling to Claire, feeling his oats, no doubt. He remembered the days when he had passed Blaze's women on his way to the fields. It was the time of year to bring in the cane and Chane thought it would be good to get permission from Mr. LaForge to go out and work like the others. If he worked especially hard he would drop off at night with no trouble. There were no women that needed covering anyway.

As he lit, buck nude, on the floor of the cabin, he heard the women greet old Gusty.

"What you doin' down here, house nigger?" Claire yelled out. She was always filled with venom.

"Here to speak to Chane," he heard Gusty reply.

Chane was getting himself into his denims as Gusty entered. The old man was in the new house livery that Mr. LaForge had bought in New Orleans. He looked fancy indeed, except for the hunch in his back. Gusty had come up in the world, too. For him it was the second time.

"Now look at Mr. Gusty," Chane found himself saying sarcastically. "Ain't he the pretty one. 'Cept maybe for his flappin' ears and bent back."

"Good mornin'," Gusty replied evenly.

"What Mr. LaForge want of me he can't come and tell me

hisself?" Chane asked.

"He comin' all right," Gusty said.

Chane looked at the little man with the steel gray hair and powerful long arms, and then walked past him into the light of day. Gusty followed as Chane approached Claire and took the plate of grits she extended. He sat down on a stump and began to eat with his fingers, keeping his eyes on old Gusty's.

"Is that so?" Chane said from around his fingers.

"You women git," Gusty ordered, but none of the three moved. Anne-Belle, the youngest of the three, shooed a child away that had been clinging to her skirt, but didn't move an inch herself.

When Gusty repeated his order Claire said, "Who do you think you are, nigger? We ain't goin' nowhere. You got somethin' to say to *baas*, say it or git."

Chane laughed and swallowed another handful of the hot grits. Gusty looked abashed.

"You are comin' up to the house," he said to Chane. "Mr. LaForge, he comin' to tell you that soon enuff."

"That so?" Chane said.

From off in the fields Chane heard a foreman's shout. Anne-Belle had come closer to him and was looking hard at his face.

"You goin' to git livery like this, and be made butler, but you goin' to take orders from me, that clear?"

"Who says all this?" Chane demanded.

"Never mind. You find out soon enuff," Gusty said heartily.

Chane could see the women were fuming. Claire came up behind Gusty and nearly blew him over she shouted so. "Listen here, house nigger. You explain yourself right quick, or I'll smear a frypan o' grits in your fancy clothes."

Gusty tried to back off but she had him pinned against the wall and to each of his sides another of Chane's women waited to hear what he had to say. They were not about to let him go until they had.

"The man's comin' back," he said.

"Huh?" Chane said. He had stopped eating but was still perched on his stump like a king of the woods.

"What that you say, you?" Anne-Belle nearly shouted. She was from an old French family that had died off in New Orleans and she spoke with the intonation of the city blacks.

"The Dutchman," Gusty said pulling back on his gums. He hadn't any teeth left. "The *maitre* is comin' after all this time."

"Dear God!" Claire said, lifting a hand to her red bandana. "Maybe some o' this gonna stop now."

"Chane, he is to come to the house to be a handservant to the *maitre*," Gusty continued. "Not enuff of that kind on this place since old Mr. LaForge done sold it, and not enuff time

to buy some fancy-ass out of town—too expensive anyways I
'spect."

"Me!" Chane barked. "I ain't no hand servant, I's—"

"I guess you is what you is told to be," Gusty snapped.

The women were silent. Claire looked more serious and
less virulent.

"Lord," she whispered. "Dear Lord! There be somethin'
odd 'bout all this. What has that Mr. LaForge done got up
in his head now, takin' a stud and show nigger for the house?"

Chane rose and placed his tin plate on the stump; he
walked back to the cabin. Gusty walked past Anne-Belle, who
stepped aside, to say to him, "What I came to tell you is you
best know whut it is like up there. You goin' to be axed to
do things you ain't never been axed to do before. And you
don't even look sideways at no white woman neither, you
hear!"

Chane stepped in the threshold of the cabin and looked
down at the wooden floor. The cabin had a good smell to it,
a smell he had become accustomed to. He hoped that
wherever it was he was going to be put he wouldn't be in a
place where he would have to do any thinking.

He didn't want anything coming into his head, anything
at all.

2

"No, Mathews," the big man said. "Things aren't faring
well for my friend Jameson Cowley. The last time we were
in Louisiana his wife, Almira, was almost clean out of her
mind. I tell you I do not want to see her worse, but I fear
she may be."

"You can't know that, sir. Best not even think it. Wait until
you see for yourself."

Hugo-Jim Morocco coughed, snorted, and moved off five
paces down the deck, only to return to the side of his valet.
Occasionally he watched the face of the young Dutchman
standing amidships, staring north, just as he had been staring
north for the last hour.

"I say, sir," Mathews began.

"Aye, Mathews?"

"I haven't properly thanked you for taking me on this trip.
I know you didn't have to, and, well, sir, I just want you to
know how nice it was to see my family in Liverpool."

Hugo-Jim just grunted in response and Mathews looked
down at the swelling sea.

"It was nice for me to be back, too," Hugo-Jim said at last.
"There was a time I thought I'd never see England again."

Behind them, from the topside dining room, the chief
steward exited with his small bell. He rang it softly and its

tender tinkle made Hugo-Jim belly laugh.

"Ah, Mr. Morocco, sir," the steward said. "It's time for luncheon, sir. The last of the voyage, I expect."

"I expect you're right, steward," Hugo-Jim replied. Then, as an after thought he said, "Look man, ask that young Opzeeland to our table this afternoon. He looks so morose I'm sure he could use with a bit of cheerin' up."

"Yes, sir," the steward said.

Mathews and his master moved away toward the dining room and entered. Their table was directly under one of the fancy new portholes and they seated themselves in luxury. Mathews had never been told about his master's experiences on the high seas in sailing ships very much unlike the one they were crossing in, when the fare had been salt pork and not good American beef.

After Hugo-Jim and Mathews were seated and the former had poured from the wine carafe with hands so rough, red, and hairy they might as well have belonged to an ape, the young Dutchman entered with a crowd of other passengers and made his way to their table.

"Good day," he said and Hugo-Jim looked up at him darkly. Mathews smiled and returned his greeting.

"I wish to thank you for your invitation to luncheon, but I am afraid—"

"*Verdomen, youngen,*" Hugo-Jim growled a Dutch vulgarism that had been in his vocabulary since his days aboard the *Zeebaas*. "Sit down and have a bit to drink. I'm sick to death of watching your forlorn face on this crossing. At least spend the last day of it slightly drunk."

The young boy was startled, then angry. He looked from Mathews, who was staring rather forlornly himself into empty space, to Hugo-Jim whose great red face was blazing sternly straight at him.

"Well."

"Sit down," Hugo-Jim commanded.

Opzeeland finally laughed and relieved, Mathews joined in. Hugo-Jim smiled, slapped the blond boy so hard on the back that the sound of it resounded across the fancy dining room, and turned over his water glass which he promptly filled with wine and handed to the young aristocrat.

Eli took it gratefully and with a laugh said, "*Prost,*" and drank heartily. The big man's merriment was contagious.

"My master is a crude man," Mathews murmured.

"What?" Hugo-Jim barked.

"Where do you come from young man?" Mathews said more loudly.

"Curacao, originally. I've been in Holland recently, and England."

"Studying?" Hugo-Jim queried.

"Yah, studying. And now—"

"And now you seem to be bound for the state of Louisiana. To find passage back to the Antilles no doubt. You've a woman waiting breathlessly for you in Williamstaat, and you are not sure you want to marry with her, isn't that it, lad?" Hugo-Jim laughed loudly. The other passengers who had not become accustomed to his boisterous ways made faces and stared at their empty plates or neighbors.

"Oh no! Nothing like that, Mr. Morocco."

"Well, boy," Hugo-Jim whispered. "What weighs so heavy on such young shoulders then? It can't be as serious as all that."

Hugo-Jim leaned even further forward after swallowing the remainder of his wine and out of Mathews' hearing whispered, "When I was your age . . . or a little older . . . I was due for a noose, lad, my back was scarred from the lash, I thought sure I'd never get a loved one again, and sure I didn't look as somber as you do," he finished shouting the last phrase jocularly.

The young Curacaoan laughed and raised his glass, holding a shy smile on his face. "My problem's not weighty at all," he agreed.

"Liar," Hugo-Jim snapped back. "I may be a gross sailor what has struck it nouveau rich in a vulgar colony but I'm a good judge of character. Come on, my boy; get it off your chest. Do you good. Best thing in a sea voyage, take it from me. Never see any of us again."

Eli laughed and was about to reply when the steward approached. As loudly as he could, Hugo-Jim instructed him to bring everything there was, and to bring it in abundance, not to ask damn foolish questions, and shooed him away.

Poor Mathews, slight and wan, cringed under the porthole seat.

"Let's not talk about me, sir," Eli said when the steward had gone. "What of yourself? Are you bound for New Orleans?"

"Just a stop, same as yourself," Hugo-Jim declared conspiratorially. "I've got business up the great river in the territories. I'm in importing," he shouted.

"Importing what?" Eli asked.

"Silks, finery from English factories, tea, manufactured goods, and wenches off the streets of London," Hugo-Jim joked, stretching his last few words in a broad cockney accent.

"So you have been doing business in England?"

"Aye," Hugo-Jim agreed, lapsing into sea talk as was his wont when his mind wandered. "I've been doin' business. And I've been seein' to the new laws."

"Eh?"

"Nothin' lad," Hugo-Jim said. "Well, look here, a decent meal for a change. Blasted cook must have broken out his last stores now that this terrible, terrible crossing is near over."

"Terrible?" Eli asked as he looked at the approaching waiters. Then catching Hugo-Jim's eye, and seeing the jest in it, he began to laugh heartily. And before they were halfway through the second course, he was explaining what had been at the back of his mind that morning and for the length of the entire voyage back to the new world.

". . . so you see, he might be anywhere. And although it's something I haven't thought about since my boyhood, it's heavily on me now. It was a promise I made, after all. Now my poor father's followed my mother to the grave and the money is mine. Now that I've come of age, I feel I must do something about it, although—"

"Although what, sir?" Mathews said, interrupting for the first time.

"Although I expect it could take me the rest of my life and I'd never find him, or find that he's dead, or no longer cares to be freed."

Hugo-Jim poised a fat piece of savory meat an inch before his mouth; staring down at it he said to the Dutch lad, "His name was what?"

"Chane," said Eli. "From the Dutch *hein*. His mother refused to name him, you see."

"No, I don't see," Mathews interjected.

Hugo-Jim bit down on the piece of succulent meat and chewed it for a moment before muttering, "Well, no one expects you to, you jackass."

Mathews cleared his throat.

"I remember a crossing to Louisiana, twenty years ago," Hugo-Jim began in a vacant tone. "On a slaver known as the *Zeebaas*. A child was born and heading for Curacao via New Orleans."

"And what were you doin' on a slaver, sir?" Mathews asked, astonished.

"Crossin' the ocean, you idiot!" Hugo-Jim shouted. He paid no attention when comments began to rise at the next table. A gray haired American woman had just said, "Oh dear," in quite the fashion of London.

"Mr. Morocco," Eli said, "what do you think I ought to do?"

"Why, it will do no harm to ask after him in New Orleans, lad. It seems to me I was present when once a group of slaves were sold there from the Antilles—it was illegal, of course," he finished, whispering.

"Oh," the handsome young Dutch lad said.

"Yes. I'll look into it myself when I go up river. And I'll ask some friends above New Orleans that might know. Aye.

What did you say the name was again, lad? It would be good for you to discharge the promise you made him to my way of thinking," Hugo-Jim said, thinking about a resolution of his own that he had made a long time ago—longer ago, in fact, that *Minheer* Opzeeland was alive.

His wine glass was poised beneath his heavy lips and his forehead was furrowed as he thought back.

"Chane," Eli repeated.

Suddenly there was a commotion on deck. They had made their first landfall. Hugo-Jim drank his wine and poured himself another.

3

Chane stood before the mirror in the downstairs bedroom that was to be his new quarters. Lulu had finished tailoring his new suit and had helped him on with it. It was the first time he had ever worn shoes and socks.

"It looks fine," Lulu said. She had grown into a beautiful black woman and had been in service in the big house for almost two years. The black people knew she was LaForge's favorite but did not hold that against her.

"Yessuh, *baas*," Gusty razzed. "That sho look fine. Never thought a dirty fightin' nigger like you so take to clothin'."

"Don't you bad ass me, Gusty," Chane shot back. He sucked his chest in further so the white silk shirt and all its frills showed a wider expanse beneath his black jacket. His tie and cummerbund were bright red, as were the pocket and collar trimmings on his suit. His shoes were shined to a spit polish and made a sharp noise on the marble and hardwood floors.

"Well, boy, you just about ready?" Mr. LaForge asked, sticking his head into Chane's room.

"Yessuh, Mr. LaForge," Chane replied stiffly.

LaForge grunted.

"He done know everythin' I could git in his black head, Mr. LaForge, suh," Gusty said.

LaForge nodded and withdrew. It gave Chane a bad feeling to know that LaForge could come in to his new room at any time of day or night. In the cabins there had been little more privacy but the presence of the other slaves had somehow helped.

"I guess now you git to find out how it is to be a house nigger here on the Dutchman's place," Gusty said with a toothless grin. He too was in livery and Lulu was dressed in a black frock offset by a white maid's smock, a white collar and cuffs:

"But it ain't goin' to be like that no more, now the master back," Lulu said.

"Like what?" Chane asked.

Neither Gusty nor Lulu made reply. They didn't have to. Chane knew well enough what went on in the master's house while LaForge was overseer and completely in charge. He knew it wasn't just darkie talk. He knew LaForge.

"Gusty!" LaForges' sharp voice came down to the servants' quarters and Gusty raced for the stairway, went up with a clatter and disappeared, leaving the door to Chane's room wide.

"Well," Lulu said. "You best git out of those before you ruin them. You goin' to need them for the master's comin' tomorrow."

Chane looked at himself once and smiled. LaForge had made him bathe and taught him to stand with his feet together and what to say when a guest came to the door. Gusty had seen to the rest of his education, about carrying a tray and laying out the Dutchman's clothes.

Chane looked hard at Lulu who looked, in turn, down at the floor. She pouted. There were ways she still reminded him of Kitty but he had become so good at keeping his thoughts from himself he scarcely remembered that.

"You goin' to stay with me and watch?" he joked.

She was gone out of the room in a flash, moving unlike any of the field hands, moving just like the white women that came to the games, or like their body servants, all of whom had airs.

Chane slipped out of his livery and folded it all neatly on the small bed. He got back into the fresh pair of denims they had left for him and sat down on the soft down. At the cabin his mattress had always been on the floor and in the first cabin, which he had shared with the other young bucks, it had been on a single layer of pine built over the bed of the man below him.

Here he had not only a mattress on a real bed but a bureau and an armoire in which to hang his livery. He had several white shirts, ties, cummerbunds, and socks, a change of shoes, and another suit that Lulu was still working on for him.

Back in the kitchen the cook and her helpers were already beginning the preparations for the feast scheduled for the next day. The Dutchman was to arrive after lunch and the party was to begin before dinner. Everyone in three counties and many influential people from New Orleans would be there. Among them would be Judge Riley and his manservant Boon, whom Blaze had beaten so badly. Mr. Cowley from The Willows would bring his wife and his ward and he would be attended by Big Mac, the high-talking eunuch.

"Chane!"

Gusty's voice came down from the top of the stairs. Chane went to the door and looked up. The white-haired old man was looking down, leaning over like a baboon in a tuxedo. Chane wondered whether he had misjudged his own looks; whether he looked that stupid in livery as well.

"What you want, Gusty?"

"You go outside 'round back and git a horse. Mr. LaForge done already sent for it."

"A horse?"

"Yes, a horse. Whut you expect to ride, a geeraff?"

"What for?"

"You has got to go to Mr. Bandeaux, Mr. Clem Bandeaux, with a message. Cain't you ride a horse?"

"Course I can," Chane replied.

"Well, git."

"Well, what the message?"

"Quail."

"That all?"

"That's all."

Chane went out through the back and around to the stable where a horse was standing with only a bridle. It was a good horse, too, a tall chestnut mare.

"You is to hurry," the boy that was holding the horse explained, "so Mr. Bandeaux can git out into the bayou if'n he ain't already."

"But what if he has?" Chane asked looking straight at the big animal.

"Then it is all right."

Chane swung up in an easy motion and locked his legs as he had seen others do. It was with a great deal of difficulty that he managed to keep his balance, however, and once in the heavy brush of the bayou lands he cut his face sharply on the branches into which the mare ran him. It took a quarter of an hour to learn to keep the animal controlled.

He felt lighter and freer than he had since he left home, since he left Curacao. He let himself be lifted by the hope that things on the plantation would change when the Dutchman took over, that the tight rein of LaForge would let up. That the niggers would be able to live in families as they wished and that the goings on at the plantation house would stop.

The horse seemed to know the way as well as he did. It had probably been there more often. When Chane was unsure of which path to take the horse made its own decision and it proved correct. It was difficult to tell during the day, but Chane finally recognized a huge weeping willow by an inlet of the bayou that he had seen one night when he and another young black had gone exploring.

He dismounted clumsily in front of the big cabin. He was surprised that no one had come outside to meet him when the horse had clobbered up. He took the opportunity to get down and find his land legs again before attempting to ride back.

He walked onto the firm wooden porch and knocked on the door just as Gusty had told him was done between white folks.

There was no sound and he shrugged and was about to go off back when he heard a twig crack in the wood by the side of the cabin.

"I thought I heard someone comin' this way," she said.

It was the Bandeaux woman, Mr. Clem's wife. He had seen her at the games when she had stared at him like none of the other white women. She had cheered most loudly when he did well. She had dark hair and even dark skin for a white. When she moved he could make out the full skin beneath the neckline of her calico frock.

She was smiling very broadly and when she walked she placed her hands on her hips and swung toward him as though she were doing a dance. He figured a white woman just didn't know how to rouse a man without making a fool of herself.

"Why, it's Chane, isn't it?" she cooed.

"I got a message for Mr. Clem," he said, humbly affecting an even heavier nigger talk than usual. "'Bout quail. You tell him that, won't you, Ma'am?"

"No need to be nervous, Chane," she said softly, coming even closer to him. "Mr. Clem's back in the woods. He figured you all would need some bird for the feast tomorrow."

Chane nodded and said, "Yes, Ma'am," and made for his horse, but he waited too long deciding how best to get back on.

"Don't you move, boy," the young white woman said. "Jes' you turn right around."

Chane obeyed her and found her not more than an inch away.

"Oh, but don't you smell nice for a nigger," she sighed. "Ain't you never been alone with a white woman, before?"

Chane backed away from her extended fingers which had begun to trace the line of his bare chest.

"No hair, neither," she was saying sweetly. "Such soft black, hard skin."

Unfortunately he stepped back into the horse and found himself pressed hard against the dark-haired woman. She purposely shrugged her right shoulder and her small white breast popped out like a bird. He felt hot and lost, not from the presence of the woman but because of the reminders that went with it.

"No, Ma'am," he managed to say firmly. He damn sure wasn't going to get into trouble with a white woman he didn't want.

"Oh no? Now, you best hurry and do my bidding, boy," she whispered straight into his ear. "My husband will be comin' home before too long and if you don't I'll jes' tell him that you tried and that I fought you off. You understand, boy? He'd kill you sure."

She had freed her upper body from her dress and hung her bare arms around his neck, almost dropping the entire weight of her body from him. He looked back into the bayou quickly. The horse whinnied and shied away and Chane grunted, lowered himself on top of the whining woman and did his duty by her, just as he had done his duty by the wenches at the Dutchman's, according to LaForge's orders.

He prayed to God that no one heard her laughing, whining and screaming when she let herself be satisfied for a second and then a third time.

4

The Dutchman's mansion was aglow in the early twilight. The eight piece white-jacketed band from New Orleans was playing soft music to accompany the fish course being served at the long table in the dining room. Each of the fifteen candles on the five chandeliers over the table was lit, and additional light from lamps on the sideboards and buffets was reflected from the mirrors on the walls, from the shining silver and expensive bone china. There was a constant tinkle of working silverware and light conversation.

The Dutchman sat at the head of the table beaming. Beside him were his guests of honor, Mr and Mrs. Jameson Cowley of The Willows. Next to Jameson sat the wife of Judge Riley, and next to the Judge, himself, Julius LaForge ate quietly, almost broodfully, dressed to the teeth in a black silk evening coat and a frilled shirt.

Lafayette and Lou-Ellen were not seated together as they had not yet announced. Mr. McKenzie was not there, nor were any of the other overseers or common people, other than LaForge, for whom the Dutchman seemed to have a special kindness. The Bandeauxs, of course, were not present.

Chane and Gusty stood silently at either side of the great double doors which led out of the dining room into the marble hall, where all the candles were lit as well. Even the wall lamps on the second floor were so bright that the entire wide stone staircase, and its brightly scrubbed bright brown walnut balustrade shined.

Gusty had greeted the ladies and gentlemen as they descended from their phaetons and small carriages and had shown them through the wide portals of the mansion. Chane had led them into the main hall beyond the Dutchman's den and the sitting rooms. They were introduced to the Dutchman himself by Jameson Cowley. Many of them had met him before, when he bought and moved into the old LaForge plantation, but many had not. As he had come to stay for life it was only proper that the important Creole society of New Orleans and the three counties be invited to his home.

Everyone had accepted his invitation. Judge Riley and the Cowleys had offered their household help and had their offer accepted. Iwana was helping in the kitchen and the serving maids of three households hurried around the great table, seeing to everyone's pleasure.

Almira Cowley placed her knife and fork lengthwise on her plate and took a deep breath. She wore an almost constant smile, but it was a thin, social smile. She was upset and she could not finish her pheasant. She knew it was probably one provided by the Bandeaux brothers and she felt it all the more repugnant. She despised both Clem and Pierre Bandeaux thoroughly, without a reason or a bit of evidence to support her feelings.

She felt Jameson's stare on her bare back. She had dared a low-backed gown although her chest was fully covered. She had done it for Julius, of course. She looked up once, turned to Mrs. Riley, a very heavy, jovial, freckled, snub-nosed woman in her early fifties and said, "Joan, I never have seen such a lovely gown."

Mrs. Riley smiled and replied "Yours is so charming, too, Almira."

The exchange, of course, was out of place. But Almira had to say something to keep her thoughts away from her husband and to prevent him from scolding her for not eating her bird. If only she had married Julius, and Julius still had the plantation.

She turned, smiled in the direction of her host, whom she suddenly hated, and looked down the table at Lou-Ellen. Her ward was watching Iwana's son who was dressed in the Dutchman's new livery. Almira let her eyes brush across Julius' face.

The fact that they had had their last meeting over three months before did not make her suspect that the Dutchman's overseer was through with her. Nor did it change the place he had in her mind. She covered him with love, respect and attention there, as she knew she ought to cover Jameson.

The Dutchman himself was as well lit as his house. His red face was aglow and his eyes were shining. The red ball he wore on the end of his nose looked as though it had been buffed along with the marble floors and bone china.

He was laughing at something the judge had said, and from the twinkle in the eye of her husband she suspected the whisper had been off color. She blushed and felt angry at their impertinence.

The Dutchman's laugh was awful. It came from his lower stomach through congested lungs and out a rasped throat. It was rough and vulgar and evil. He was no gentleman. His laugh was enough to give that away. What did Jameson see in the rough-looking old seaman that drew him so to the man? It could not have been only a question of money.

Finally a child came and took away her bird. She caught Julius' cold eye on her and returned the glance, lifting her left eyebrow ever so slightly. But he turned away. She could not understand his behavior either.

At last they were bringing the dessert. The wine was changed and the new glasses used. The ugly Dutchman was refusing to give up his glass, downed its contents, laughed and then handed it with an all-too-familiar look, Almira thought, to the young maid of Judge Riley's. Again, Mrs. Cowley was deeply insulted.

And Lou-Ellen could not take her eyes from that Chane!

She looked again at the aging Dutchman. Jameson had not told her his age but he was certainly in his middle sixties. His dissipated face and heavy jowls gave evidence of his having once been of much greater weight. His bald pate shone in the brilliant light and the strange angular shape of his large skull made Almira despise him even more.

Dessert was a French pastry, in honor of the Dutchman's new home, a millefieulle, prepared especially in the patisserie in New Orleans. It was delicious but Almira ate only half her portion. At last it was time for the men to retire to the smoking room and for the women to gossip. In an hour there would be dancing.

Lafayette had gathered a large group of young Creole men around him and was talking flamboyantly at the other side of the room. She couldn't imagine what that silly young man might have to talk about. But he was from good family. That was what counted.

She caught Julius' eye and rose, excused herself to Mrs. Riley, and went out into the main hall between Gusty and Chane. She found her way to the Dutchman's den and went in, closing the door behind her. Luckily, none of the men had gone in there.

Of course, that would have been impolite, Almira realized. That was such a silly idea! How could one possibly be impolite in the house of such an obvious boor? He was an incorrigible foreigner.

The room was exactly the same as it had been several years before when she had her first honest talk with Julius. What a long time Jameson was taking in making up his mind about the Lafayette boy! He had been courting Lou-Ellen for years!

Even the lights in the room were dim. It was just exactly as it had been. Except for the fire, of course, there had been no fire in the hearth that day.

At last she heard the door open behind her and turned to find Julius facing her. He hurriedly entered and closed the

107

door behind him. He stood right against it with his back on it.

"I went to town," she blurted. "You weren't there."

"I'm a fool to come in here, Almira. Stay right there, woman! Right there!" he commanded. "I've only a few words. There's to be no scene now, not tonight, especially when the Dutchman's just back. Later on you can do what you damn well please. Tonight there's to be no scene!"

"But whatever do you mean, Julius?" she whispered.

"Oh, *mon dieu,* Almira. You can't tell me you don't understand. It's over, quite stone dead."

He stayed only long enough to stare into her amazed eyes with enough ferocity to frighten her. Then he left and closed the door behind him, leaving her alone in the Dutchman's den. She could hear the roar of the blaze behind her and the crackling of the logs in the fire.

Jameson left the men standing in the smoking room and walked out into the main hall. Julius LaForge was talking to Gusty who had gone to the front entrance. Iwana's son, Chane, the stud LaForge had chosen for the Dutchman's body servant, for reasons the boy would find out soon enough, was also there.

Julius saw him, seemed momentarily startled, and then came over.

"What is it, Julius?" Jameson said as he approached.

"It's your man, Mac, he wants to talk to you."

"Eh?"

Jameson came to the entrance and stepped out on the front porch.

"I thought I told you to stay with the carriages," he snapped.

"Yessuh, Mr. Jameson, suh, only Timony, he come from The Willows with a message, suh," the big eunuch replied from the dark at the foot of the stairs, where he stood, hat in hand.

"Well, what is it, Mac?"

"It's your friend, Mr. Morocco, what has come off a sailing ship today and is on his way here."

"Here," Jameson yelled. "Not here!"

"But yessuh, Mr. Jameson, suh, he heerd 'bout the doin's and he is comin' straight away."

Jameson's countenance darkened. He shooed the servant away and backed into the hall behind him. Gusty and Chane closed the doors and Julius asked, "What is it, Jameson?"

He didn't like Julius' tone. It was even colder than usual.

"Nothin'," he replied.

Then he saw Almira exit from the Dutchman's den. She didn't see him but walked quickly toward the dining room where many of the women were still sitting, spreading their gossip.

"You," he sneered, turning to Chane and looking the big black straight in the eye. This was the black Lou-Ellen had been staring at. He couldn't understand it. Blaze had partially flattened his nose; his lips were thicker than they had been when he was younger. He didn't see what the ingenuous little girl saw in him. "When Mr. Morocco comes, you send him to me, in there, straight away," he commanded.

"Yessuh, *maitre*," Chane replied.

Jameson stared at the black a moment longer. Not even his own slaves called him *maitre*. Then he marched away into the room from which Almira had just exited and where he had instructed Chane to send Hugo-Jim.

There was a fire roaring in the hearth. The captain's sextant was on the big oak table; his globe was nearby. Old Mr. LaForge's books, bound in Morocco leather, lined the walls. What could Almira have been doing in there? Just when he thought she had taken a turn for the better, too.

Through the window he saw the shadow of a carriage pass and heard the muffled clatter of horse's hooves. He went to the door and opened it a few inches. He watched the main entrance.

Gusty and Chane did their duty. When the big man arrived they spoke softly to him and Chane led him quickly toward Jameson. Jameson opened the door wide and Hugo-Jim came in in a rush, embraced him, and pounded him upon the back with his heavy hands.

"Hey Jamie boy, how are ye? Ye are lookin' fit, lad, still fit."

Jamie was forced to smile broadly. He warmly returned his friend's emotion and greeting.

"And you too, you cockney oaf. How's your business?"

"Well, well, Jamie, and yourn?"

Jameson shook his head, looked down at the floor and turned his back on his old friend.

"Why, what is it, lad?" Hugo-Jim complained.

"Close the door, Hugo," Jameson said softly. A hush fell about them as Hugo-Jim complied. Jameson heard the door come to as he walked closer to the fire.

"Then it's true," he heard Hugo-Jim whisper hoarsely behind him. "I hadn't wanted to believe it of ye, Jamie. Truth to tell, I hadn't."

Jameson approached one of the big leather armchairs and sat down in it. He watched the blaze burn before him and, reaching forward, he grabbed a poker and turned a heavy log.

From outside in the main hall he heard a group of women pass, giggling and laughing and shrieking something incoherent at the top of their voices, probably something asinine.

"Sit down, Hugo," Jameson said.

His big friend came over to the neighboring chair and sat

109

on its arm. The man seemed in good health; his face was red from his recent voyage and he held himself as powerfully as ever. The only signs of age were his baldness and his increasing wealth, told by the quality of his clothes and his jewelry, a diamond stick pin in his tie and a cluster of rings on his right hand.

"It is him, then, is it not, Jamie?"

"Yes, old friend, it is him. As you suspected all these years."

"Hasebos," Hugo-Jim pronounced the assured name sarcastically and spit in the fire. "I'll kill him."

Jameson looked hard at his friend and simply shook his head. His jaw pushed out jackel-like and he could feel the place where his teeth touched.

"No," he finally said. "There'll be no killing, not of the Dutchman, not of Hasebos, or Van Zachten, if you prefer his real name. He is too valuable to me, Hugo. Do you hear me?"

Again his big friend spat in the fire. The spittle hissed. His friend stood and began to pace the room.

"You would come between me and what I promised to bring to this man—"

"Revenge?" Jameson shouted. "He never did you any harm! You've twisted him in your mind with the captain you ran from that black day in Gibraltar. Those were blacks that Van Zachten killed, not English sailors! White English sailors!"

"White!" Hugo-Jim snorted fiercely. "White!"

"And do you see no difference then?" Jameson shouted. Then, realizing he was making too much noise, that he might be doing the reverse of what he intended, riling instead of calming Hugo-Jim, he stood and approached the man whose life he had twice saved.

He came straight up to him and took the huge man by the shoulders.

"Leave it be. I ask you as a favor to me, Hugo. Leave it be. This man is both a friend and a business companion of mine . . . and more than that; more than I care to speak of. It's like . . . Remember the house in Tangier? It's better than that here for me. I would go mad at The Willows," Jameson pleaded. "Almira is . . ."

Hugo-Jim broke away and walked toward the window. He stared out into the night for a full minute.

"How is it with Lou-Ellen?" he asked softly.

"Well."

"And her man. Are they to be married?"

"No. But I have given up trying to stop them. The next time he asks I fear I will give my permission."

"Despite her birth, aye, despite her birth," Hugo-Jim laughed, posing and answering his own question. "It has

110

always been a source of wonder to me that it made any difference to you at all. A person is what they are and that's all."

"I know how you feel about that, too," Jameson said.

"I wish ye had told me at once, instead of hiding it from me all this time," Hugo-Jim said, returning to the question of the Dutchman. "Telling me the man was another and not that slimy Van Zachten. If you had only come straight out and told me then, and begged me then."

"Begged?" Jameson barked.

"Aye. And what would you call it, Jamie?"

Jameson put his hand to his forehead and stared deeply into the fire. Then he turned and looked at the big man again.

"Mathews and I arrived this afternoon from England. It's an easier crossing than it once was," he laughed. "This evening we leave for the upper Mississippi country."

"There's no need to go. Stay at The Willows as long as you—"

"This evening we leave," Hugo-Jim snapped, interrupting. "I cannot tell ye, Jamie, just how much it is ye are askin' of me."

The Englishman slapped his thigh with his heavy hand and started for the door.

"Hugo, I . . ."

But Jameson had nothing more to say. He followed the man into the hall, watched him stare at the wide staircase for a moment, knew he was thinking that Van Zachten was back there somewhere, and then watched him walk quickly to the door in that wide posture he had that had served him well on the rolling ocean.

Jameson watched Gusty come alert and snap at Iwana's son, "You, Chane, get Mr. Morocco's hat, quick."

Hugo-Jim, who had his hand extended for the hat, stopped suddenly and stook stark still. Jamie heard him ask, "What's your name, boy?"

"Chane," the black said.

Jameson watched them exchange a long, peculiar look, saw but did not hear, Hugo-Jim whispered something to the Dutchman's new body servant, saw the black straighten suddenly and seem to come alive, and then watched his old friend leave through the great portal of the captain's plantation.

7 : LAFAYETTE

It was a cold winter. In the middle of January there was a snow that stayed on the ground for over a week. It was the coldest winter Jameson could remember.

In the three months since the Dutchman's party, Almira had entered a decline as bad as any Jameson had foreseen. He permitted only Lafayette to call at The Willows and consulted with doctors in New Orleans. They all agreed that there was nothing wrong with her physically. Still, she would sit in her downstairs room in front of the cold fireplace and work endlessly on her petit point. She did not speak to him when he addressed her, but communicated only with her servants, and with Lou-Ellen when it pleased her. She was far worse than she had been before.

The wind had increased and rattled the window behind Jameson's desk. In an hour the work gangs on the wharf road would be sent home and McKenzie would ride by with the daily report. It was already dusk. Lou-Ellen was spending the week with the Judge's daughters in New Orleans. Lafayette, Jameson's constant plague, had not been to The Willows in days.

The lad's innocence and foppishness disgusted Cowley. When he had been Lafayette's age he had already been to Europe and Africa, had fought and loved boldly, and ridden out storms on the high seas. Everything was too soft for Lafayette's generation. They would never be men of quality.

Jameson rose, crossed to the sideboard, and poured a brandy for himself. He removed a cigar from the box and made the motions appropriate to preparing and lighting it. Then he returned to his desk, hoisted his feet to it, and made himself comfortable.

It was quiet in the house without Lou-Ellen, but it was also a relief. He had more time to visit the Dutchman and more freedom. The accounts were in order. The combined profits of twenty years were working quietly in New Orleans banks. His slaves were content and generally cheerful. There was but one thing he wanted that he could not have: a son to whom to pass on The Willows.

Unfortunately Lou-Ellen was as determined as she was naive. Lafayette seemed destined to come into the plantation, regardless of how little Jameson liked the lad.

The day darkened quickly as less light filtered through the window behind Jameson's head. His cigar burned down inch

112

by inch as he thought about his wife and what he could do about her. Word was bound to get out after a while. He would not have her damage the reputation of The Willows by bringing a pall of insanity over the great house.

He rose finally and stretched, stubbing out his smoke in a jade ashtray, a souvenir of his days in England. He went to the door, opened it, and walked out into the great hall. Big Mac, who had heard his door open, came out of the sitting room and waited as Jameson walked toward the front doors. Jameson stopped and looked back.

"Where is Mrs. Cowley, Mac?" he asked.

"In her sewin' room upstairs, suh," the big eunuch replied.

Jameson nodded darkly and continued to the door. He opened it and stepped out on the porch. The cold air that assaulted his senses revived him. He had not realized how drowsy he had been feeling.

For a time he paced the porch with Almira in the front of his mind. He could see her up there, over his head, working away on her damn petit point, or staring stupidly out into the dusk. For a long time he stood on the cold porch, staring toward the wintering fields, wishing she were dead, dead and buried. It was not too late for Jameson to marry again, to marry someone who might bear him a son.

He was not unattractive. He had seen to it that his body remained in good condition. He had not put on weight, nor gone bald. He was only forty-five years old. His dress was impeccable, it always had been. He carried himself with style on foot or on horse. There was no reason why—after a decent amount of time had passed—he couldn't marry again.

Judge Riley had a sporty young daughter that took well to the games. She did not gossip much and simper quite as much as the other Creole wenches.

The sun had gone completely from the sky and a night wind had come up off the river, whipping past the house and howling around the corners of the big building. For a moment Jameson thought he saw a horseman way off at the bayou road but by the time he blinked and looked hard there was nothing there. It was possible to see that far only because the high cane in the close fields was down. The land lay fallow, awaiting spring planting.

Soon he heard an owl somewhere and then the sound of McKenzie's mare coming up from the river with the wind. The horse's hooves hit the hard ground, giving off a different sound than they did in the other seasons at The Willows. The wind rushed through the long line of heavy trees to the entrance road and a beam somewhere in the old house creaked as if the house were a ship and night wind were pulling at her sails.

McKenzie's mare turned the corner of the building and

Mr. McKenzie nodded to the booted figure astride the porch who held a black thong in his right hand and stared bleakly ahead of him.

"Evenin', sir," McKenzie said loudly, to be heard over the wind. "Shall I get down and come in?"

"Is there any need?"

"No, sir, everything is all right at the work."

"Good."

"Ought to be done in a week or so. The new road will make the hauling easier, all right. That much is already clear."

"Good. You might as well get home. Your woman has a hot meal for you, no doubt."

McKenzie nodded and looked thoughtful. He looked up at the second floor, probably at the light in Almira's sitting room, and then returned his glance to Jameson.

"What is it?" Jameson demanded. He too had to raise his voice over the howl of the wind.

"Place is quiet with Lou-Ellen off to town."

"Yes it is."

"Mr. Cowley?"

"Yes."

"Something strange has been going on in the bayou."

"What?" Jameson shouted. He felt a sudden threat, as if McKenzie connected whatever it was to the strangeness over their heads.

"Someone has been watching my woman from the trees. I found tracks a couple of times now."

"A nigger," Jameson stated.

"Mule tracks. A runaway maybe, though I know of none that's recent. Maybe someone from the Dutchman's, or . . ."

"Or what?"

"Might be Bandeaux."

"What for?" Jameson said intently, stepping closer to McKenzie's mount so that he was looking straight up at the man.

"Don't know, but Clem's the onliest one with a mule sneaks around in the bayou. Just wanted to tell you."

Jameson nodded and waited.

"Didn't want to pick up a scatter gun without you knowing about it."

"Blast him to Mississippi," Jameson said, spat off the porch onto the cold soil, and turned to go into the empty house.

It was at least two hours later, after he had eaten by himself in his study, that he ordered his stallion saddled, mounted up, and rode off through the cold night to the Dutchman's.

2

It was even colder near the sea reach of the great Mississippi. The levees did not help much against the wind that had come up out of the Gulf of Mexico, bringing the waves to white caps on the usually quiet river.

All the lights were lit in the judge's house so that it looked warm and especially hospitable from the cold street. Lou-Ellen, who had disentangled herself from the judge's daughters in order to be alone with her thoughts, watched from the window of her upstairs room. The women had spent the evening talking about the engagement of a silly Creole woman of no real money and no charm to a gentleman of high birth and wealth. Lou-Ellen was furious.

She saw the darkie return to the judge's house as he had left, through the front door. She had sent him because she liked and trusted him and because he was so cute. He was twelve years old and the son of the judge's kitchen woman and Boon, and he was chocolate brown and so sweet Lou-Ellen felt she could crush him to her. She had always wanted a flock of young colored boys to wait on her. Well, someday she would get that wish.

There was a gentle rap on her door and she turned from the curtain just long enough to say, "Come in."

The lad entered but she did not look. Her eyes were back on the street.

"Miss Lou-Ellen, Maam. Ah done whut you said."

"That's good, honey. That's real good. Did he say somethin'?"

"No, Maam."

"Then I expect he will be right along."

"Yessum."

"But I declare. I don't see him, angel. I jus' don't—wait, here he comes now."

Lou-Ellen turned in a flurry of petticoats and rushed to the child who had closed the door behind him. "He is comin'," she said excitedly.

She could not help herself and bent down in a warm rush of emotion to kiss the small boy on the cheek. She blushed for a moment, looked coyly at him, and then sent him running from the room, patting him sisterly on the rear and saying, "Thank you, angel. You did jus' fine."

When he was gone she gathered herself together, took a deep breath and began to walk slowly and stately toward the top of the staircase.

Everyone else was in the smoking room listening to the judge or still talking about that stupid engagement. She would soon give them something to talk about.

She heard the sound of the knocker and then the footsteps of the judge's door man as he hurried to see to the visitor. She started to descend the stairs.

The butler opened the heavy door and bowed slightly as

Lafayette entered the house. She was just in time to come up to them both. The wind in the street rushed in through the open door with Lafayette and blew her dress up over her ankles.

"My, that wind!" she exclaimed in a high voice. Then she settled down quickly and said seriously, "Jarvis, you tell the judge nothin', you hear? I want to talk with Mr. Lafayette alone for a few minutes."

"Yes, Maam, Miss Lou-Ellen."

"What is this, Lou-Ellen?" Lafayette queried.

"Soon enough, Lafayette," she answered. Then, turning to Jarvis, a small coal black man with long, white, elegant mutton chops, she asked, "Jarvis, do you think we could use the library?"

"Oh yes, Maam, Miss Lou-Ellen. Right through here."

The colored man led them to the judge's library and closed them into it with a smile. He was a good-humored darkie, Lou-Ellen thought. She knew black people liked her.

"Now, why have you called me like this, Lou-Ellen?" Lafayette demanded petulantly.

Lou-Ellen walked to the other side of the judge's long table, putting it between herself and Lafayette, and then raised herself up on her toes an inch and came down with decision. She knew she looked her best; she had spent a full hour in front of the mirror after deciding to send for him. Her blond hair was perfectly sculpted to her head, her forehead was smooth and white, her skin ripe and alive. She had been told more than once that she was one of the prettiest girls in three countries.

"I have come to a decision, Lafayette," she said firmly.

Lafayette eyed her warily. She could see he wished that table were not between them. Well, there would be more than just a table between them if he did not do what she wanted. She wanted to marry him but she was not going to wait for ever. She wanted him because of his family name and his family's place in society. She wanted him because of his good looks and because she knew she could have her way with him.

Most of the other men that had courted her or that she had met in New Orleans were too strong willed to suit her. She knew exactly what she wanted and she was not likely to change her mind about it.

"Lafayette," she said. "You asked me to marry you almost three years ago. Do you know what today is, Lafayette, do you?"

"No, Lou-Ellen," the young man said tentatively.

"Today is the fifteenth of January. It is just two months and two days before my birthday."

"But—"

"Lafayette, I am going to be twenty. Twenty," she repeated.

116

"Do you hear?"

"Lou-Ellen, I have asked your guardian—"

"I know that, Lafayette," she said petulantly. "Now I want you to ask him again."

"All right. I will next week when you go back to The Willows. I will come to call."

"No," she said decisively.

"What?"

"You will go out there tonight."

"Tonight?" Lafayette repeated incredulously.

"Yes Lafayette, tonight! You will ask once and finally for my hand."

"It's a hell of a night out there tonight," Lafayette said, spinning around and pointing out the window. His young forehead was creased with perplexity, his mouth wide open. He looked upset and cute.

"What do you mean, 'finally,' " he said very slowly, as an after thought, coming closer to her side of the table.

"What 'finally,' " he said again.

"Lafayette," Lou-Ellen began with her head high and her hands folded across her midriff. "I said I had come to a decision."

"What are you driving at, Lou-Ellen?"

"If my guardian will not grant you my hand in marriage tonight, yes, this very night, Lafayette, we are going to elope."

The young Louisianan's jaw fell a foot.

"Now, now, Lafayette! You stay right there!" she commanded weakly for he had let a wicked gleam come into his eye and his open mouth had become a beaming smile. "Right there."

But he rushed around the table to her and grasped her in his arms. It was just as she had planned it. He kissed her passionately on the mouth. She felt her heart beat, felt the blood rush through her breasts, and her loins weaken. It was just as she had imagined it all.

"No, Lafayette. Go now. Hurry."

"Yahoo!" he shouted so loudly it was probably heard down at the road, let alone in the sitting room. Lafayette's eyes still held the wicked gleam she knew she could inspire in them and she let hers reflect it as well as he looked once more at her longingly, before rushing from the room.

He was calling for a horse even before he was out the front door and the cold night wind rushed in again and played with the hem of her skirt.

3

Lulu came into the dark room and closed the door quietly behind her. She lifted her hand to her kerchief, removed it,

117

and shook her hair out. Chane did not change his position by the window or in any way acknowledge her presence in the room; still, he knew she was there.

She folded her kerchief neatly into a diamond shape and put it in the hip pocket of her uniform.

"Mr. Cowley jus' came by," she said softly.

Chane turned at last and looked at her a long time. She always felt odd under his glance. There was more power in it even than in LaForge's whip or the Dutchman's orders. Chane was so broad, so tall, and so black. His muscles rippled under his skin when he did nothing, nothing at all. His eyes flashed always, no matter what his mood. His bearing, even when he was trying to be humble or shuffling in front of the masters, was always somehow regal. It frightened her and filled her with hope.

"Go to him then," Chane said. His voice was like the sound of distant thunder. It was deeper than the preacher's she had heard outside the church in New Orleans when she had been a child.

"When they send for me . . . or for us," she replied.

He looked at her and then reverted his gaze out the window. He was not staring at anything in particular. He could not have been, as it was black out there, and cold.

"He leaves us be two, three days, then he is on us again," she said slowly, coming over to Chane's bed and sitting down on it.

Chane snorted in response.

"You goin' to go tonight?" she asked.

"Leave me be, woman!" he snapped.

She fell silent and looked down at the floor. Then she said, "You want me to go now? I will go and leave you alone."

He made no answer so she did not move. She was just too tired to get up unless he told her to. It was not from the work that she was tired, but from the fear and the prospect of another session with the Dutchman and Mr. Cowley . . . though it was better when Mr. Cowley was there.

"They will tire of us soon and find others," Chane said, softly.

She smiled but she did not believe it. They would go on performing for the insatiable and impotent old man until he died, she knew it in her bones—till he died, or they did. She knew that they were something special together, she and Chane; she knew the Dutchman valued them highly.

She still burned to know whether Chane would sneak off that night to visit Iwana, who had sent word that she had a message for him. If he went to see Iwana he would probably see Clarissa as well.

The cold wind rattled the window pane beside Chane but he still did not stir. She could sense the terrible strength that was building inside him. The others, Blaze and Gusty before him, had all done the master's bidding easily, knowing it was their place to obey. Chane was different. She could see that much even if LaForge and the other white folk could not.

"How is it," she asked finally, "that you have never spoken to me of the place you came from?"

For the first time since she had come in Chane looked at her fully. Although it was dark in the room he could see clearly enough, the thick bones of her face which reminded him of the Opzeeland girl, the quick way she seemed to have with her shoulders. For a moment he felt something within him that had not moved for a long time. For a moment it was as if the thousand and one times he had forbidden himself to think had never occurred. She saw it in his eyes, although she did not know what it was.

She moved by shifting forward; although there were ten feet between them in the room, it was as if they were much closer.

"What?" she asked.

He made no reply but she saw from his smile that something, some thought or memory or thwarted wish, or perhaps all three and more than the three together, was giving him a great deal of pain. Still smiling, he turned his gaze back out into the bleak night and again the window pane rattled.

Strangely, Lulu felt relieved. She had not wanted to have that thing out. She intuited that somehow it would be terrible. She sighed and rose and went toward the door.

She was about to reach for the knob when she heard the footsteps outside. She sighed again, this time with resignation.

Gusty knocked. She opened it so that he could not see Chane at the window.

"What you doin' here, gal?" the old man snapped.

She made no answer. She did not have to answer to him.

"Where he at?"

Again she said nothing. The old man was filled with much hate for her, for Chane as well. Once he had been the favorite of the white people. That was a long time past. It had been before Blaze and before the one before Blaze. Like the Dutchman, Gusty was envious of those who had what he no longer had; youth, lust, beauty perhaps.

"You gonna answer me, gal?"

She looked into the old man's face and frowned. Finally he said, "You first. You tell him he is to come up when I call, and to be ready. Git undressed," he snapped, spun on his heel, and walked away. His long arms reached almost to his knees, his ears protruded from the sides of his white scalp like birds about to take off.

"It's time," she said to Chane softly and heard him grunt in answer. "You gonna go over to The Willows after?"

"Uh huh."

"It's cold out there tonight."

"I got my coat," he said.

She sighed once again and moved off. Her room was down the hall. She entered it and slipped her black maid's uniform over her head and left it, and the rest of her garments, folded neatly on her calico bedspread. Then, entirely nude, and cold, she started up towards the Dutchman's den.

She walked slowly with her shoulders thrust back to make her breasts come up, the way she had been instructed. She walked with her head down but without shame. She had done it a hundred times before.

There was no one in the great hall. The door to the Dutchman's den was slightly ajar and she could smell the smoke from their cigars. There was no sound of voices or of movement.

She did not look to either side as she entered. She had instructions about that as well. The chaise longue was ready before the fire and she went to it and sat down. She could see their feet then, the Dutchman's pink fat ones and Cowley's, still booted. The young boy was ready at the Dutchman's feet but Cowley, as usual, had no one. As usual he would wait until she was all but dead and then use her.

She lay back on the chaise longue and spread her legs so that one dropped over each side. Then, slowly, she brought her hands down her sides, fingers spread wide as she had been told, to her vagina and spread it with her fingers. She breathed heavily, as she had been told, so that her large breasts swelled and sank. The Dutchman's boy knelt and tried to excite him, but he was an old man, an old, old man.

She continued to work at herself and to do the deep breathing. She could not help but feel dizzy after a time and she began to rock slightly to and fro and up and back. She was only a few feet away from the old man. Her head spun so that she could see his flabby paunch and his useless white sex and she quickly brought it back straight so that she could see only the ceiling. It was too late, however. He brought his heavy hand down hard on her breast and she bit her tongue to stop from screaming out.

"Faster," she heard the Dutchman say. She did not know whether he meant her or the boy. She moved faster.

"Hum," master Cowley ordered softly, without passion, as if he were asking for a box of salt in a store.

The Dutchman was laughing. She made no external manifestation of it but she was extremely relieved. Even with Cowley there he was capable of using a hot poker on her skin, or at least of beating her viciously with a cold one. She had endured both of these pastimes of his in the last months. But recently, after the experiment with the boy, the Dutchman had been able to become excited after some time and he was happy to let Cowley conduct the sessions.

Her long legs were bent so that her thighs were taut. Her arms were close to her breasts so that the motion of her hands also moved them slightly. She could see her nipples swaying and heard master Cowley begin to breathe faster. She let herself sigh for him so that it would be soon over. Her foot nearest the flame was becoming uncomfortable.

"All right," Master Cowley said.

She knew Gusty was going for Chane, that soon he would be standing as nude as she, with his head down, waiting at the door, all his sex strong and ready to do anything asked of it for as long as it was asked. She was entirely without shame and shuddered then at the prospect of his arrival. After Chane, master Cowley would be easy to endure. She could even be grateful to him for the little bit of pleasure he would add to what Chane would do to her. It was only because by himself that he could never suffice, that she hated it when he tried alone.

"I found the door o—What in God's name!"

She did not understand what was happening but suddenly there was someone else in the room, another white man. She was so startled she looked up. Beyond Master Cowley, who was red faced and trying to cover himself, the young master Lafayette stood completely dumbfounded.

She could hear the wind from the outside beyond the open door in the great hall as the roaring in her loins stopped.

"Get him out of here! Gusty!" The Dutchman yelled at the top of his voice. He stood completely naked over the small colored boy, trembling with rage, such that she gasped and hid her face and lay back and began again.

She felt his kick in her side and grabbed for air through the pain and heard him shout again, "Gusty! Get him out of here! Gusty!"

4

Chane took advantage of the situation. He did not care one way or the other about Mr. Lafayette. Whatever happened among these white people was their business, and their problem. In the fields, and in the cabins behind the house, the black people might still think the Dutchman's welfare was worth their worry, but Chane knew better.

He had stood at the top of the stairs and watched the young white man run out of the house, mount, and ride off into the wind. He was there, looking at the open door, standing next to muttering Gusty, when Mr. Cowley ran out after him putting himself back together, called for his stallion, and rode off in just the opposite direction. Then Chane went back on downstairs before the raving Dutchman could come out into the hall too. He went back downstairs and got dressed again.

It was a good fifteen minutes before Lulu came down and went into her room. He thought he could hear her sobbing but he did not go in to see to her. She had sobbed before and there was no damn thing he could do about it.

He put his coat on and looked out into the night. Then he raised his window. He stuck his head out and looked up. The Dutchman had not yet put his bedroom lantern on. He closed the window and began to pace slowly.

It occurred to him again to pity poor Mr. Lafayette, whose horse would be too tuckered to run all the way back to New Orleans. And run it would have to. He paced and wondered what Iwana wanted to tell him. He thought about Clarissa and he thought about not thinking.

It was about a half hour later, after the commotion, that the Bandeaux brothers rode up to the front door to be shouted at by the Dutchman, and then rode off into the night. He saw them approach from the window, coming up out of the black bayou like evil spirits, carrying long guns, their hunting knives gleaming in the moonlight. He shook his head once again for Mr. Lafayette, raised his heavy eyebrows, and waited.

Finally he heard a sound on the upstairs landing. He raised his window and waited. When he saw the light go on he threw one leg out, brought the other after it, and jumped. He was in the cover of the trees within three seconds.

It was a long walk to the bayou and hard going against the wind. Once he thought of turning back but decided against it, lowered his head, and kept walking. Once he got within the shelter of the bayou it would be easier.

The cane was down in the fields. The earth was frozen from the snow that had just about disappeared. Hunks of ice sometimes came down the river and knocked against each other or against the shore so that you could hear them way up from the wharfs. The work gangs at The Willows had been ordered to stop work on the road and buoy up the docks against a freeze, and they had not gotten back to work on the road until way after the snow.

Once in the bayou it was easier going. There was plenty of light too, although it came unevenly as the strong wind blew the branches of the willow and cypress trees back and forth across the face of the moon. The wind howled through the Spanish moss and the old trees shook like demons loose in the world, but Chane did not believe in demons, or in the voodoo.

He could see the overseer LaForge's house through the trees. There was a light in his bedroom which went out even

122

as Chane watched. Chane thought that he would have gone too, but apparently not. The fewer the better, of course.

It was funny how transparent white people were. Even back in Curacao . . . but once again Chane stopped himself from thinking and just lowered his head and increased his speed.

He could see Mr. Cowley's tracks, the fresh ones, going back to The Willows. He saw where they had left the road to go toward Bandeaux's, and where they had come back on to it. It was slippery there on the old moss-covered logs and Chane looked ahead carefully to make sure Mr. Cowley was not ahead.

It was a good hour later that he arrived at the west cabins of The Willows. None of the lights were on that could be seen from outside. He approached the nearest and listened carefully at the door. There was nothing to be heard over the sound of the wind.

He knocked, lightly at first, then louder.

"Who dere?" someone finally yelled. Chane had not been there for a long time and the male voice surprised him.

He knocked again. A yellow light went on inside the cabin and then the heavy curtain was drawn over, closing it off from the dark night again.

The door opened and a skinny young black man stuck his head out. Chane did not recognize him.

"Come to see Clarissa about a message," Chane explained.

"Message? Message? You Chane, ain't you? Who you think you are, message?"

Chane frowned and said, "You ask her."

"You crazy? Who you think you are, you?"

Behind the man he heard Clarissa's voice. "There's a message from his mother. Invite him in, Henri."

He saw her come up behind him. She had wrapped a calico blanket around herself for the cold. Henri was also bundled up.

"This is my man, Henri," she said by way of introduction. Chane nodded.

The young man stepped aside and let him in. He went over to the cold furnace and sat beside it. Clarissa still looked very good to him, but he was too tired to really care that she had taken a man.

"What has been with you, Chane?" she asked.

"I am in the Dutchman's house," he explained softly.

The couple looked at each other, then back at Chane, but made no reply.

"You wait here," Clarissa said, "Ah'll git yo ma, you."

She went to the back of the cabin and dressed. Henri was worried that Chane would look but he didn't. Chane just watched the light in the lamp flicker and listened to the wind and tried not to pay too much attention to Henri. He was a runt of a man, not much good for anything, probably.

Clarissa went out hurriedly and left them alone. He looked at Henri, then leaned back and asked, "Don't you offer nothin'?"

"Nothin'," Henri replied.

Chane snorted and relaxed further. It was good to be in out of the cold.

"You killed a boy once, you," Henri stated.

"That so?"

"At the Dutchman's games."

Chane nodded. Henri made him feel very tired. Yes, he had once killed another fighter.

"He was mah brother, you," Henri said.

Chane didn't answer. He looked over at Henri and just nodded. Henri stood up and went to the back of the cabin, clasped his hands before him and returned to sit by the clumsy wooden table. He didn't say anything else.

Finally Clarissa came back, alone.

"She is comin'," she explained hurriedly and also went to the cold furnace for heat, and also found none. Chane looked up and their eyes met for a moment.

Iwana finally came in. Chane was tired but he rose humble and went to her and embraced her. He could not remember a time when he had been able to get his arms around her. She was so huge, so monumentally large.

"*Youngen,*" she said. "*Het is zo hoot.*"

"Yes, Wana," Chane replied. "What is it, Wana? What was so important, Wana?"

She was crying. Great tears rolled down her majestic black face and over her thick cheeks. She was also smiling broadly.

"It is master Eli," she said. "Mister Hugo-Jim sent word with his man. Master Eli is coming. Oh youngen," she said, "We have to hold on. *Wie moot wachten.*"

5

The wind was high over the flat bottom land between Bayou Chien and the lights of New Orleans. It brought clouds quickly over the face of the moon. Lafayette's horse whinnied and tried to break away from the cypress tree to which he was tied. The sound of footsteps coming up from the river across the hard ground spooked the horse again and Pierre Bandeaux had to go over to it and swat it between the ears.

Pierre's thin frame and hard profile stood in silhouette against the gray light. It was not until he was directly upon him that Clem could make out the cruel depth of his features.

"Nope," Clem muttered. "No place down there."

"Didn't I say so?" Pierre responded coldly.

"We could dump him in the river; the current would take him out to sea."

"Chancy," Pierre replied sternly.

"Take him on back then."

"I reckon."

"And the horse?"

Pierre stood and scratched his scalp as Clem spat into the road. "Better whup him up, send him back."

"This is good bay," Clem said looking the animal over. He stepped over the body of the dead Lafayette to get a better look at the saddle.

"Better set him loose, you," his brother repeated.

"Good saddle, too, fancy bridle."

A gust of wind came up off the river and hissed across the grass toward them. The bay tried to back away from the Frenchman.

"What people goin' to think when Mr. Lafayette's horse comes back with an empty saddle?"

"What they goin' to think if they find him on your place?"

Clem spat again into the road. "That Cowley is goin' to have to give me a horse, now," he said sternly.

He reached over and untied the animal which stepped back into the underbrush in fright. Clem pulled it out again into the dark road, over the body of its former master, and smacked it on the rump so that it raced away. Pierre held the reins of the mule and the borrowed mare.

They watched the frightened bay race off toward town. He would return to his stable and the word would be out by dawn that Mr. Lafayette was missing. They had work to do.

Pierre looked up and watched the clouds race across the moon. He felt the chill wind coming up over the river and he bent down again and removed Lafayette's wallet. He split the money within it with his brother, took the watch for himself, gave Clem the cufflinks and the tie pin and the belt and hoisted the thin body of the dead man onto the mule. Then he mounted behind it and rode off.

He did not look back. Clem was checking the hard ground to see if there were any signs for the law to find. When he was satisfied that there were none he mounted the mare and rode off after his brother.

The animals were exhausted after the hard ride to catch up with Lafayette, and the pace was slow. The mule was especially stubborn under the heavy burden, although it was a good mule, as fast as a horse when under the whip. The two brothers made an eery sight on the dark road in single file.

After several miles they cut away from the road in a line for the deepest part of the bayou, across the uncultivated wooded land of the Dutchman's place. The path through the woods was wide, as it was used for hauling timber, and the brothers were soon riding abreast, slouched and grumbling in their saddles.

"Man has to pay if'n he gits another man up out of the night."

"Out of his wife's bed," the elder added laughing.

"Got to pay well, eh?"

"Yes, yes, Pierre. Oh yes."

"A horse too, from our Mr. Cowley."

"Uh huh. I reckon Mr. Cowley will have to be a mite more friendly now. And his man McKenzie jes chasin' me off the plantation, too. Yes, I reckon Mr. McKenzie will have to be a mite more friendly too."

As they approached the dark bayou the sound of frogs became audible and the hooves of the horses made a softer, steady sound on the beaten grass.

"You best stay away from McKenzie, you," Pierre said.

Clem made no reply. He rocked slightly in his saddle and watched the way the dead man was sprawled in front of his brother. There was blood all over the back of his jacket but it was not dripping on the road.

"That Scot will kill you sure if he catches you with his colored."

Clem laughed and took a deep breath. He let his mare's head sag as the pace slowed even further. There was no hurry. There wasn't a living soul in twenty miles, outside of the plantation people and Clem's woman. By the time the winter sun came up the body would be well hidden and they would be safely home.

"I reckon Mr. Jameson didn't like the boy much," Pierre said after a while.

"I reckon."

"Put him in the bayou?"

"Nah. He'd jes come up."

"You mean we got to bury him?"

"What then?" Clem asked.

"Drop him in a gully."

"This ain't no nigger, you," his brother replied.

"So?"

An owl hooted somewhere to the north; the borrowed mare picked up her head and tossed it. Somehow Lafayette's right arm shook loose and tumbled down alongside his left one.

"So we better bury him."

It was becoming light enough to see ahead and Clem spotted a water moccasin slip across the grassy path toward the water. Almost anyplace along the bayou from there on would be all right. Just to be on the safe side he thought they had better go in a bit deeper, however.

"In here," he finally said.

Turning the mare, he led Pierre down into a gully that ran

straight into the swampy ground near the water. There digging would be easy. He dismounted and walked slowly along until he found a patch of mud free of stones and roots.

"You find a place?" Pierre asked.

"Come on."

Pierre dismounted and tied the animals. He looked once enviously at Lafayette's boots, shook his head, and came over.

"Dutchman is gonna give me a pair of boots too, he is," he muttered.

Clem spat because he hadn't thought of that himself. He pointed to the spot he had found.

Pierre nodded and kicked at it with his foot. It seemed all right to him too. He turned and went back to Clem's mule. He got his rifle and came back. Clem had already begun to work.

Holding the rifles like spades they slowly hollowed out a section of the muddy gully. It took a long time and they stopped often to rest.

"Should of brought a shovel," Clem muttered once.

"Next time."

Then they fell to work again. Down in the gully, far into the wooded bayou land, the cold river wind couldn't reach them and didn't penetrate far enough to howl in the tree tops. The only sounds were those of cicada and frogs and an occasional night bird.

"I reckon Miss Lou-Ellen is goin' to have to find herself another suitor," Clem said laughing, as Pierre went back for the body.

"I reckon," he said.

He tried to carry it so that the blood didn't get on his clothes but failed. He carried it over and dumped it into the hollow.

"*Merde*," Clem cursed and started kicking the soft earth back over the body.

"You think the spring rains will wipe loose all this, you?" Pierre asked when they had finished.

"Spring?" Clem said. "Spring ain't hardly here yet."

He was dead tired.

8 : ALMIRA

Although spring had arrived, and although some of February and all of March had been warm, the women of The Willows kept the windows of the upstairs sitting room closed. If they ever spoke except to the servants. Cowley never heard them. Almira's look of condemnation and disgust which Cowley had suffered for twenty years persisted, but something had been added to it which was far worse.

If Lou-Ellen suspected Cowley's role in the disappearance of Lafayette she never said it in so many words, but she stared at him hatefully whenever he entered the room, and her hate was far more impossible to bear than was Almira's. This was true not simply because Cowley felt more for Lou-Ellen than he did for his wife, but because Lou-Ellen was made of different stuff. Her hate was thorough enough to wither the spring oleander on the vine.

Almira sat in the same chair, day after day, continuously and to the point of insanity, working on her endless petit point. It was a great Louis Quatorze armchair with red and white upholstery and it had once been his father's favourite.

Lou-Ellen sat opposite her, often on the couch, sometimes in the smaller mate of Almira's chair. The servants brought them their food there and were especially solicitous of their every desire, few as they were. Iwana was especially kind and often Cowley thought that if any one were able to bring either of the women around it was she. The great Negress exuded such health, vitality and maternal life, exuberance and joy, that Cowley hoped it would be contagious.

Iwana was the one bright spot in the house. Clarissa had been doleful since her marriage to Henri whom Cowley had purchased for her from Judge Riley, and Big Mac had fallen into a silence almost as complete as that of the women. He had never again tried to talk seriously to his master.

Cowley felt more alone than he ever had before. It seemed all his friends had deserted him. Even ever-faithful Hugo-Jim had not written since coming upon the true identity of the Dutchman. He had sent his manservant once, while he and Mathews were passing through New Orleans on the way east from the frontier, to ask after Mrs. Cowley's health. That was all Jameson had heard of the big cockney.

The Dutchman, too, had become more exclusive with his time. He had finally tired of Lulu and sent her back to the fields. Chane had been kept on only because there was no one like him on either plantation, if anywhere in the state. But the evenings at the Dutchman's had become less frequent since the murder.

LaForge kept to himself in the overseer's house in the bayou. Cowley knew he had some of the black women with him but he still wondered why he stayed on. There was nothing in it for him and he seemed to have had a serious falling out with the Dutchman.

Cowley could not even go to town without causing talk about Almira's absence. In short, he was hard pressed to keep his wits.

The elder Bandeaux, Clem, had attempted to befriend him

after rendering him the service of his gun. But although Cowley had half succumbed to his blackmail and given him a horse, he shooed him back to the dark recesses of the bayou where his sort of trash belonged.

Only tight-lipped McKenzie remained faithful to the days before the disappearance, but he had always kept to himself.

On a Thursday morning in the last half of April, Cowley mounted the stairs to the upper landing after having break-fasted alone below. He had been going to go out and ride the cane fields with McKenzie but something in him finally snapped and he took the stairs quickly.

The door to the sitting room was slightly ajar and Cowley stepped in boldly, without bothering to knock. Almira, of course, was in her chair and did not even so much as look up. Lou-Ellen raised her eyes but lowered them again as quickly.

"For the love of God," Cowley stated with exasperation. "I can no longer endure this condition, Almira, Lou-Ellen."

He strode forward purposefully, reached for the lower strut of the window frame and hoisted it high, letting fresh air into the room for the first time since the previous fall.

"There," he said with finality, turning his face to the women and found himself biting down hard on his lower lip. They had not stirred.

He was dressed in his riding boots and held his short whip. He had been all but outside when he had been seized by the impulse which had brought him upstairs. He snapped the whip against his thigh and recovered his composure.

Once again he strode forward purposefully, this time toward the door, spun about and began pacing in that fashion between the two women, increasing the speed and the steadiness with which he brought his whip down against his thigh.

"I am going to say something now and I expect to be heard; is that clear? At least I fully expect to be heard by you, Miss Lou-Ellen. I have known for some time that I can no longer expect much of my wife."

He stopped full in the center of the room, blocking Almira from Lou-Ellen's view as if trying to block the influence of the older woman as well.

"But you, my dear, are quite young and quite a bit healthier, even in your mourning poor Lafayette's disappearance."

Cowley spoke rapidly and loudly. He was aware that he had closed the door so that the servants in the house were unable to hear. He did not want a public scene.

"You have not spoken ten words to me since the day it happened. One would suppose you blamed me for it. In fact I was not here that night as you have already been told. For all you know, my dear, the young man may have given up on ever getting my permission and simply left the territory."

He watched her face carefully. He was purposely leaving her a wide opening. What about his horse? What about Lafayette's horse? Cowley wanted nothing more than to get her to speak even if her speech contained an accusation.

But Lou-Ellen said nothing nor did she change her expression. Finally she did look up and stare into his eyes for a full minute, but when he began to speak again she again lowered her glance, a glance which had told him nothing. It had been as blank and meaningless as the back of a playing-card.

"Lou-Ellen, you are to obey me! By this afternoon I expect you to pick yourself up, to go to your room, dress for riding and go to the stable. Your mare will be saddled. You will spend the day riding by yourself." Cowley shouted the last two words to make his point completely clear. "By yourself, wherever you wish to go *on* the plantation. You are not to stray off the property!"

He did not himself understand why he had made that restriction. Perhaps, again, it was to get her to disobey, to bring her naturally violent independence to the fore. Perhaps he did not wish her to find anything that would further distress her. He had never asked Clem or Pierre about the body.

"Now, let me tell you what will happen if you do not obey me. I shall come back this evening and close that window and nail it down. I shall instruct Big Mac to bring two field hands here to restrain you from ever leaving this room. You and my dear Almira shall be interred here forever, forever, Lou-Ellen, at my order. And I shall go to New Orleans and not return except to see to the harvest. I implore you to think about the alternatives. Living here in this condition forever is one of them!" he hissed purposefully. "You may have my wife, this woman," he gestured with a sweeping motion of his right hand, stepping aside to surprise the blank-faced Almira, "or that!" he shouted, pointing meaningfully out the window.

There the air was fresh and cool, as inviting as any spring day in Louisiana had ever been for a young woman. The birds were in full voice, the sky was light blue, a small flock of cirrus were crossing the heavens in formation, and the fragrance of the garden was in her nostrils for the first time since a nebulous sense of revenge and fury had turned her against him.

Cowley saw that she had at last turned her gaze out into the spring day and he spun on his heel and left her for a final morning with Almira.

2

Jameson Cowley was not present when Lou-Ellen went to the stable. She took the old bayou road across to the Dutchman's. From the shelter of the trees she could make out the McKenzie family working in their garden, the stately mulatto woman and the three children. They saw her and stood still, then the woman raised her hand in greeting and Lou-Ellen could not help but respond. The colored loved her so!

She crossed the old bridge and watched as her horse brought her across the old wooden road to a place where she could see Julius LaForge's place. It seemed dark and deserted but she knew he lived there now that the Dutchman was back. She heard the sound of frogs and of their jumping into the bayou waters and of the birds. It was almost with difficulty that she was able to regain her sense of purpose and spur her mare forward.

She could not be seen crossing the cane fields. The stalks were already that high. Down a wide avenue between the fields she saw a gang of the Dutchman's naked workmen and felt a sudden stirring. She kicked up her mare before she could see too much.

By the time she came upon the mansion she had forgotten what the sight of the naked colored men had done to her. She dismounted and climbed the stairs and knocked on the thick oak door. It was strange that it should be closed. The place had an air almost as morose as that of The Willows.

It was not old Gusty who answered her knock but Chane, and again, quite suddenly, she felt flushed and hot.

"Good day, Miss Lou-Ellen," he said with surprise. Evidently he not only knew who she was but that she had not been out in quite some time. "What can I do for you, Miss?"

He was a huge, stunning brute. She found she could only control the sense of elation his presence gave her with a firm expression backed by a meaningful will that he obey her.

"Why, I have been out riding, Chane," she said. "It is a fine day."

Obviously the young buck negro was perplexed. If she did not know better she would think him capable of intelligent thought; but then his expression changed, leaving the rapid, brutal dullness she was accustomed to.

"Yes, Miss," he said softly.

She was not quite sure herself why she had come. Something forceful had driven her but she did not yet understand what it was.

She stepped back on the porch and ordered, "Come out here, Chane."

He obeyed her readily but left the door behind her ajar. She had not even looked inside. The Dutchman's presence was not of interest to her.

She looked closely at the great black man. His livery was tight, outlining not just the long muscles of his chest, but those of his limbs as well. He had the appearance of a stone wall.

"He was here that night," she stated suddenly, turning on him and approaching very closely so that she could smell him and knew he could smell her as well. He did not falter but she saw it in his eyes. Lafayette had been there all right!

"Lafayette was here that night, looking for my guardian, wasn't he, Chane? You answer me boy and you answer me quick!" she hissed.

She was boiling angry, suddenly full of vituperation and a strange but undeniable power. The black man was going to answer her.

"Miss?" Chane said.

"Don't you play the fool with me!" She raised her hand and slapped him brutally across his cheek. Her hand rang with pain. Her eyes sparked fury and she felt saliva gather in her mouth. She had never, never felt that way before.

"Say it!"

"Yes, Miss," he said. "If you say so, Miss."

He was almost smiling. She became perplexed. She knew something was going on that had never gone on with her before. She was not just interested in the truth of Lafayette's disappearance. Almira had probably been right about that, she knew that then. She was suddenly after something far greater, something that could elevate her entire dull, vapid, righteous life. So that was why she had been stewing for so long! She was not going to marry anyone!

She looked at the handsome black man long and hard, smiled again, as softly and sweetly as she knew how, and brought her hand up across his face again, far harder than she had before.

He stood his ground, made no move either forward or back, his expression changed only minimally. He seemed to sense the same feeling of relaxation.

She nodded, just that. She was not sure what she meant by it. Then she went down the stairs of the porch, mounted her mare, and rode off. She looked back once as she galloped back toward the bayou. She raced straight for the old road through the cane break. When she passed the spot in the field where she had seen the naked men working they had been alerted by the hoof beats and were staring in her direction. She heard LaForge's voice behind her as she continued ahead. She did not slow down until she was within the quiet shade of the Bayou Chien.

Her heart was racing wildly. When she had been a small girl riding through the fields on her pony, accompanying her guardian, she had often admired the colored men working the rice, and later, the cane. She had a joke with Jameson Cowley and although it was not especially funny it was something between them and part of her early childhood. She had always wanted a male instead of a female body servant. That, of course, had been before she knew the difference between men and women. She had asked her guardian for one and his laughter, a laughter she could still remember with clarity, had made the joke out of it.

In the shade of the bayou as she stopped her mare and listened to its heavy breathing and to the sound of the spring and the beat of her own heart, Lou-Ellen resolved to have her childhood wish after all. There was a burning desire building within her for that black man, and one way or another she was going to have him. She asked herself why she should not and could not find an answer that satisfied her.

Lafayette and her plans for her life were gone. She would not give in to her guardian and marry someone else. She would not let Cowley do to her what he had done to Almira. She would not be broken!

Lou-Ellen heard the sound of the horse behind her and spun about. When she saw that it was not a horse but a mule, and that it Clem Bandeaux heading into the bayou from the Dutchman's side, she stiffened. She hated Bandeaux's blood.

He saw her and smiled a wide, toothless grin.

"*Bonjour,* Miss Lou-Ellen," he called as he spurred his animal forward. She spun her horse about to face him politely.

His glance was disgusting. He was laughing at her, belittling her and lusting after her all at once. She would not let this white trash Frenchman get the best of her.

"Good day, Clem," she said haughtily.

He came up alongside her but she turned her mare so that he could not approach closely.

"Been out riding, I see," he said sarcastically, smiling that same evil smile.

"Quite right," she said proudly. "I see you are heading up the bayou for bird."

"Bird?" he said questioningly. "Oh, no, Miss Lou-Ellen, not bird. I am jest goin' on in for recreation."

"Recreation?" she repeated. "Very nice, very nice. Do give my best to your wife," she said and kicked up her mare who clattered onto the old wooden road and over the bridge and away from the laughing white man.

As she rode to The Willows she saw Jameson Cowley, mounted on a rise near the river road, watching her. She stopped her mare and stared at him but he did not move to come toward her. He stood his ground and watched. Apparently he was keeping his word. She would ride alone on the first day.

3

Lou-Ellen went out again after dinner. Cowley felt so

relieved that she had snapped out of her cold trance that he poured himself an extra deep brandy and sniffed it happily. It had been the first time he had not eaten alone since Lafayette's removal.

She had said she wanted to walk along the river and, as it was still light, Cowley had no objections. As long as she was still recovering he would permit her what she wanted. He had sent Big Mac after her to see that she went undisturbed.

He cut a cigar and lit it up, then left the den. He decided to have a bath drawn and to refresh. Perhaps later, after Lou-Ellen went to sleep, he would ride over to the Dutchman's. He climbed the wide staircase with his cigar and his brandy snifter in hand. He was almost singing.

He caught sight of Almira when he came to the top of the stairs. He had not seen her on her feet in a week. She was out of her chair at last and standing at the door. Perhaps she too would finally come around. He had to do everything within his power to help her.

"Good evening, my dear. Did you dine well?"

Iwana was removing his wife's dishes. She smiled to him sweetly as she took them out of the sitting room and down the flight of stairs. He did not know what had come over the gigantic black woman of late, but he liked it.

When Almira did not respond to his question he repeated it. He tried to summon some warmth for his wife, toward whom he felt no warmth, and from whom he had received none, in years.

Again she made no answer. He turned and headed for his bedroom. He had his hand on the latch when she screamed. He spun about so quickly he nearly spilled his drink. His wife was standing in the middle of the hall at the head of the stairs, her hair in disarray, her arms flailing wildly, and an awesome, high-pitched, terribly loud wail emanating from her throat with no promise that it would stop until her very lungs gave out.

He stepped forward quickly, placing his cigar in the same hand with his snifter. He had intended to clasp his free hand over her mouth but he found himself slapping her brutally across the face with his open palm.

His wife spun about and fell against the wall but she stopped screaming. He leaned over the bannister and shouted at the servants who had gathered below. Little Hanny, Iwana's boy child, was staring boldly up, open mouthed.

"Back to the kitchen," he shouted.

He turned his attention back to his wife who had regained her footing and was staring at him hatefully.

"Get in there," he ordered.

She backed away from him into her sitting room and went to the window, cowering.

"You fool," he hissed. "You know how I detest a scene in front of the servants. All New Orleans will know what I have to contend with in a week. You fool!"

"Cowley," she pleaded. It was the first word she had said to him since the winter.

"Cowley, please."

He slapped her again, almost as hard as he had the first time. She fell against the window, but did not break it, righted herself, grabbed a statuette off a base near her chair, and raised it over her head threateningly. He suddenly realized he liked it far better when she was silent and confined than he did when she was up and about.

"You bastard!" she hissed. "You trash bastard."

Cowley was horrified.

"You killed him, didn't you? With your own two hands, Mr. Jameson Cowley. You did away with Lafayette because you couldn't bear to have anyone take her from you."

He felt an incredible fury build within him because she had hit a vital nerve. He felt blood rush to his face as much in shame as in fury. Yes, he had wanted her. He placed his cigar and snifter down carefully on an end table and stood before her trembling.

"You thought you could drive me mad, didn't you, Mr. Cowley? Taking Lafayette away from Lou-Ellen, and Julius away from me."

"What?"

"Well, I shall have him back, do you hear! Or I shall disgrace myself before you in such a way that it will never be forgotten. I shall take Big Mac to my bed. It would be rather than you."

Cowley silenced her raving with another slap. He was perplexed as well as enraged.

"What's this about Julius?" he shouted.

"We are lovers!" she shouted. "Every weekend in New Orleans."

He laughed and turned his back on her. Then he turned again and watched her carefully.

"You haven't left this house in half a year," he exaggerated slightly.

"No. Not since you made him give me up. But I shall have him back."

Cowley tried to keep some modicum of control. He steadied his voice as he approached her closely.

"You are trying to tell me that you have been Julius LaForge's lover," he hissed. "You have become a raving lunatic."

She looked up at him and laughed in his face. Whether he believed her, or was so enraged by her laughter or simply exasperated by the perpetuity of the insanity around him, he never knew. He simply closed his long fingers around her neck and went into a blind rage.

He knew he was strangling her but he never even heard the sounds behind him. He remembered only, standing above her withered body, watching her face, finally peaceful in death, her entire head at an odd angle from her body, her eyes open wide and her mouth ajar, and he remembered hearing, "Uncle Jameson. In the name of G—"

Lou-Ellen was standing behind him staring in horror.

He sunk with finality into Almira's chair. He was completely exhausted. He stared bleakly at the dead woman, then up at his ward. There was a constant humming in his ears.

Lou-Ellen spun quickly and shut the door behind her. She knelt over the body of Mrs. Cowley and quite coldly lifted an arm.

"She is dead," he remembered her saying.

He sat there as she began to pace the room, very much as he had paced it once, recently or very long ago; it was unclear. The humming in his head would not stop. It struck him as strangely fitting that he should be sitting in her Louis Quatorze armchair. He said as much to Lou-Ellen.

"Shut up!" she commanded. He stared up at her dumbfounded.

"We shall have to get Mac up here," she said, thinking aloud. She found the statue of Venus on the floor and lifted it, testing it for weight. "We shall have to get him up here and hit him, kill him. Then we shall have to call McKenzie and explain that he did this, and that the others . . ."

"The others?" Jameson remembered asking incredulously. He had never felt so weak, so sapped of sense and strength. What was that humming and why was Lou-Ellen taking charge?

"I will be able to handle McKenzie," she said softly, still pacing, still testing the weight of the Venus statue by slapping it against her open palm. She was not a skinny woman; she was strong as well as strong-willed. He must not let her do this.

"Lou-Ellen," he began.

"Oh don't you fret, Uncle Jamie. I am not doing this for you. I know you had Lafayette killed. Oh yes, I am sure he is dead," she said callously. "You needn't even say anything, Mr. Cowley."

Mr. Cowley. She was calling him Mr. Cowley, just as Almira had, with that same sarcastic voice. That humming had to stop!

"I will not have this house covered with scandal. It is to be my house now!" she hissed.

"Your house?"

"I will not, I will never become like that—or like she was

136

before—I will have my way!" she exclaimed. "Call Mac up here!"

"What?" He was dazed. Why was he so grateful to her for becoming his mistress, for ordering him about? What did she intend to do?

"Call Mac I say." She moved off behind the door to strike the eunuch when he entered.

He could not understand why she should wish to do that. She had known Big Mac all her life. Why should she wish to hit him? Would that humming never stop? What did she intend to do about the others?

"Call him," she hissed again, so ferociously this time that he tingled. But he could not find his tongue. He looked down from his new place in his wife's chair at her dead body and watched her blank, ceiling-aimed stare, her open mouth.

"All right," he remembered her saying from behind the door. "I will call him myself!"

4

"It must be done quickly," Lou-Ellen said stiffly. "Right away, this evening."

"Yessum, but the—"

"I shall send word to Judge Riley who shall support us in this matter. It is Mr. Cowley's wish."

Horrified, McKenzie turned again to look at his employer. The thin man was seated in one of the big armchairs staring blankly ahead. McKenzie looked again to the dead woman and then to Big Mac who was sprawled on the sitting room floor, near the woman he had murdered, in a pool of his own blood.

"Yessum," McKenzie said again. He found himself shaking his head and looking at his own hand for want of another place to put his eyes.

"It was a revolt of the entire household. The others, even the small boy, are cowering below in the kitchen. Clarissa, Iwana, and the rest, all the body servants—"

"All," McKenzie said, aghast.

"Every black who was in this house at the time!" Lou-Ellen declared with finality. "They are all to be hung."

"Yessum."

"To forestall a general revolt of the slaves."

"But Miss Lou-Ellen," McKenzie began to protest. A general revolt was unthinkable. Who should know better than he?

"You have been duped," she shouted. "You have been softened by living with one. Do you want your own woman and children involved in this?"

"No, Miss Lou-Ellen."

137

"Then you had best begin. Clem Bandeaux was in the bayou earlier; but now he is probably home. Get him, get Julius LaForge, and get this thing done by this evening. I shall myself send for the judge."

"Yes, Maam," he whispered. He felt incapable of action. Of course, Miss Lou-Ellen was right. But he could not believe what he saw in Jameson Cowley. His wife's murder had completely broken the man. Who would have thought it?

"It was lucky," he murmured, "that you arrived when you did, Miss. Else the crazed fool might have done in his master as well."

"He wasn't crazed, I tell you, McKenzie. He knew quite well what he was doing. It is a plot I have felt afoot in this house for some time. Have you noticed nothing strange these past weeks?"

"No, Miss."

"We have been living in fear of our blacks. Now go," she commanded regally.

McKenzie turned and went out of the room. He heard her closing the door behind her as he descended the stairs. None of the other household servants were visible, and he was glad. He had no idea of how Lou-Ellen had managed to order them all to the kitchen.

It was still light in the sky when he mounted and rode off toward the Bayou Chien. It would take an hour or two to gather the men he would need in case there was trouble. He would not use any of the colored in the hanging.

They would use the trees at the front of the house as Miss Lou-Ellen had said. It would be a further shroud on a terrible, terrible day. He thanked God that none of his family had been inside when it had happened. He spurred his horse and brought it to a trot between the growing rows of cane.

He found Bandeaux at home. Clem, like the mighty fool he was, came out to greet him with his rifle in the crook of his arm. He told him straight out what had happened, and what had to be done. Clem nodded, said he would get Pierre, and went to saddle his mule. Mrs. Bandeaux remained silent, leaning up against the door frame of her small house, her calico dress showing pretty much everything she had to show.

Neither she nor her husband showed a moment's grief at the news, nor a moment's hesitation at what was to be done. For Clem it was a job of work, and for his white trash wife it meant something to talk about for the next few weeks.

He turned his stallion and went on toward Julius LaForge's place. After he had given him the word he stopped home, told the children and his woman to go inside, to bolt the doors and not to open them for anyone but himself, and met Pierre and Clem coming through the thick wood.

Pierre was mounted on the new horse Jameson Cowley had

sold him. Both the brothers were heavily armed. They had been thoughtful enough to bring two lengths of rope as well, and although McKenzie could not understand why, Pierre had a shovel with him, stuck behind his saddle.

Silently the men turned toward the avenue between the cane that led toward the high ground and the plantation mansion. Julius LaForge soon caught up with them and the four white men rode at a walk, thoughtfully, as the sun began to go down over the river.

They cannot be still in that room, all four of them, McKenzie thought. He summoned more determination and continued ahead. The loss of the mistress of the house grieved him. He was a loyal man, and he grieved also for the condition in which he had seen Jameson Cowley. The man had become temporarily ineffectual. In time, McKenzie thought, in time he would come back around.

"Where is it to be done?" Pierre asked quietly, in a businesslike voice.

McKenzie did not immediately answer. It ought to have been obvious. The only trees near enough were the willows lining the main avenue. He let his horse keep to its own pace and stared blankly ahead at the big white house. The sun had gone behind a row of clouds low in the western sky, burning them bright red and diffusing its rays over that whole portion of the heavens.

"Right at the front of the house," he finally said. "Mr. Cowley has instructed me to use the willows themselves."

"Can't imagine what come over them niggers, me," Clem Bandeaux remarked.

"Well, this will put a stop to any thoughts of rebellion they may have grown back in the bottom lands," Julius LaForge added.

McKenzie took a deep breath. Just to be on the safe side he withdrew his pistol from his belt and checked the charges. Behind him he heard the Bandeaux brothers doing likewise with their long guns. Only LaForge seemed controlled enough not to expend his nervous energy preparing his firearm.

"She must look a sight in death, eh?" Clem Bandeaux muttered and McKenzie heard Julius click up his steed in response but thought nothing of it. It was probably just a job of work for him too. McKenzie was not so naive he did not know what evil Julius LaForge perpetrated on the Dutchman's. But he would need him. He had to accept help as ordered.

Miss Lou-Ellen was waiting for them on the porch. The sun was well down behind the house so she was well in the shade. She had already changed into black. The men dismounted, removed their hats and approached the stairs, but did not venture up them.

"We are terribly sorry," Julius LaForge said and the other murmured something as well.

"Let's get on with it. Mr. Cowley would be pleased if you would also hang the dead man. He wants to have them all on these trees as a sign to God, and to the other coloreds."

"The dead man—but he is already dead, Miss?" LaForge said with surprise.

Lou-Ellen made no answer and McKenzie was the first to walk up the stairs onto the porch. She looked very beautiful in mourning.

"Yes, Miss," he said. "We will hang the dead man as well."

The coloreds were sitting in the kitchen in complete silence. There was no protestation as they were led out of the house. Then, when they realized what was to happen to them, Clarissa began to scream and the young Hanny made a rush for the cane. Clarissa screamed until it was all over for her. The child cried, protested his innocence in a rush of hot tearful words.

When Iwana was lifted by the Bandeaux mule, and her thrashing body was finally tied above the ground even as the last breath of life went out of her huge body, McKenzie nearly fainted. His eyes filled with tears and his knees began to give way. He could not forget the madness of the woman's last words. "And I was nearly free!" And he could not get the sight of her awful eyes out of his head. He would find he would never be able to forget that brilliant, inexhaustible, bottomless gaze.

Finally they hoisted the dead man. The coloreds from the cabins below the house had gathered. There was complete silence. The sun had all but set. The families of coloreds from the north end of the plantation began to arrive with open mouths and heavy hearts. A general wail went up and did not stop. One by one the field help were allowed to come into the house and view the body of their murdered mistress.

The wailing increased. Miss Lou-Ellen stood in the shadows of the porch with a bent head and at no time did Mr. Jameson Cowley appear. Once McKenzie saw a curtain in the upstairs sitting room draw back and he thought the master was watching, but then he saw it had been nothing but the spring breeze rushing in through the open window.

In all, ten slaves were hung that day and their bodies were left hanging until morning. The greatest wailing was done for the small boy and when the judge arrived late in the night it was with great grief and a rent heart that he condoned the executions.

5

A somber hush had fallen over the two plantations and over

Bayou Chien that divided them. Chane followed Henri across the moss-covered bridge and through the trees on the Cowley side of the boundary, and up to the first fields of cane. A slight spring breeze came up off the river and made the standing rows of young crops whisper in the night. A full chorus of bright stars in the Louisiana sky screamed a plaintive funeral dirge into the ears of the big black man.

"Where?" he asked.

"From de willows front de *maitre's* house," Henri answered in a high, broken voice. The thinner man was quaking with fright in the warm night.

"Come on."

"Dey find us, de Dutchman do de same thing to you, *Maitre* Cowley, he stretch my neck too, him," Henri pleaded.

"Come on," Chane repeated. His voice betrayed both the depth of his anger and the strangely determined calm in which that anger lived.

Henri moved out across the fields toward the big house. The night was bright enough to make out the white structure by the river wharf far ahead. Chane could see the square pillars on the front of the porch, and the flat roof. His thick black nostrils flared and his long muscles tensed, relaxed, tensed and relaxed again.

"Someone comin'," Henri whispered and broke into the cane for cover. Chane followed him and hid behind the tall stalks. Soon he could hear the hoofbeats approaching.

Three men passed. One was Clem Bandeaux, mounted on his mule; his brother followed him, on his new mare; a little ways behind, Julius LeForge, the Dutchman's overseer, rode his stallion proudly. The moonlight revealed the deep scars on his left profile as he made his way south, toward the bayou. Each of the three white men was heavily armed. Chane watched their faces intently from the depths of the cane.

When the men had passed he grabbed Henri by the shoulder. He could feel the man shaking beneath his grasp. He pushed him back out into the avenue between the fields.

Henri turned with fright and looked at Chane. The big man thought the other was too close to tears to be trusted near the master's house. His lips were tightly pressed as if he were in pain and the whites of his eyes were moist.

"Clarissa, she made me a good wife, Chane," he stammered.

"Where are the other folk?" Chane asked.

"Back to the cabins. Some done gone to the bottom land to the north to make the voodoo. Some hidin' in the cane lookin' up at the dead folk, maybe."

"Maybe it's best if you go back to the cabin," Chane suggested. "I will go on myself."

Chane felt the warm spring air fill each square inch of his

lungs and he heard the deep sound of his own breathing. He was conscious too of a great deal of saliva forming in his mouth, and of the steady, hateful, beat of his heart.

"I don't want to go back there, you," Henri explained pitifully. "Dat cabin goin' to be dead lonesome without Clarissa."

Chane nodded and pushed him ahead. They walked quickly. Chane kept his eyes on the house ahead. He could not tell whether any of the front windows were lit until he saw the darkness at the front of the big building get suddenly darker and he knew the lamps had just been damped out. None of the side windows were aglow.

"Dey goin' to bury Miss Almira by the grave of the old *maitre* Cowley, near the river," Henri said softly.

Chane pushed the thinner man on. He did not care what they did with the body of the white woman.

The cane grew within fifty feet of the house on either side and within fifty feet of the willows to either side of the main drive. The two black men cut into it about a hundred yards before the house and started through it toward the trees. Chane heard sobbing deep within the cane and cried out in a hushed voice.

"Who dere?"

The sobbing stopped.

"Who dere?" Chane repeated more loudly.

The cane broke ahead on them and a small black girl emerged. She was dressed in a calico frock and a bright red kerchief. She was no more than twelve.

"You is Mister Chane," she breathed heavily.

"Diss is Bess, Chane, Clarissa's sister," Henri explained.

"You is de prince mister Chane, you has got to do somethin' 'bout all dis horror, mister Chane," the young colored girl sobbed.

"Shh!" Henri exclaimed. "You want to git us all hung, you?"

Chane took the girl in his arms and quieted her.

"Where?" he asked.

Henri looked through the cane break in the direction of the Willows. He gave the sobbing child to Henri who tried to comfort her, and walked slowly through the cane. He went easily, as if expecting treachery; his great hands in front of him separated the stalks until he was at the edge of the field.

It took him a long time to steady himself after he first saw it. He felt grief swell his chest, felt blind rage fight for release, and could not keep his balance. He fell through the cane break to his knees and listened to the river breeze rustle the crop. He stayed quite still for a long time.

Henri and Bess came up behind him but he did not know it until they were touching him on the back.

142

"Come back into the cane, you," Henri said softly, tearfully.

Chane felt a roaring in his head, felt the blood of his mother rush through his arteries, pumping fury and despair.

"Come in here, man," Henri insisted.

He looked up into the dead face of the great woman whose weight threatened to topple the limb of the tree from which she was hung. He looked to the body of his youngest brother and wailed long and deep into the still night.

"Come in," Henri hissed.

A light came on in the big house as Chane wailed again.

"Dey gonna come wit' guns, you," Henri pleaded.

"Chane, Chane," the girl said placatingly, sweetly and reminding him of her sister for whom he shook with rage.

"Come in, Chane," the girl said.

Ten in all. Ten black bodies swaying from the young willows of the main drive.

The lights were lit downstairs and the front door opened. Chane looked in time to see McKenzie, the big Scot, come onto the front porch. He stood up and walked into the center of the avenue of trees and faced the man.

From the cane to his left he heard Henri gasp and beg him to come back, and he heard the girl sob. McKenzie raised his rifle from his hip and pointed at Chane with his free hand.

"Who is that?" the overseer yelled in a booming voice.

Chane made no answer.

"Is that you Chane? Big Chane? Get on back to the Dutchman's before he skins you alive," McKenzie roared.

"Or before I am hung here?" Chane bellowed and the fury of his voice carried a thunder with it that hung in the air when the words had died.

"Chane," Bess called from the cane. "Wana said to be patient, the last thing she said to us, Chane," the young girl pleaded, aware that she did not know what force those words might have on the huge black, aware that she did not know what Iwana had meant.

Chane watched the porch of the great house. Miss Lou-Ellen rushed out draping a frilled black blanket about her shoulder even as McKenzie raised his rifle and brought Chane within his sights.

"Get back home, Chane, and all will be forgiven," the big Scot called.

Miss Lou-Ellen raised her hand to McKenzie's long gun and forced him to lower it. She came down the stairs and took three steps toward the buck along the avenue of willows.

"Come back here, Miss Lou-Ellen," McKenzie ordered. "I have seen that boy kill a man with one blow."

"Chane," she called to him. In the spring night her white skin seemed to glow, so much like the skin of a young girl he remembered vaguely, to whom he felt his heart crying beyond Iwana, beyond the gulf, beyond the Caribbean.

"Go back, Chane," she called. " Please."

He felt his head drop to his chest. He had no control over it. He felt nothing but the weight of his own flesh on his muscle and heard nothing but a dull roar behind his head. He walked back into the cane and let Henri and Bess lead him silently back toward the bayou.

An ancient, atavistic violence searched for an outlet. He tried to quell it. He knew that if he did not succeed it would only be worse in the end.

9 : CHANE

On an exceptionally hot day in the middle of summer, Mathews approached the enormous desk in the ornate lobby of the City Hotel in New Orleans and cleared his throat several times. Finally the piebald desk clerk looked up and approached him.

"Oh, yes. There is a message for Mr. Morocco. One moment," the man said turning to the wooden boxes behind him for the letter.

He found it and handed it over to Mathews, who nodded, looked once at the official stamp on the envelope, turned quickly and made for the door.

Mathews ran up Charles Street to the saloon, went through the swinging doors, and straight into the back room. Hugo-Jim was just finishing a large stein of frontier beer.

"It's come," Mathews said anxiously. He held out the envelope to his employer.

Hugo-Jim wiped his mouth with the back of his hairy hand and smiled. There was a gleam in his eye that Mathews recognized and enjoyed.

He tore open the envelope and unfolded the sheet of paper.

"Aye, Matey," the big man stated. "We are to go immediately to the British consulate. Well, come on lad, what's keepin' ye?" he bellowed, already halfway to the door.

Mathews ran to keep up.

"Then this is it?" he asked.

"It would seem so, matey, it would seem so," the large man replied. "But let's wait till we talk to the man before we go off 'alf cocked."

At the corner of Canal Street they found a cab and climbed aboard. In a few minutes they were at the door of the consulate and there they disembarked.

Hugo-Jim paid the driver, wiped his hand across his mouth again, as if to remove any possible stain of drink, and strode purposefully forward toward the embossed doors of the big building.

They were ushered in immediately and led up a wide curving staircase to a landing off of which there were many thick wooden doors. They were brought to the closest of these and shown in. Behind a wide desk a balding man whose pate shined like a polished white fruit, who wore thick mutton chops and thicker glasses, was signing a folio of papers.

"Sit down, sit down," the man ordered without looking up.

Hugo-Jim cleared his throat and complied, and his man did likewise.

After a moment the consul looked up and smiled shallowly at Hugo-Jim.

"You would be Mr. Morocco, I take it," he said in an Oxford accent.

"Aye," replied Hugo-Jim.

The man frowned and said, "Well, well, well, well."

He lowered his head and returned his attention to his papers.

After another moment he looked up again and said, "And who might this be?"

" 'e's my man," Hugo-Jim explained avuncularly.

The consul cleared his throat. "Quite," he said.

"Are those the papers?" Hugo-Jim asked bluntly.

The man looked up still once again, this time in an attempt to wither Hugo-Jim with a glance. Failing that, he cleared his throat, said, "Quite," again, and looked back down.

Finally he said, "These papers name the intended bearer, Mr. Hugo James, now known as Mr. Hugo-Jim Morocco, as a full agent of her majesty's government in these United States. They clear him of any and all charges that he may or may not be subject to owing to indiscretions on his part while a sailor in the British navy, and empower him to apply to the federal government of the United States for a writ of habeas corpus on the person of Hans Van Zachten, now known as Hans Hasebos, for delivery before her majesty's court in London on charges of piracy."

"Hear, hear," said Hugo-Jim.

"Quite," said the consul.

"Furthermore, these papers," said the bald little man distinctly, holding up another set and handing them across to Hugo-Jim along with the first ones, "are directly from Washington D.C., from the office of the Secretary of State, enabling the aforementioned agent of the British Government to arrest and imprison the aforementioned Dutchman on charges of piracy and escort him out of the country."

"Hear, hear."

"Quite."

"Quite," Mathews mimicked under his breath.

"These papers are to be handed to the federal marshal in this county, to be served on one Julius LaForge for complicity in the swindling of Heeren Broth und Bahuis Maatschaapi, the famous Dutch slaving company."

"Hear, hear!" said Mathews.

"And at the request of Mr. Morocco," the consul continued, "no warrant for the arrest of Jameson Cowley in this same matter has been or will be issued."

When he had finished speaking he handed Hugo-Jim the papers, folded his hands on his desk in front of him, and allowed the barest corners of his mouth to turn up in a smile.

"Now," he said, "Would you care to tell me what this is all about?"

"Of course," Mathews was so excited he spoke out of turn.

"Aye. I'll tell ye," Hugo-Jim declared in a voice far too loud for the consul's comfort. "These here men swindled this here Dutch firm out of thousands of blacks and made a fortune doin' it, only to mistreat those same blacks quite vicious like."

"Oh," said the consul.

"Word came to me just last month that ten of 'em 'ad been put to death, to death, mind you."

"Quite," said the consul.

"Quite," Mathews repeated softly.

"And this here Van Zachten is a pirate under the new statutes concerning slavery."

"Quite," said the consul. "All this is imminently clear. But would you care to explain what part you have in it all."

"No sir, I wouldn't," Hugo-Jim said flatly.

"He wouldn't," echoed his man servant

"Quite," said the consul. "In that case our business is at a close."

"I will say this," Hugo-Jim stated. "If, many years ago I hadn't been so selfish as to protect my own hide, most of this here would never 'ave happened."

The consul nodded, shrugged, and returned his attention to his desk. Hugo-Jim folded the papers, tucked them into his waist coat, and rose. Mathews rose as well. Without so much as a good day the two men left the room and the building.

They were joyful as they walked along the street toward the old quarter. Mathews remarked, "Will we wait now, sir, for Mr. Eli I mean?"

"We will try," Hugo-Jim said. "He's 'ad trouble at home and been detained. But we shall give him a few weeks more before going out to that infested bayou."

"Yes, sir."

"And clear it out once and for all."

"Yes, sir," Mathews repeated.

"He couldn't fool me, after all these years. Him just sittin' there like that."

"No, sir."

"He killed Almira sure as we're standing here."

"Yes, sir."

"And then put the blame on those poor colored."

"Yes, sir."

"Too much for a man to stand, it is," the big man stated.

"Yes, sir."

"Never should 'ave stopped watchin' over 'im. Stupid young pup."

"Quite," Mathews said.

2

Several weeks later a colored boy led a mule along the river road between the two plantations. Sometimes the mule got stubborn and tried to turn back toward the marsh. When it did the boy would walk up to it and clout it between the ears with his small fist.

"Hey, what you got there, you?" another tiny colored lad yelled, appearing out of nowhere from the cane stalks along the road.

"Who you, you?" the first boy asked.

"Me, I'm Clyde, who you?"

"Brash," the other replied.

"Who you belong to, Brash?"

"Who you belong to?" the other insisted.

"The Dutchman," Clyde responded proudly.

"Me, I'm a Cowley colored," Brash declared even more proudly.

"Well, what you got there, Cowley?"

"What it look like, a steam boat?"

The other child laughed and slapped his thigh, straightened up and with a terribly somber face said, "I know what you got."

"Oh, yeah?"

"Yea. You got the Bandeaux mule what died."

"Ain't got no dead mule end o' this line," Brash said, implying by his tone that the other was stupid.

"Didn't say that. Said Bandeaux what died."

"So what?" Brash said.

"So nothin'," said Clyde.

Brash continued to lead the mule along the road and Clyde fell in step. After a while the first one said, "Where you think you goin', you?"

"Along," Clyde answered obtusely.

"Along?"

147

"Yep."

"Dutchman or Mr. LaForge catch up with you whup you sure, nigger," Brash said.

"Ain't nothin' compared to mule thief," Clyde retorted.

"Ain't no mule thief. Done following orders."

"Oh yea, whose orders you followin'?"

"Mr. McKenzie's, whose orders."

"Oh," the second child said, rebutted.

"Now, where you goin'?"

"Along."

" 'Long where, damn it?" Brash said loudly, stamping his foot on the dirt road.

"See that Mr. Chane."

Brash stopped in the middle of the road and looked hard at the other young Negro. "Ain't you never seen Mr. Chane when he was by you?" Brash asked.

"Once, maybe," Clyde said.

"So?"

"They say he is different, now."

"Who they?"

"They," Clyde explained somewhat incompletely.

"Well, he ain't. He jus' Mr. Chane and he don't want no nigger chillun starin' at him."

"Won't stare," Clyde said but too late, for Brash had moved off, apparently satisfied that he had made his point and the other child would remain behind. The other child did not, however, and they were soon walking abreast again.

"They all say," Clyde began, "that after Mr. Chane hid out in the marsh for a full month he went right out o' his head."

"Do they?" said Brash.

"Yessuh, best believe it."

"Well, I don't believe it," said Brash.

"They say he come back to the Dutchman's right crazy, rollin' his eyes, and talkin' nonsense. They say he couldn't find no way safe out o' that marsh so jes' stayed in there and come out crazy."

"Shut up," said Brash.

"They say then the Dutchman was right happy to sell him to Miss Lou-Ellen."

"Shut up," Brash said more loudly this time.

"They say that, they do, you," Clyde remarked positively.

"Now you listen here, nigger," Brash began. "Fust off Miss Lou-Ellen don't buy nothin'. Mr. Jameson does the buyin'. Secund off, Chane is as right in his head as I am. So shut up!"

Clyde made no reply for a time but continued to walk along, keeping the other company.

Finally Brash said, "Whut else they say?"

"They say," said Clyde, and then paused to savor the victory he had won over the other boy. "They say."

"Whut?"

"They say that every one roun' here knows that it were Mr. Chane whut killed them white folks in the bayou whose mule you got right there."

"That so?" said Brash caught between anger and disbelief.

"And they say, that every one roun' here knows he ain't dead now 'cause Miss Lou-Ellen takes a special favorin' to him."

"Shut up you, or I bust you in the mouth," Brash said adamantly. He stopped in his tracks and the mule stopped behind him. Little Clyde also stopped but continued speaking.

"They say that she done the Dutchman some big favor and got Chane off the hook and all for herself," Clyde stated boldly. Then he looked both ways and leaned closer to be even more confidential.

But Brash would have none of it. He made a tiny fist of his little black hand and swung wildly at Clyde. He missed entirely and the other laughed, stepping away to the side of the road.

"Hee haw, hee haw," Clyde mimicked.

"Tell you what boy," Brash said inspired. "You git off Cowley land and you git off now or I go back and tell Mr. Chane jes whut you been sayin' 'bout him and Miss Lou-Ellen."

The other boy stared silently for a moment, mouth agape. "You wouldn't, you," he whispered.

"Goin' right now to Mr. Chane, tell him everythin'. He could throw you across the Missip, I reckon."

"No. No. All right, I'm goin'," the other said hurriedly and not without fright.

"Git!" Brash yelled and watched with relief as the other took off through the cane back toward the Dutchman's property.

The child continued to lead the mule toward the main drive. Finally he walked with it under the boughs of the beautiful weeping willows and toward the front of the main house. Mr. Chane was standing on the front porch in his house clothes, what the white folks called livery. He looked mighty elegant.

"Mornin', Mr. Chane," Brash said as he came up to the porch.

"What are you doin' with that mule?" Chane asked blankly.

"Mr. McKenzie said to git it," the child explained.

Chane looked at the boy a long time, and then at the mule. He made a face that Brash did not like and then began to say something. Before he could, however, Miss Lou-Ellen's voice came from inside the house.

"Chane," she called. "Chane!"

"You git that mule where it's supposed to be, boy," Chane

said and disappeared inside the big white house. Brash lowered his head and started the mule walking toward the stable. Mr. McKenzie was standing with his foot on the anvil, looking out over the fields with that same expression he always had, the one that seemed to say he wished he were a thousand miles away but didn't much think he'd ever get there.

"Suh," Brash whispered. He wasn't supposed to talk to white folks unless they talked to him first but Mr. McKenzie was kindly.

"Yes, boy," he replied.

"How come Mr. Jameson, he never come down stairs any more, suh?"

"Take that mule inside, boy and tell the smithy to see to shoes for it. He's been out in the marsh for quite a spell."

"Yessuh" Brash replied.

He walked off into the dark dank stable to wonder about the strange ways of white folk.

3

Chane stepped into the dark hallway of the big house and went to the office, the former den of Mr. Jameson, where Lou-Ellen sat behind the large mahogany desk checking the accounts.

"Yes Maam," he said.

"Close the door, Chane," Lou-Ellen ordered.

He closed the door and faced her again. He had learned a new calm, a new temper. Combined with the trick he had long since mastered of keeping all thoughts from his mind, he found he was never bothered either by the rush of angry blood that white people inspired after the hangings, nor by the roaring in his head that preceded unthinking acts of violence.

"I want your advice about something, Chane," his mistress said sweetly.

"My advice, maam?"

"Yes. I didn't pay three thousand five hundred dollars for you just to have you answer the door," she said with an odd smile.

"I know that, Maam," he replied.

He knew it well enough. He knew it every evening when they retired to the same room and he allowed himself to forget that she was kin to Mr. Jameson who had caused him so much grief, when he allowed himself to treat her white flesh as he had once treated the white flesh of a girl named Kitty.

"Don't be smart," she said familiarly. "Come here."

He went to her side of the desk and looked over her shoulder at the accounts. He could neither read nor write and

150

so the inspection was somewhat purposeless.

"You see here," she said softly, pointing to a row of figures. "these are the number of acres in cane each year, these in rice, and this column," she explained, "is the yield, and this one, the important one, is the gross profit."

Chane laughed. He could understand nothing of what he saw.

"You would like to learn to read and write, wouldn't you?" she asked, again using her sweetest voice. Chane had heard all her voices and sometimes he thought he disliked that one most. In the past few weeks she had become bored with his gentleness and he sensed that she was building toward something. He had become somewhat bored with her as well, although her firm white flesh still sparked him to action.

"Yessum," he replied softly.

"I want you to do something for me, Chane, do you hear me?" she whispered.

"Yes, Miss Lou-Ellen."

"I want you to cover me right here, right now, and I want you to use . . . to use force, Chane. And then," she whispered the rest to him for shame of speaking loudly what any of Chane's black women would have screamed at the top of their lungs if they had a mind to.

"Yes, Maam," he replied. He was ready to do anything she liked. It was not just because he found her flesh exciting. She could turn him in at any moment for the murder of the Bandeaux, then Eli would never be able to buy him free. Chane did not think about that but he knew it, and he operated with that knowledge firmly in his mind.

"But you must do it now, Chane!" she said with a shaking voice. The stupid white woman somehow got a bigger kick out of being covered in her guardian's office.

"But Mr. Jameson is liable to come in, Maam," he teased.

"He hasn't stirred out of that chair since . . . since God knows when, Chane."

The sudden reference to the time when Miss Almira had been killed burned through him. He straightened and looked out the window at the fields of cane. Just beyond them he could see the trees that shaded the marsh lands. Somewhere out there Pierre Bandeaux had tried to ambush him as he went north, and forced him to return to the marsh or to the plantation. It was deep in that swamp that he had tried to outwit Bandeaux, but the other had never ceased his vigil. While Chane lived on frogs and roots and bayou water, Pierre did likewise. Finally Chane had given up and returned. He had counted on the Dutchman's lust for him as a performer to save him. He had not counted on Miss Lou-Ellen.

Lou-Ellen stood and walked away from the desk to the door through which Chane had entered. She turned the latch so that they were locked in.

"There," she said trembling, "does that make you feel easier about it?"

Chane turned to inspect her. She was wearing a yellow cotton frock and a red ribbon in her blond hair. There were dark lines under her blue eyes and lines had formed about the corners of her mouth giving her something less than a girlish mien. When she frowned she sometimes looked absolutely deadly.

"Yes, Maam," he lied. It made no difference to him whether the whole world watched.

"Take me," she ordered.

He looked down at the heavy carpet. She approached slowly, moving her hips beckonly, but he did not feel inspired. She whispered her plea again and he grasped her with one heavy hand the way he had grasped the Bandeaux woman, by the back of the head, and thrust her easily to the floor.

She smiled just as the other white woman had smiled and began to pull furiously on her clothing to free herself of it. He stood over her and did likewise, but taking his time, enjoying the imprecations of the sighing white woman.

"Come on," she squirmed below him on the soft carpet as he took off the last of his clothes. He bent to her and ripped the dress from her back exposing that which she had not herself exposed. Again she sighed deeply and he saw a look of satisfaction come to her face. He grabbed her by her hair and pulled her lips down to him. She had to squirm to get in position because his leg blocked her from pivoting, but he made her do what she had asked him to make her do.

She worked at him with wide eyes and he enjoyed it. He felt the air pierce his chest as he took deeper and deeper breaths and knew that he would be able to spill his seed where she wanted it spilled from the way his sense of balance began to fail him. He watched his great black body with hers contentedly. She was able to make him forget far better than his own disciplines. He raised his heavy hand and slapped her hard on the rump.

She began to cry and let go of him. "Not so hard, you blasted fool," she cried. She bit her lower lip and stared at him. Then she rushed to cover his sex again and he waited. When she stopped again her eyes were moist and she was trembling.

"I want to watch it happen," she said.

She used him as though he were a giant toy, examining him and testing. When he remembered that she wanted to be treated violently, and he pulled her hair and slapped her softly, she smiled . . . just so long as he did not really hurt her.

"Now it's my turn," she said sweetly and slapped him across the face. He hardly felt it and the surprise of her move made

152

him laugh. She slapped him again harder and positioned herself as only a mistress could before her slave.

When they had finally finished and she allowed him to dress again he felt light hearted. He had done many things for the Dutchman's vicarious pleasure, far worse than anything Lou-Ellen's imagination could conceive, and he was to be paid well for his treatment of this young white girl . . . or so he hoped.

From where he stood rearranging his clothing he could see out the window to the first of the great weeping willows.

"All right," she said softly. "Git now. I'll call you if I want you again."

He remained motionless. "I thought you were going to teach me to read and write," he said.

She smiled at him. "Not today. Perhaps some other time, Chane."

"Miss Lou-Ellen?"

"What is it?" Her tone was becoming increasingly short-tempered. He sensed she wanted him gone. She wanted to have her thoughts to herself.

"How much would it take to buy me away from you?"

"Why, Chane, who is going to buy you? Everyone knows you are mad. Everyone is afraid to have you about. Who would buy you?"

"Suppose someone came along," he suggested.

Lou-Ellen approached him. She kept her mouth partially open. Her eyes were narrowed slightly making her look even more evil and even more old beyond her years.

"You are not for sale," she stated flatly.

"Plenty of other bucks in the fields," he said.

She reared back and slapped him harder than she had ever before and spit in his face.

"White woman," he said as he felt the spittle run down his nose, "can't make up your mind what you want. Love too, eh?" he hissed.

"You talk to me in that tone of voice one second longer and I will have you hung like I had your mother hung, boy," she shouted. Then she lost her breath, realizing what she had done, then lost her control entirely.

Chane sensed she was about to use her anger at what he had said to make a confession he did not want to hear.

"Yes, I had it done. Not my guardian. Yes me, you fool! I did it, not that enfeebled excuse for a man sitting upstairs! Mac didn't kill Miss Almira, he did!" she pointed up to the second floor.

Chane stepped back aghast. He felt his breath come more quickly and his nostrils flare. He had tried not to think about that. He had mourned her and tried to forget her. He had tried to find peace, not in forgiveness for Jameson Cowley, but in an understanding that the time was not yet ripe for him to take revenge. But the idea that this woman was responsible was too much for him to bear.

He killed her as he had killed Clem Bandeaux, by breaking her body. He used Mr. Jameson's sideboard, spilling his brandy and scattering his cigars over the thick carpeting of the tidy room. No one came when she screamed. Obviously the other servants thought that passion had caused them and not fright.

4

Julius LaForge raced his stallion over the moss-covered bridge and through the trees to the Dutchman's place. He ran his horse at break-neck pace through the cane break. It was night, and although the moon and the stars were bright in the Louisiana heavens, the brightest light came from the north. The Willows was afire and had been since early evening.

There was no longer a chance of saving the house or either of the Cowleys, Lou-Ellen or Jameson. The latter, still grief stricken, had never left his wife's room when the fire started and it became impossible to reach him. Miss Lou-Ellen was nowhere to be found and was certainly dead somewhere inside the blazing inferno.

He dismounted as his horse approached the house and raced up onto the porch. Old Gusty greeted him with an open mouth and asked him what had happened. Most of the other slaves had been rushed over to help with the fire fighting.

"You can forget that place," Julius shouted, his face wet with sweat and the moisture accentuated the ugliness of his scarred profile. "It's gone, dead gone."

He rushed inside the house and called out, *"Minheer* Hasebos, *Minheer* Hasebos!"

"Up here," a hearty old voice bellowed from above in a thick Dutch accent. Julius rushed up the flight of stairs and stood winded before his employer.

"Vat is it?"

"The Cowley place is gone! Jameson is dead and so is Lou-Ellen."

"Yah," said the Dutchman. "I have been vatching from der vindow."

"But that's not all."

"Eh?"

"Do you know a man named Hugo-Jim Morocco?"

"No. Never heard of it."

"Well, listen. He is at The Willows fighting the fire. He and a young Dutchman named Opzeeland. Opzeeland," LaForge repeated. "Does that ring a bell?"

"No."

"Listen to me. They were riding here when news of the fire reached them on the river road and they passed us to help."

"Here? Vy here?" the Dutchman demanded.

"They carry warrants for our arrest."

"Vat?" the Dutchman screamed. His face, weak and thin in contrast to the thick power it once betrayed, went red and his mouth fell open revealing his toothless gums.

"You heard me! The marshal warned me. It was just luck the fire happened. It—"

"Der marshal?"

"Yes, the marshal, they've brought the marshal. I'm clearing out. Give me some money."

"Vat?"

"Listen, you old fool. I'm clearing out," Julius screamed. "You're through keeping me around here. You're through, period! Give me what's due me!"

"Yah, yah," the Dutchman said, nodding quickly. "First get Gusty, tell him to go for Pierre. I am too old to run. Der marshal, he is on our side?"

"I don't know. He warned me. I don't know what would happen if it came to a shooting."

"Get Gusty, I go to the office to get some money for you."

Julius hesitated for a moment but then flew down the stairs and raced for the front door, calling for old Gusty. He found the slave on the porch, looking to the great blaze in the northern skies.

"Gusty, take my horse, get Mr. Pierre, and hurry. Tell him to come armed."

The old man hesitated for less than a second, leaped from the porch and mounted, with surprising agility, and hurried off into the night toward the bayou.

Julius turned and rushed back into the house, leaving the door wide open. He raced in to the Dutchman's study to find him counting a large number of bills in several currencies.

"Dere is not much," he said.

"Then I'll take it all!" Julius shouted and pulled his derringer from his side pocket pointing it directly at the Dutchman's navel.

"Julius, Julius, don't be a fool! Of course you take it all. I have all I vant here. Ve have been partners too long, Julius. You shall have this and more if you stay to fight. I promise you der place vhen I die."

"No," Julius stated flatly. "Not me. I know when it's time to get away. I should have left here long ago."

The aging sea captain frowned and pushed his money toward the overseer and leaned on the table that supported his sextant. Then he turned and faced the window so as to provide no threat whatsoever to his former partner.

"Take, take," he said. "But tell me, Julius, how soon do you think before they get here?"

"There's no telling," Julius said in a rush. "Damn it!"

"Vat is it now?"

"I gave Gusty my stallion. He's worth five hundred dollars."

"So, vait. He'll be back in a few minutes. He is a fast horse. You are too nervous."

"I'll saddle another."

"Julius, please stay," the Dutchman pleaded. "Help me against these men, for they must be your doing. I have never heard of either of them."

"Morocco is Cowley's friend. You mean you really never heard of him?"

"No, never—ah, vait! The big one! Yes, yes! Many years ago. He was distressed at how I treated a ship's freight on a passage to Curacao," the Dutchman remarked in a tone that suggested he had all the time in the world, even time in which to reminisce about old voyages.

"Goodbye," LaForge said with finality. He replaced his derringer as the Dutchman turned.

"Dag, Julius," the old man said as he fired. He had removed a small pistol of his own from his blousey shirt front and sent both barrels into Julius' chest. The overseer was thrown into the hall by the force of the blast and up against the far wall.

He clutched his stomach and was about to reach into his pocket again for his derringer when death rushed in and covered him with blankness, as it had done to his father in the same house many years before.

The Dutchman came out of the room shaking his head and bent to retrieve his money. It was then that he saw the huge body of the giant slave framed in the doorway.

"Chane," he stammered.

Chane said nothing but approached slowly. The Dutchman raised his revolver. He fired twice before realizing that he had already discharged both loads. He stooped to pick up Julius' derringer too late. The big man was upon him.

Chane lifted him from the ground bodily with both his hands and held him over his head. He walked with him slowly toward the stairs. Behind him he heard hoofbeats of the approaching stallion and close behind it, another horse. He had been watching when Julius LaForge sent for Pierre and so he knew what to expect, but he did not hurry. He no longer cared very much one way or the other. He thought there would be enough time to start another blaze.

He carried the squirming, cursing Dutchman up the flight of stairs to the top, and turned so that he could see the entire first floor below him, the great hall and the dining room beyond it, the long hall to the outside. He heard voices and men dismounting.

The Dutchman cried for help in his own language. It was so strange, hearing Dutch again after so long. He recalled how pleasant it had been to speak it to Eli. He thought of Kitty and of an overseer whose name he no longer remembered who had worked for a man named Corver. It all seemed so long ago.

Pierre rushed into the house toward the Dutchman's voice. He stopped at the bottom of the stairs and looked up.

"No white woman goin' to buy you off this hook, Chane!" he screamed in a hateful, bitter voice.

Chane agreed. He lifted the Dutchman high and sent him hurtling through the air, out over the plantation mansion he had worked so hard to steal enough to buy.

The shot went off at much the same time. Pierre was good with a pistol. The charge sent the projectile into Chane's left eye, killing him.

5

By early morning The Willows was a heap of smoldering beams and ashes. The black people of the plantation, and those of the Dutchman's who had let their curiosity overcome their fear of LaForge's whip, gathered around the hollow place where the house had stood and began to chant.

The song they moaned took Hugo-Jim back to the time when he and Jameson Cowley had shipped together out of the slave port of Tangier. He remembered the buck that had been hung from the yardarm by Van Zachten and the girl he had whipped and raped. He remembered the woman who had been brought to the deck to witness the execution and how she had been stained with the afterbirth, and how she had held her son close to her bosom to protect him from the fiendish wrath of the Dutchman.

The big man felt suddenly old, extremely tired, sore in the muscles of his back and his arms, weary in his mind, and in his heart. When he looked up he saw the row of weeping willows illuminated by the first clear light of early morning and he shuddered.

The marshal, Mr. McKenzie, Eli Opzeeland and the man-servant Mathews were gathered together at the back of a buckboard that had been employed to haul buckets of water from the river. The mule that had been used to drag the heavy contrivance over the new wharf road had been freed of his harness and had wandered back to the stable. White folks from town had begun to arrive but they stayed as far away as the river road, getting the news they wanted from the closest blacks, and then returning to town rather than intrude on the privacy of those gathered around the smoldering ruins.

An old slave in the Dutchman's livery approached slowly. He had large floppy ears and steel gray hair, his arms hung low and his expression was at once stupid and inscrutable. Hugo-Jim watched him approach the marshal and sensing news, he stood up, put his weight on his toes, pushed his shoulders back for a moment, and then wearily walked along to the buckboard where the old slave had just sat down as though wearier, even, than those who had spent the night fighting the fire.

As Hugo-Jim approached he watched the face of the young Dutchman. It was too bad, for Chane had surely been lost in the blaze, along with the Cowleys. Well, there was still his job to be done. He felt in his waistcoat pocket for the warrants as he approached.

"Gusty," the marshal said. He was an old man too, and slightly bent. His hair was thin and white, his nose flat and indistinct as if from the wear and tear of years. It was a morning for old men.

"Mornin' " Hugo-Jim heard the slave say to the gathered white folks.

"How things up the Dutchman's?" the marshal asked and something in his tone made Hugo-Jim wary. He had not mentioned a word of his warrant to the marshal before actually going to get him to ask him to come along. But the night before, while they had fought the blaze, the marshal could have warned LaForge—if he had a mind to.

"Not good, marshal, not good at all," the old black man moaned.

"Eh?" the marshal said.

"Mr. Hasebos, he done shot Mr. LaForge," Gusty remarked, opening his hands plaintively.

"Hugo-Jim straightened and came to attention. "What's that?" he demanded of the black man.

"Yessuh, *maitre*," Gusty continued, almost in tears. "And big Chane, oh that bad nigger, oh that bad nigger."

"What is it, man?" Eli shouted at the old man jumping up and grasping him by the shoulders. It was his first indication that Chane might be alive "Is Chane alive then?"

Gusty looked wide eyed and open mouthed at the strange young Dutchman and muttered finally, "Oh no, suh. Mr. Pierre done shot Chane after he killed the *maitre*."

"Killed the *maitre*?" Hugo-Jim repeated.

"Yessuh. He done hurled Mr. Hasebos right through the air from the top of the landing. I nearly fainted dead away, suh. I never seen a man thrown so far or thought it possible."

"Then it was Chane who set the fire," the marshal said thinking aloud. Turning around he looked for a long time at the row of willows leading to the main house. "I told Miss

158

Lou-Ellen not to take him in. I told her he was crazy with grief."

The white men stood huddled around the old slave, the old man whose use and abuse had wearied him far beyond the others of his age, beyond the marshal and even Hugo-Jim who had worked hard on land and sea for almost forty years.

"Who is this Pierre?" Eli finally asked.

"That would be Pierre Bandeaux" the marshal explained softly. "His brother and sister-in-law were the ones killed in the swamp a while back. Some thought it was Chane that did it, but Mr. Hasebos—Van Zachten if you prefer," he deferred to Hugo-Jim, "—and Miss Lou-Ellen convinced me it could not have been him."

"What sort of man is this Bandeaux?" Eli asked in a dull broken tone.

"Oh he is an evil man, *baas*, an evil man," Gusty murmured into the ground.

"Don't be speakin' ill of white folks," the marshal suggested.

"Oh, an evil man," old Gusty moaned, and as if they had caught the feeling of his heart, the black people who were gathered about the smoldering house raised the level of their chant, their eulogy to their dead master and his ward. Their voices carried far across the plantation to Bayou Chien at the south, to the voodoo bottom lands to the north, to the river, and to the marshland.

"What will you do now?" Hugo-Jim said to Eli, placing a friendly, fatherly hand on his back and looking intently at the young man.

"I will go bury him."

"And then?"

"And then I will go after Mr. Pierre," he said softly.

"I wouldn't suggest that if I were you, son," the marshal interjected. "Pierre Bandeaux is a marsh man. Many is the slave he's brought back dead or alive that tried to get past him in the country. You wouldn't stand a chance against him out there alone," the old law officer crooked a finger toward the south east where the bayou and the marsh land bordered the two plantations.

"I guess I'll come with you," Hugo-Jim said. He had once before committed himself to helping a young man. This time he was gladdened by the sureness of his feeling that he had made a better choice.

"Mathews!" he said. "See to horses."

"Horses, sir?" Mathews said hoarsely. He had lost his voice the night before, shouting for the blacks to hurry with water. He had been a ferocious worker.

"Aye man, horses! There won't be gettin' a carriage through that swamp!"

159

"Yes sir," Mathews said.

"We'll bury him under the willows near his mother," Eli whispered.

"Aye," Hugo-Jim responded .

The marshal, old and embittered, turned away from the men and walked toward the stable. Hugo-Jim looked after him once and withdrew the warrants from his waistcoat. He looked at them, at the long line of willows that led to the river road, and he walked over beyond the line of black people, still chanting softly, to the smoldering house. There was still a tremendous amount of heat rising from the smoking ruins.

The early sun behind him cast his shadow over the length of the foundation as he tossed the white papers from the British and American governments into the ruin. They must have landed on a glowing ember for within a few minutes they had caught fire, and brushed gently by the morning breeze, their quick, flaming life whispered and died.

In
1935 if you wanted to
read a good book, you needed
either a lot of money or a library card.
Cheap paperbacks were available, but their
poor production generally mirrored the quality
between the covers. One weekend that year,
Allen Lane, Managing Director of The Bodley Head,
having spent the weekend visiting Agatha Christie,
found himself on a platform at Exeter station trying to
find something to read for his journey back to London.
He was appalled by the quality of the material he had to
choose from. Everything that Allen Lane achieved from that
day until his death in 1970 was based on a passionate belief
in the existence of 'a vast reading public for *intelligent*
books at a low price'. The result of his momentous vision
was the birth not only of Penguin, but of the 'paperback
revolution'. Quality writing became available for the price of
a packet of cigarettes, literature became a mass medium
for the first time, a nation of book-borrowers became a
nation of book-buyers – and the very concept of book
publishing was changed for ever. Those founding
principles – of quality and value, with an overarching
belief in the fundamental importance of reading –
have guided everything the company has
done since 1935. Sir Allen Lane's
pioneering spirit is still very much alive
at Penguin in 2005. Here's to
the next 70 years!

MORE THAN A BUSINESS

'We decided it was time to end the almost customary half-hearted manner in which cheap editions were produced – as though the only people who could possibly want cheap editions must belong to a lower order of intelligence. We, however, believed in the existence in this country of a vast reading public for intelligent books at a low price, and staked everything on it'
Sir Allen Lane, 1902–1970

'The Penguin Books are splendid value for sixpence, so splendid that if other publishers had any sense they would combine against them and suppress them'
George Orwell

'More than a business ... a national cultural asset'
Guardian

'When you look at the whole Penguin achievement you know that it constitutes, in action, one of the more democratic successes of our recent social history'
Richard Hoggart

Lady Chatterley's Trial

EDITED BY C. H. ROLPH

PENGUIN BOOKS

PENGUIN BOOKS

Published by the Penguin Group
Penguin Books Ltd, 80 Strand, London WC2R ORL, England
Penguin Group (USA) Inc., 375 Hudson Street, New York, New York 10014, USA
Penguin Group (Canada), 10 Alcorn Avenue, Toronto, Ontario, Canada M4V 3B2
(a division of Pearson Penguin Canada Inc.)
Penguin Ireland, 25 St Stephen's Green, Dublin 2, Ireland
(a division of Penguin Books Ltd)
Penguin Group (Australia), 250 Camberwell Road, Camberwell, Victoria 3124,
Australia (a division of Pearson Australia Group Pty Ltd)
Penguin Books India Pvt Ltd, 11 Community Centre,
Panchsheel Park, New Delhi – 110 017, India
Penguin Group (NZ), cnr Airborne and Rosedale Roads, Albany,
Auckland 1310, New Zealand (a division of Pearson New Zealand Ltd)
Penguin Books (South Africa) (Pty) Ltd, 24 Sturdee Avenue,
Rosebank 2196, South Africa

Penguin Books Ltd, Registered Offices: 80 Strand, London WC2R ORL, England

www.penguin.com

The Trial of Lady Chatterley first published in Penguin Books 1961
This extract published as a Pocket Penguin 2005

1

Copyright © Penguin Books, 1961
All rights reserved

Set in 11/13pt Monotype Dante
Typeset by Palimpsest Book Production Limited
Polmont, Stirlingshire
Printed in England by Clays Ltd, St Ives plc

Contents

Regina v. Penguin Books Ltd
October 1960, Old Bailey

The following extracts from the trial, drawn from C. H. Rolph's classic *The Trial of Lady Chatterley*, are designed simply to give a flavour of the proceedings rather than pursue all the trial's ins and outs, and it is hoped that it is reasonably fair to both sides.

The Opening Address for the Prosecution

Mervyn Griffith-Jones

'If your Lordship pleases. Members of the Jury, I appear with my learned friend Mr Morton to prosecute in this case. The defendant company, Penguin Books Limited, is represented by my learned friends Mr Gerald Gardiner, Mr Jeremy Hutchinson, and Mr Richard du Cann.

'This company, as you have just heard, is charged with publishing an obscene article which is, in effect, the book *Lady Chatterley's Lover*, written by D. H. Lawrence some time about 1928 and now published, or proposed to be published, for the first time in this country.

'Members of the Jury, Penguin Books Limited need no introduction to you. They are the well-known and, let me say at once, highly reputable firm of publishers incorporated in 1936 and publishing Penguin Books. It was learnt earlier this year that that company proposed to publish this book, *Lady Chatterley's Lover*. As a result of that the company were seen in August by the police, and as a result of the conversations which took place it was arranged that prior to the actual release of this book, which at that time was planned for 25 August, the company should, in effect, provide evidence of a publication of the book in order that it should be brought before a jury really as a test case, so far as a criminal case can be a test case, in order to obtain a verdict from a jury as to whether or not this book was an obscene book within the meaning of the law. And so it comes about that you are now in that jury box to give your verdict upon this book, *Lady Chatterley's Lover*.

'Let me emphasize it on behalf of the Prosecution: do not approach this matter in any priggish, high-minded, super-correct, mid-Victorian manner. Look at it as we all of us, I hope, look at things today, and then, to go back and requote the words of Mr Justice Devlin, "You will have to say, is this book to be tolerated or not?", in the sense that it must tend, or may tend, to deprave and corrupt. Members of the Jury, when you have seen this book, making all such allowances in favour of it as you can, the Prosecution will invite you to say that it does tend, certainly that it may tend, to induce lustful thoughts in the minds of those who read it. It goes further, you may think. It sets upon a pedestal promiscuous and adulterous intercourse. It commends, and indeed it sets out to commend, sensuality almost as a virtue. It encourages, and indeed even advocates, coarseness and vulgarity of thought and of language. You may think that it must tend to deprave the minds certainly of some and you may think many of the persons who are likely to buy it at the price of 3s. 6d. and read it, with 200,000 copies already printed and ready for release.

'You may think that one of the ways in which you can test this book, and test it from the most liberal outlook, is to ask yourselves the question, when you have read it through, would you approve of your young sons, young daughters – because girls can read as well as boys – reading this book. Is it a book that you would have lying around in your own house? Is it a book that you would even wish your wife or your servants to read?

'Let me at once – because not for one moment do I wish to overstate this case – let me at once concede that D. H. Lawrence is a well-recognized and indeed great writer. Let me at once concede, but perhaps not to so great an extent, that there may be some literary merit in this book. I put it no higher. Certainly let me concede that some of his books have great literary merit. All that I concede. But, again, you have – have you not? – to judge this book, balancing the extent of the obscenity (if you so find it is obscene) against any interests of literature, art and so on, and you have to say in the end, balancing the whole thing, the one against the other: is its publication proved to be justified for the public good?

'And so we come, members of the Jury, to the book itself. And you must forgive me if I have occupied too much of your time in preliminaries. The book has been passed to you. It is a book about – if I may summarize it in literally a word almost – Lady Chatterley, who is a young woman whose husband was wounded in the First World War. They were married at the beginning of the war; he comes back wounded so that he is crippled and paralysed from the waist downwards and unable to have any sexual intercourse. Members of the Jury, other views may be put before you; I invite you to say that, in effect, the book is a book describing how that woman, deprived of sex from her husband, satisfies her sexual desires – a sex-starved girl – how she satisfies that starvation with a particularly sensual man who happens to be her husband's gamekeeper. And you have the episodes of sexual intercourse. There are, I think, described in all thirteen throughout the course of this book. You will see that they are described in the greatest detail, save perhaps for the first. You may think that this book, if its descriptions had been confined to the first occasion on which sexual intercourse is described, would be a very much better book than it is. But twelve of them certainly are described in detail leaving nothing to the imagination. The curtain is never drawn. One follows them not only into the bedroom but into bed and one remains with them there.

'Members of the Jury, that is not strictly accurate, because the only variations, in effect, between all thirteen occasions are the time and the *locus in quo*, the place where it happened. So one does not follow them into the bed and remain with them in bed; one starts in my lady's boudoir, in her husband's house, one goes to the floor of a hut in the forest with a blanket laid down as a bed; we see them do it again in the undergrowth in the forest amongst the shrubbery, and not only in the undergrowth in the forest, in the pouring rain, both of them stark naked and dripping with raindrops. One sees them in the keeper's cottage, first in the evening on the hearth rug and then we have to wait until dawn to see them do it again in bed. And finally, members of the Jury, we move the site to Bloomsbury and we have it all over again in the attic in a Bloomsbury boarding-house. And that is the variation – the time and place that it all happened. The emphasis is always on the pleasure, the satisfaction, and the sensuality of the episode. And, members of the Jury, when one talks about the book as a whole one reads those particular passages against a background in which you may think sex is dragged in at every conceivable opportunity. The story of this book, apart from those episodes, again you may think, although it is true there is some kind of plot, is little more than padding until we can reach the hut again and the cottage or the undergrowth in the forest. You have that background. You have drawn into it the premarital sexual intercourse that took place between our heroine as a girl and the German boys in Germany where she was studying art.

'The book abounds in bawdy conversation. Even a description of the girl's father, a Royal Academician, has to introduce a description of his legs and loins; and, members of the Jury, even the old nurse who is eventually employed to look after her husband, the heroine's husband, without any point to it whatsoever, without adding anything at all, you may think, to the story, has to have her breasts felt while she is looking after him in his bed. Members of the Jury, not only that type of background, but words – no doubt they will be said to be good old Anglo-Saxon four-letter words, and no doubt they are – appear again and again. These matters are not voiced normally in this Court, but when it forms the whole subject matter of the Prosecution, then, members of the Jury, we cannot avoid voicing them. The word "fuck" or "fucking" occurs no less than thirty times. I have added them up, but I do not guarantee that I have added them all up. "Cunt" fourteen times; "balls" thirteen times; "shit" and "arse" six times apiece; "cock" four times; "piss" three times, and so on. Members of the Jury, it is against that background, as I say, that you have to view those passages.

'Now let us look at the book. You see, the normal Penguin cover on it. Let us open the front cover. There we have a short description: "Lawrence wrote of *Lady Chatterley's Lover* '. . . I always labour at the same thing, to make the sex relation valid and precious instead of shameful. And this novel is the furthest I've gone'."' Members of the Jury, you may think that nobody could go much further. "'To me it is beautiful and tender as the naked self . . .' This story of the love between a game-keeper and the wife of a crippled intellectual is therefore one of 'phallic tenderness'" (Members of the Jury, for those of you who have forgotten your Greek, "phallus" means the image of the man's penis) "and is never, in any sense of the word, pornographic. Unfortunately, the critics and censors who bitterly decried the book concentrated their attacks on the language and ignored the tenderness. Lawrence knew that he would be attacked. 'It will bring me only abuse and hatred', he said, and it did. It has taken over thirty years for it to be possible to publish the unmutilated version of the book in this country." Members of the Jury, it is for you in effect to say now whether it has taken only thirty years or whether it will take still longer.'

The Opening Address for the Defence

Gerald Gardiner

'Members of the Jury, you have now heard from my learned friend Mr Griffith-Jones the nature of the case for the Prosecution. He has told you in general terms what this book is about and the grounds on which the Prosecution contend that it is obscene. He has told you it is full of repeated descriptions of sexual intercourse, and so it is. He has told you it is full of large numbers of four-letter words, and so it is. And you may have asked yourselves at once how comes it that reputable publishers should publish, apparently after considerable thought, quite deliberately, an appalling book of the nature which has been described to us.

'So perhaps I should start by telling you something about the defendant company. Because when anybody is charged with any crime their good character, it has been said, is like credit at the bank, something you can draw on in a time of trouble.

'In 1935 there was a man called Lane, in his thirties, who had been in the publishing business, and he thought it would be a good thing if the ordinary people were able to afford to buy good books. The ordinary book was expensive then, as it is expensive now. He himself had not had the advantage of being at a university. He had a passion for books. He left school at the age of 16.

'Of course, people can get books from libraries, but it is not the same thing as having one's own books. Of course, there were those who thought he was mad. They said it's no good giving the working classes good books, they wouldn't understand them if they read them. The next year he formed this company, Penguin Books Limited, to publish good books at the price of ten cigarettes. (The cost of publishing books has now gone up even faster than the cost of cigarettes.) It was 6d.

'He started off with novels and detective stories. Then there were the Penguin Classics, translations from Latin and Greek, masterpieces of literature of other countries. Penguin poetry, Penguin plays, Penguin art, some called Pelicans which were non-fictional: economics, sociology, in fact every subject.

'Whether he was right or wrong in thinking the average person would buy good books if they had the chance is perhaps shown by the fact that since then this company has made and sold 250 – perhaps I might repeat that – 250 million books.

'It was not their intention to seek to publish new books, but substantially to republish, in a form and at a price which the ordinary people could afford to buy, all the great books in our literature. The whole of Shakespeare's works, Shaw (ten volumes of Shaw were published on his ninetieth birthday), and by 1950 they had published four books by D. H. Lawrence. In 1950, that being twenty years after Lawrence's death, they published a further ten of his books, and in 1960, thirty years after his death, they endeavoured to publish the rest, including this book.

'This book has, unfortunately, had a chequered history. It was not published in this country at the time. It would I think be conceded that as the law was thirty years ago it would have been against the law to do so. Of course, there are many books in London now circulating freely which nobody would think ought to be prevented from publication and which have been banned in earlier years – say twenty years ago. This book in English, you will hear, was published on the Continent. No doubt many copies found their way to this country, so it has never been unknown to anyone.

'I shall be calling a great number of witnesses. I think you will find nearly all of them read the unexpurgated edition years ago. The book that Lawrence wrote has never before been published in this country. There has been an expurgated edition and there would have been nothing to stop Penguin Books from publishing an expurgated edition years ago, but they have never thought of doing so. Because, whether they could have made money or not, they have never published a mutilated book.

'The expurgated edition, you will appreciate, is not the book that Lawrence wrote. You can, of course, have an expurgated edition of *Hamlet*, which no doubt has things in it which are, *prima facie*, obscene. You can have an expurgated edition of the *Canterbury Tales*, which would not be the book which Chaucer wrote. They have always refused to publish any work unless it was the work of the author.

'Before this Act the law had three defects which Parliament has now recognized. The first was that the Prosecution could pick out particular passages from a book and say "Just look at those. Don't bother about the rest." Whereas if one is to be fair to an author when one is considering whether a work tends to deprave or corrupt, one must, of course, judge by the whole book. Secondly, the question used to be whether the work had a tendency to deprave or corrupt those whose minds were open to such immoral influences. That at once made everyone think of young people, and referred to nothing but young people. If applied literally it would have meant that our literature would be such as was suitable for a sixteen-year-old schoolgirl. So Parliament got rid of the words about "those whose minds are open to such immoral influences". Thirdly, there was no distinction between pornography and literature. Pornography means literally the writings of prostitutes, but it is now used in a much more general sense, and you may think the best definition is "dirt for dirt's sake" – works which we have all seen and can see on book-stalls, not excepting our Sunday papers. That which is put in for the purpose of selling them has no art, no literature. Mr Justice Stable [in a judgement referred to earlier in the case] said: "I do not suppose there is a decent man or woman in this court who does not whole-heartedly believe that pornography, the filthy bawdy muck that is just filth for filth's sake, ought to be stamped out and suppressed. Such books are not literature. They have got no message; they have got no inspiration; they have got no thought. They have got nothing. They are just filth and ought to be stamped out."'

The Defence Witnesses

Rebecca West examined

'It has been suggested,' said Mr Gardiner, 'that this is a book which sets upon a pedestal promiscuous and adulterous intercourse?' – 'Er, yes,' replied Dame Rebecca. 'It has been suggested, and that on the bare facts is true; but it is not a recommendation of such intercourse. It shows a broken life, and what somebody did with it, but it does not suggest adultery. It could not, because Lawrence was a man who spent all his life working out the problem of how to make a good marriage: he thought a good marriage was perhaps the most important thing in the world.'

'It has been suggested that sex is dragged in at every conceivable opportunity, and that the story is little more than padding. If that was true would it obviously be an attack upon the integrity and honesty of purpose of the writer?' – 'Yes. The idea that the story is padding cannot be true because as a matter of fact the book has that story because it was designed from the first as an allegory. Here was culture that had become sterile and unhelpful to man's deepest needs, and he wanted to have the whole of civilization realizing that it was not living fully enough, that it would be exploited in various ways if it did not try to get down to the springs of its being and live more fully and bring its spiritual gifts into play. The baronet and his impotence are a symbol of the impotent culture of his time; and the love affair with the gamekeeper was a calling, a return of the soul to the more intense life that he felt when people had had a different culture, such as the cultural basis of religious faith.'

'Is Lawrence's message any less valid in today's circumstances than in the circumstances of 1920?' – 'No, I think it has more bearing on them. Since then we have had a war which was due to something that Lawrence feared very much. Lawrence was a very practical and realistic man and he did see that in every country in the world there were vast urban populations who had lost touch with real life, and that they could be taken in any direction. They have been taken in the direction of evil by their obedience to leaders such as Hitler. Lawrence was talking about something quite real. He was not a fanciful writer. He did write about reality. Talking to one, he was governed by the fear that something would happen, and he did want to get back to something which would save us.'

'Is there anything else you would like to say as to the literary merits of the book?' – 'The great literary merit of his book is something that readers accord by reading him in such large numbers, and his critics accord by writing so much about him. But it is not an easy matter to define the literary merit. If you take individual sentences of his, you can find passages which appear to have no literary merit at all; but the same is true of Shakespeare and Wordsworth, who have some terrible lines both in verse and prose, and of Dickens. But if you take Lawrence's books as a whole they are books of great literary merit. If you take all his books together he was a great writer.'

'Don't trouble about these other books,' said Mr Justice Byrne. 'We are only dealing with one. What is the literary merit of this book? I think that is what Mr Gardiner is asking you?' – '*Lady Chatterley's Lover* is full of sentences of which any child could make a fool, because they are badly written. He was a man with no background of formal education in his home. He also had a great defect which mars this book. He had absolutely no sense of humour. A lot of pages in this book are, to my point of view, ludicrous, but I would still say this is a book of undoubted literary merit. After all, a work of art is not an arbitrary thing. A work of art is an analysis of an experience, and a synthesis of the findings of the analysis, that makes life a serious matter and makes the world seem beautiful. And though there are ugly things, though there is this unsuccessful attempt to handle the ugly words, this is still from that standard a good book in my opinion.'

The Bishop of Woolwich examined

'Has the Church,' said Mr Gardiner, 'always had a special interest and a special concern in human relations?' –

'Clearly, that would be one of my chief interests in this whole case, the effect upon human relations and the effect upon Christian judgements and Christian values.'

'What do you say are the ethical merits of the book?' – 'I would not want to be put in a position of arguing this primarily on its ethical merits. Clearly, Lawrence did not have a Christian valuation of sex, and the kind of sexual relationship depicted in the book is not one that I would necessarily regard as ideal, but what I think is clear is that what Lawrence is trying to do is to portray the sex relationship as something essentially sacred. Archbishop William Temple . . .'

Mr Justice Byrne interrupted:

'Before you talk about Archbishop William Temple, he was trying to portray – what?' – 'The sex relation as essentially something sacred. I was quoting Archbishop William Temple. He once said that Christians do not make jokes about sex for the same reason that they do not make jokes about Holy Communion, not because it is sordid, but because it is sacred, and I think Lawrence tried to portray this relation as in a real sense something sacred, as in a real sense an act of holy communion. For him flesh was completely sacramental of spirit. His description of sexual relations cannot be taken out of the context of his whole, to me, quite astonishing sensitivity to the beauty and value of all organic relationships. Some of his descriptions of nature in the book seem to me to be extraordinarily beautiful and delicate and portraying an attitude to the whole organic world of which he saw sex as the culmination, which

I think in no sense anybody could possibly describe as sordid.'

'Would you make any difference', Mr Gardiner asked, 'between the merits from that point of view of the book as it is and those of the book as it would be if the descriptions of sexual intercourse and all four-letter words were expurgated from it?' – 'I think the whole effect of that would be to suggest that what Lawrence was doing was something sordid in putting it before the public, if these things were eliminated. I think that is a false suggestion, and neither in intention nor in effect is this book depraving.'

'It has been suggested that it places upon a pedestal promiscuous and adulterous intercourse.' – 'That seems to me to be a very distorted way of looking at it. It is dealing with sexual relationship, and many books do that. I think it has artistic integrity. It is not dealing with intercourse for its own sake, and it is not dealing with sexual promiscuity. If the Jury read the last two pages, there is a most moving advocacy of chastity and the remark "How can men want wearisomely to philander?", and I think that is Lawrence's whole approach to the subject, and that the effect of this book is against rather than for promiscuity.'

'Have you one son and three daughters?' – 'I have,' said the Bishop; and this concluded his evidence-in-chief.

'I must just point out to you,' said Mr Griffith-Jones, rising to cross-examine after lunch, 'that I don't propose to discuss with you what Lawrence intended. Did you